Accidentally in Love on Purpose

Accidentally in Love on Purpose by Hosanna King

Published by Chapters Publishing
Queensland, Australia
www.chapterspublishing.com

Cover by Chapters Publishing Graphic Design Department
First Edition

You can't go back and change the beginning, but you can start where you are and change the ending.
C.S Lewis

One

He had always been a little peculiar. Perhaps he's the one from whom I inherited that particular trait. His life had consisted mostly of him sliding between one adventure and the next, with a few brief respites when he would pop back to England, mostly to visit me. Once, at a family gathering, he had arrived wearing the traditional dress of a Korean king from the Joseon Dynasty. He hadn't been at the party longer than five minutes before he shouted "Tally-ho!" and jumped into the pool, fully clothed, drenching my surprised family members.

Despite feeling somewhat out of place in the chaos of my family, I had always adored him. Somehow, despite my awkwardness and general gawkiness, he had deemed me to be his favourite nephew. My mother's brother was, without a doubt, my favourite person in the entire world.

Oswald Basil Montgomery.

What a name. I had asked him before if Oswald was his real name, given my mother's only slightly more usual name of Petal Petunia. It was. Mum had lopped the Montgomery off the end of her name and adopted Alvey when she married my Dad, George.

Unfortunately, they saw fit to name me Alfie.

Alfie Alvey.

As you can probably tell, I didn't start my life with much of a chance at anything even remotely resembling normality.

I had tried to escape the tyranny that followed me in my hometown of Doddinghurst in Essex, by making the move to London, much like countless other people from small towns looking for something bigger. That was over three years ago, which brings me to the precise moment that I am exactly six months away from finishing my law degree, sitting at my desk with a monkey named Aslan perched on my shoulder.

Aslan was a gift for my last birthday from Uncle Oswald. As I said, he had always been a little weird.

My twenty-fifth birthday was rapidly approaching. Uncle Oswald was currently in the Czech Republic, or perhaps it was Russia, or Romania. He was gallivanting around, doing whatever it was that he actually did. He was constantly jumping from country to country, missing hundreds of important family events, but he always, without fail, made it back to England in time for my birthday.

Each year he did something ridiculous and completely inspiring. Last year he brought me a toga from Greece, along with a scroll he claimed was once in the lost Library of Alexandria. I added it to my growing collection, which included a missing Van Gogh, the helmet of Leonidas and a chess board that had once, apparently, belonged to Elizabeth. As in, Queen Elizabeth. The Second, to be precise.

Oswald Montgomery was an archaeologist, technically, but if ever I asked him about his profession, he would claim to be more akin to a male version of Lara Croft. A Tomb Raider. Minus the very small shorts. Or at least, I hoped.

He had more money than he deemed necessary, and so, instead of cashing in on many of his findings, he gave them to me. He kept numerous artefacts for himself, of course, and he even gave the occasional piece to a museum, but he said that nothing gave him greater joy than leaving his discoveries with me.

I kept excellent care of everything, obviously. I had had to move out of my dorm room at University, as pets – particularly monkeys, for some reason – were strictly prohibited. My best friend, Hugh Dabney, and I moved into a two-bedroom apartment in Wandsworth. Number 323A. It was a narrow blue house with a white door and the smallest kitchen in the history of all mankind.

Hugh had been a friend since I first arrived in London. We were dorm mates and classmates, and soon after, actual mates. I supposed that's what happened when you spent as much time together as Hugh and I did. He was an odd fellow, who always wore jeans and a t-shirt, most of which were either stained with cheese sauce or sported some kind of mathematical equation or geeky image. I, personally, tried to keep as low on the public radar of humiliation as possible. Years of torture in school had forced me to harness my unfashionable geekiness, but Hugh, with his shoulder length greasy hair and stringy beard, had never been one to be swayed by the opinions of others.

He accepted me for the way I was, and I returned the favour. Most days, this seemed to be to my detriment.

Aslan jumped off my shoulder and onto the desk. I looked at her and sighed, the half-finished assignment, which sat stagnant on my laptop screen, giving me a stress headache. I had named her Aslan before Uncle Oswald told me that she was, in fact, female. I hadn't looked at her undercarriage to respect her privacy, but decorum had never been a burden under which Uncle Oswald had ever truly toiled. I had kept the name, deciding it suited her black and white face. She was a capuchin monkey from Argentina, who was – most of the time – well behaved, if not ever so slightly odorous.

I scratched the top of her head. "Want to finish my assignment for me?"

She cocked her head to the side, as if she were trying desperately to understand me.

"You do?" I continued. "That is so kind of you. It's supposed to be five thousand words on ethics in law. Go right ahead. Just slam your face on the keyboard. It'll probably be about the same quality as if I wrote it."

"Are you talking to your monkey again?"

I hadn't heard Hugh come into the room. I pulled back from Aslan and twisted in my swivel chair to face him. "What can I say?" I held up my hands to either side and shrugged my shoulders. "She understands me."

Hugh stared back at me blankly. "You need a girlfriend, mate."

I scoffed. "You're one to talk. How long has it been since you went on a date?"

"As a matter of fact, I have one tonight." Hugh dropped his bulky frame down on the sofa, his legs spread wide, with a sloppy grin on his face.

I blinked in shock. "You? You have a date?"

"Try not to sound so surprised, Alfie."

"Oh, but I am," I said as I watched Hugh pluck an old potato chip from his beard, then pop it into his mouth. "Who are you going on a date with?"

"Vanessa Chadwick."

"There's only one problem with that story, Hugh. It's total bollocks." Vanessa Chadwick was the most beautiful woman in our ethics class. The chances of her dating Hugh Dabney sat somewhere between none and zero.

"It is not." He grinned again. "I'm helping her study. She needs me."

It all made sense now. "Helping somebody study isn't a date."

"I think you will find that it actually is."

"I see. And how many other people will be in this study group?" I asked.

Hugh was hesitant to answer. He tugged on the ends of his white t-shirt, suspicious stains covering the front, as per usual, and remained silent.

"Hugh?" I pressed.

"Okay, fine." Hugh shoved his forefinger into his mouth and fished around inside, before pulling it back out again and consuming whatever he found that was suddenly atop his finger. "There are only four…teen. It's for the assignment."

"Why wasn't I invited?" I asked, offended.

Hugh leaned forward in his seat and expressed his most sympathetic smile. "Probably something to do with the fact that people don't know you exist."

"Oh. That. Right."

"Look, you can come if you want. Just don't go making any moves on Vanessa. All right?"

"Thanks for the… touching offer…but I'm gonna stay in tonight."

"This is why people don't know you exist, Alfie!" Hugh slapped his open palms on his knees to emphasise his point.

"Really?" I asked. "I thought they were just ignoring me because my high intellect and exceptional wit intimidated them."

"The key is to give them a chance to get to know you first. Then they'll run for the hills because of all the other stuff."

"My mistake. Anyway, I thought we were doing pizza and a Doctor Who marathon tonight. For my birthday. Because it's the day after tomorrow and I have to go home." I elongated my words, as if I were speaking to a child, trying to encourage them to remember to flush the toilet and wash their hands.

"Oh. Right. Well, hoes before bros? Right?" He hopped up on his feet and threw his arms out to his sides. "There is an actual chance I'll get to snog Vanessa Chadwick tonight!"

"Yeah. Just…" I paused, trying to search for the most diplomatic way to dash his hopes. I couldn't bring myself to do it. "Just make sure you wear a clean shirt then, eh?"

Hugh sniffed the underarms of his shirt and screwed up his face. "Yeah. Brilliant."

As he went to leave the room, he stopped and pointed a finger at me. "On the off chance though, that I do strike out with Vanessa, let's do drinks. At the pub?"

"Yeah. Righto."

"Ten-ish?"

"Ten-ish," I confirmed.

Hugh turned from the room, his thundering footsteps accompanying his out of tune mating call. "I'm gonna snog Vanessa. Vaness-ss-ss-aa-aa. Gonna snog, gonna snog. Vaness-ss-ss-aa-aa."

Aslan poked out her tongue and slapped her face with her hands.

"That," I said to her, "is my best friend. Can you believe it?"

With a suddenly vacant evening ahead of me, I turned back to my computer and actually did slam my head against the keyboard.

Two

The knock at the door was like something out of a horror film; slow pounding against the wood… once, twice, thrice. I sat up and shot a worried glare to Aslan, before remembering I was a man – a manly man who was capable of handling whoever – or whatever – was at my door.

I paused the episode of Doctor Who – the one where the Doctor finds out who River Song really is – and trotted over to the door, while feelings of bold masculinity empowered me. I opened the door quickly and came face to face with… no one.

I felt, for a moment, slightly satisfied with myself. Just my presence alone had been enough to thwart any intruder, murderer or evil alien that had managed to escape from my television set. As I was about to close the door, I noticed an envelope of thick card on the door mat.

The mailman. I should have seen that one coming. He was at least ninety and walked like a thousand-year-old tortoise. He was known for making late night deliveries.

I picked up the envelope and recognised the script immediately. It was from Uncle Oswald. Closing the door to the outside world, I plopped myself down on the lounge and turned the card over in my hand. Aslan came up to me and started pawing at the envelope. I snatched it out of her way.

"Uh, uh, uh," I reprimanded her. "This is mine."

Aslan, clearly perturbed, clambered onto the top of my head and began picking through my hair. I plucked open the tab of the envelope and pulled out a single paged letter.

My stomach lurched as I read it.

Alfie,

Sorry my dear boy, but I won't be able to make it back for your birthday. I have sent you a gift in my place — it's a good one! You're going to love it.

I am not going to tell you what it is. It simply must be a surprise. Ha! Who am I kidding? I can't keep a surprise from you!

A woman will arrive on your doorstep, expecting to be your bride! I found her on the Internet! Apparently, you can do that these days! Take care of her, now, won't you? She's a special one. I expect you to show her every courtesy, as I know you will. There's no greater gentleman than Alfie Alvey.

Must go now. Terribly busy these days! Wish that you were here with me! Think of the damage we could do!

Bye for now,

Oswald.

I read the letter twice. Then a third time, just to be sure I still spoke and read English. I felt little beads of sweet form out of nowhere then dribble down my temple.

I put the letter down and I drew in deep breaths. I looked over to the clock on the wall so fast that Aslan fell off my head and landed as a dazed mess on the lounge beside me. 9:30. Drinks. Ten-ish.

I ran into my room, threw on a clean shirt and bolted out the door, letter in hand.

Outside, I pounded along the sidewalk, up the street that never ended. I arrived at the pub slightly sweaty, despite the crisp evening letting me know that winter was on its way. It was busy inside, as usual, and I immediately spotted at least seven people I knew.

"If it isn't my favourite Ginger!"

I spun around to follow the voice, finding Hugh standing in the centre of two of his friends, who I only knew as Dark Lord and Wizard. For that reason alone, I refused to address them in public. Or ever, really.

"Hugh," I huffed out a breath. "I have to talk to you."

"Come here, you," he said as he approached me. He wrapped his heavy arm around my shoulders and bent me in half, rubbing his closed fist against my head.

I waited for his drunken display of affection to end.

He let me back up and looked at me, clasping a hand to his chest. "Would you just look at that? Magnificent, isn't it? Ginger. Gin…ger." He tasted the word on his lips and chuckled satisfactorily.

Whenever Hugh got tipsy, he became entirely fascinated by the colour of my hair. In his defence, it was extraordinarily red. I was the ginger to end all gingers. And yes, I was also ginger down south, to my eternal horror. Miraculously, I'd missed out on the accompanying freckles. I think God felt it was only fair.

"Come on, Alfie. Come hang out with the Lord and the Wizard. We have been waiting for you ever so patiently. Like proper gentlemen, we are."

"I really do need to talk to you, mate," I protested.

"You know," he continued, oblivious, "she blew me off? Vanessa. She blew me off!" He pushed out a small breath to signify her wrongdoing against him and sighed. "I really thought we had something. Something special. Something…lasting."

"Sorry, buddy." I patted him on the back as he stuck out his bottom lip in a devastated little pout. "She doesn't know what she's missing."

Hugh perked up. "True!" he shouted. "Never was a truer word spoken! Truer? More true? Which is it?" He let out a cackle. "Oh, sod it! I don't bloody care. I don't!"

"Hey, Alfie," Dark Lord said tipping his hat in greeting in my direction. Dark Lord was extremely thin and had the whitest skin of any man I'd ever met, including myself, which was saying something. His nigh-on florescent pallor was accompanied with narrow brown eyes and greasy black hair. He wore a fedora, which he no doubt tried to pass off a Rat Pack-ish, but failed when he joined it with a Metallica shirt and baggy black jeans.

"Hey," I replied. "Having a good night?"

"Slower than last night," Wizard replied. Wizard was slightly more normal looking. He wore a striped blue and white shirt with cream-coloured pants. His very round glasses were perched on his small nose, which was in the very centre of a plump face. He was trying to grow out his hair, but since he had only started a few weeks ago, it was in that ragged stage that made him look like an unmade bed. Or a member of an American pop band.

"How long has he been here?" I asked Dark Lord as Hugh started pulsating like an electrocuted ape in some sad sort of attempt at dancing.

"Since about eight. Vanessa got a better offer and left early. Broke his bloody heart."

"I can see that." I rubbed my face, exasperated. I wasn't going to get anywhere with Hugh in this state. And since I was in a bar, and I desperately desired to be drunk and forget the letter in my hand, I headed to the bar to order a pint.

I shoved the letter into my pocket; it felt about as heavy as a bowling ball. Wizard joined me as I leaned up against the sticky counter, waiting for my drink.

"You all right?" Wizard asked. "You look a little weird."

"Great," I answered a little too quickly. "It's just a totally normal, nothing-out-of-the-ordinary night."

"Right, right," Wizard replied slowly. "So, totally wigging out then?"

"Pretty much," I answered.

"Well," Wizard sighed, as our pints slid across the bench and into our hands. "Only one thing to do."

"Yeah? What's that?"

Wizard held his glass up to his face and grinned. "Get totally bol-locks-busting drunk," he said, avoiding a hit to the head as Hugh swung his arms in the air like Julie Andrews in The Sound of Music.

I picked up my drink and clinked it against his.

Looking back, one could say it was the FFD – First Fatal Drink – that ensured the evening would spiral even further into madness. There was a widely known truth amongst me and Hugh's crew of misfits. I couldn't hold my drink to save my life.

As our glasses clinked together, I should have known what I was in for, but of course I was blindly unaware of the repercussions of tasting beer for the first time in six weeks. I never drank during seasons of heavy assess-ments, and with this notable exception.

The first sip passing my lips and sliding down my throat did little to stop the shake in my hands so naturally, I required another. Two sips are incomplete without a third, and once you've had three you may as well have four. If you've had four, you may as well finish the pint, as anything else would simply be wasteful. Of course, by the time you've finished a pint, you're feeling remarkably more comfortable with the idea of just one more. How two pints turns into five, however, is inexplicable.

If the juke box hadn't played my favourite song, there would have been at least a chance of the evening ending with my head in the toilet, wishing I had had better sense, but as chance would have it, the juke box proudly played, 'I Will Always Love You', by Whitney Houston, circa 1992, and I did feel the overwhelming need to enjoy it.

"You've got a beautiful voice," Dark Lord gargled.

"Do you really think so?" I asked. "I've always been ever so shy about it."

"Like Bon Jovi meets Michael Jackson. An angel is singing before us,"

Wizard agreed.

"You know, I have an idea," Hugh said.

This really should have been the point I put a stop to it all, because nothing – and I do mean nothing – good ever follows the words, I have an idea when it is Hugh that has voiced them.

But I did not. Such is the power of the fifth pint.

"Go on," I encouraged. "You've always got such good ideas."

"I think the people in this pub would like to hear you sing. I think you should stand on the bar and sing. Put on a show for us all. Us hard working people. We deserve a show."

"Do you think so?" I asked.

"We do," they chimed in unison.

I genuinely believed in that moment that they were absolutely, undeniably right. What a monster I would have to be to deny my heaven-blessed voice to the people of Wandsworth.

Without another thought, I clambered, unsuccessfully on both my first and second attempt, onto the bench and stood, proudly and wobbly, in front of my audience.

As Whitney reached that unreachable note, I did my very best to match her. To my own inhibited ears, I sounded like her male equal. The voice the radios have been missing. But when one is drunk, the ability to both walk and sing at the same time is rather diminished. As such, when I started to strut down the length of the bar, I fell.

Ideally, I would have fallen onto the floor, shaken myself off and continued my evening. Instead, I began toppling towards the row of expensive bottles behind the counter.

Hugh, ever my rescuer, even when I don't need it, noticed my fall, which seemed to happen in slow motion. He threw himself at me, which did little but drag him down with me.

Together, we smashed into the row of bottles behind us, shattering them into a million tiny pieces. Drenched, wreaking of alcohol (from both within and without) I sat in my puddle of shame, stunned, and seeing double.

I don't know how long I would have sat there if I had been left to myself, but I wasn't. The strong hands of the chunky barman yanked me to my feet and promptly threw me over the counter into a pile of people, as though I were a bowling ball being tossed at pins.

Together, I and strangers, fell to the floor, wounded, and utterly surprised at our current state. Unfortunately, the strangers weren't the sort to allow a slight such as this to go unpunished. In mere moments, the bar was like a scene from a Wild West movie. Fisticuffs ensued. Bottles were thrown. Wedgies were given. By me, since I have no other experience in physical altercations other than those given to me by my younger sister when we were growing up.

By some strange twist of fate, I managed to knock a man to the ground. Making his way to back his feet, the man turned around and looked at me with fury in his eyes..

I decided remorse was the best option. "I am so sorry," I said. "I didn't mean to-"

My sentence was interrupted as I was yanked forward by the collar of my shirt.

"Oh dear." I squeezed my eyes shut as a closed first landed squarely on my cheek. The blow was enough to knock me out of the man's grip and send me flying backward, only to smash into another fellow bar-brawler. This caused a veritable game of 'Toss the Idiot' to occur, and I was thrown back and forth, from person to person, creating quiet the stir, until I could handle it no more.

I managed to squirm out of somebody's grip and find my balance, with my back to the wall. I had been pushed around long enough. I could take care of myself. I felt anger rushing within me and I mustered all of my will and strength. I raised my fists in the air and adopted my most ferocious glare.

"You want a piece of me?" I growled. "I am a weedy little ginger who went to high school in Doddinghurst. You think I've never been beaten up?

I was President of the Chess Club, for goodness sake! Bring it on!"

The patrons all stopped and stared at me, silenced. For a moment I thought my rousing speech had managed to tame the ravenous crowd, out for my blood. But when the leaders of the pack looked at each other and shrugged their shoulders, I suddenly regretted opening my mouth at all.

"Hugh!" I screamed, hoping he would save me.

They came flying at me, and I managed by some miracle to duck out of the way of their potent blows and deliver an uppercut to the stomach of one of the men. He gripped his stomach and coughed, bent over in pain.

What had I done?

I had hit him. I had actually punched someone! I threw my arms in the air as a hazy rush of victory came over me. "Are you not entertained?" I shouted, à la Russell Crowe.

Perhaps I had seen The Gladiator one too many times. All that was missing was my animal hide breastplate.

Stunned, the thronging crowd began to cheer for me. I was even petted on the back like a poodle who had successfully rolled over for his treat. Hugh looked at me like I was his hero. Dark Lord and Wizard, who were in the grips of muscle-blessed muppets, shouted my name.

I now understood why jersey wearing Neanderthals began bar fights, or why men defended their dates until unconsciousness. The feeling of winning, of laying that gratifying punch to slay injustice, was glorious.

I was a hero.

I was a champion.

I was…going to die.

My assailant straightened himself and glared at me while revealing a row of remarkably white teeth. He was definitely angry. I hadn't thought past laying that first punch. In fact, I hadn't even thought about punching him at all. It just sort of… happened. I had never touched a hand to anyone in an overtly violent manner, ever, and yet it was just like second nature to duck and weave and throw a punch inside this grimy pub. But now what? I had no idea what to do next. The man was clearly very unhappy. He wasn't just going to let it go. I wasn't a particularly prideful man – for that matter all of my dignity had been robbed from me slowly ever since I hit puberty – but even I knew that there was no way he was going to turn the other cheek in a room full of people who were egging us on. No. This was going to get much, much worse.

I gulped.

As the man I had punched launched himself at me, I squeezed my eyes closed and prepared myself for the pain. But the pain never came. I opened my eyes to see that Hugh had thrown himself in front of me in an act of selfless heroism. I was protected from the attack, and then one after another, Hugh came to blows for me, protecting me from the two villainous leaders. Not wanting to let my comrade down, I threw myself into the fray like a caveman.

When the police finally came to stop the fight, I was having the life squeezed out of me by a wide hand wrapped around my throat. I gave a small, pitiful wave to the policemen in an attempt to request that they save me. The hand dropped me and I fell to the floor, my face smushing against something sticky.

Three

Sitting in the gutter outside the pub, I had never felt so low. How had I, a respectable, quiet, possibly even boring, law student ended up here, covered in sticky liquid, smelling like a brewery with what I hoped was only peanuts in my hair.

Hugh was beaten to a pulp, but he smiled at me and I felt bolstered. I decided I was going to take my punishment in the same manner I dished it out.

Like a Gladiator.

Boldly, I walked over to the policeman, doing my best impression of a sober man. Utilizing everything I had ever been taught at law school, I managed to talk us out of a trip to the lockup, acting as somewhat of a representative for Wizard, Dark Lord and Hugh, who were all so incapacitated that the only words they could come up with sounded like an old man snoring.

As the barman and I came to an agreement that we would cover all costs for breakages, I reminded myself never to drink again.

I shook hands with the barman, whose angry, purple face had softened to a much calmer shade of pink. The policeman, a portly fellow who looked as though he would rather be anywhere but here, was glad to be able to get back to his evening without carting four drunk university students to the police station.

As we began the ascent up the never-ending street, back to our apartment, the cold night air made me feel woozy. Gone was the feeling of euphoria, and in its place was stomach-turning regret.

Unfortunately for me, Hugh was not yet to the stage of remorse, and frankly I wasn't sure he ever would be. Hugh wrapped his arms around my neck. "Oh, Alfie. I love you, Alfie."

I chuckled weakly, swallowing back bile. "I love you too, buddy."

"I love this man!" Hugh shouted into the empty street. "I love Alfie Alvey!"

"Shut up!" someone shouted from their window, unimpressed by Hugh's sudden declaration.

Dark Lord and Wizard, shuffling along like members of the undead a few feet behind us, mumbled their agreement.

"He saved us," Hugh said, spinning around, arms extended either side of him. "from prison! From doom! From the end of our degrees!"

"Hear, hear," Dark Load groaned.

"All right, all right," I said, waving them off. "Let's not forget we're gonna have to pay for all that."

"Alfie," Hugh said in a hoarse whisper.

"Yes, Hugh?"

"I think I'm drunk."

"Really? You're not showing it," I replied in mock horror.

"Did I-?"

"No," I stopped him, "The police arrived before you started to propose to strangers."

"Good. Last time someone broke my nose."

"I think this time someone broke your nose, mate," I said sadly.

"Really? I can't feel it."

"I don't think you'll be saying that tomorrow. I can't believe you jumped in front of me like that."

"You're my best mate, Alfie. Of course, I did."

"The whole bar was screaming your name," Wizard said wistfully.

"I think the head of our university is going to be screaming my name, as well, when he hears about this."

Dark Lord chuckled conspiratorially. "You mean if he hears about this."

"We are heroes," Hugh declared. "We should sing a song."

"Let's not," I covered his mouth with my hand as he opened it, ready to belt out a tune. "I didn't actually come to the bar tonight for drinks. I have to talk to you."

"Can it wait?" Hugh asked through my hand. I released him from my grip, satisfied he wasn't going to sing. "My head is pounding to the beat of the Imperial March right now. What did I drink? Vodka? Gin? Gin and Vodka?"

"Yeah, there's nothing like cold air to make you realise how wasted you are. But no, it can't wait. I got a letter from Uncle Oswald."

"And?"

"He's not coming for my birthday and-"

"Oh, that's a shame, innit? He always comes."

"Yeah, I know. But-"

"I mean," Hugh looked up at me with watery eyes, "you think you can count on someone, but you just can't. I'm sorry mate. Really. You need a hug?"

"No, I'm fine. I don't need a hug."

"Yes, you do. Come 'ere."

"I really have to tell you-"

Hugh reached his wide hands towards me and yanked me until I was pressed against his side. He patted my back and sobbed a little. Wizard and Dark Lord stopped, surveying the scene for a moment before attempting to join in. I held up my hand, wedged as it was beneath Hugh's sizeable arms, and stopped them.

"Really mate, it's okay." I tried to pull myself free, but Hugh had a death drip on me.

"No, it's not okay, Alfie. You don't have to be strong. He's always there. Every year. Doesn't he love you anymore?" He sniffed. "Don't worry, I still do. I always will. Always. Honest. We all will, won't we lads?"

Wizard and Dark Lord nodded. "Forever," Wizard said, placing his hand on his chest like he was taking an oath in the military.

"As much as I'm touched by this display of affection," I said, "it's really not what I wanted to-"

"We could throw a party!" Dark Lord slurred suddenly. "A big one. Just for you. Get everyone to come around."

"Oh," Hugh said, biting his lip. "We're his only friends. No one else will come."

Ouch.

"Right. True, very true," Dark Lord nodded in agreement. "We could take him to see some lady bits."

"Yes!" Wizard replied, a little too eagerly.

"No!" I said, shoving Hugh off me. "No, no, no. Everybody settle down. No lady bits are required. Thank you." I shuddered at the thought of an evening spent in a debaucherously intimidating place. I wouldn't know what to do or where to look.

"Shame," Wizard sighed.

"Hugh, please listen to me," I implored. "I got a letter from Uncle Oswald. And he told me what he got me for my birthday."

Hugh started sniffing the air. I sighed internally. It was right about now that he would be craving potato crisps. We were getting nowhere.

"I could really go for some crisps." Hugh tucked his hands into his pockets and thudded down the street.

"We've got some at home."

"No, we don't. I ate them all," Hugh protested. "I always bloody eat them all."

"Yeah, we do. I hid them from you, and I'll tell you where they are if you just listen to me for five seconds."

Hugh stopped and sighed. I manoeuvred myself until I was standing in front of him. We were almost home. The front door was just a few feet away. "What is it, Alfie? I'm listening."

I took a deep breath and let the words loose. "I'm getting married."

Hugh's eyes went wide, and he stared at me in disbelief.

I pressed my lips together, anguished, and groaned, "Apparently."

"Let me get this straight," Hugh said, a packet of half-empty crisps in his hands. "Your Uncle – Uncle Oswald Montgomery – has got you a live human being for your twenty-fifth birthday?"

"Yes!" I all but shouted, throwing my hands in the air in exasperation. "No. Wait. It's not…well, like, she's not a slave or anything, but yes, I suppose, something like that."

A snort and a huff put a momentary pause on our conversation. We looked down at Dark Lord and Wizard who were snuggled up together on our floor, entirely unconscious. Hugh pulled out his phone and took a photo of them, arms wrapped around each other, drool dribbling from Wizard's mouth onto Dark Lord's cheek.

"He bought you a wife?" Hugh spat. "A wife! As in, a woman! To marry!"

"That's what he said in his letter! Hugh, what the hell am I supposed to do! I know it's not like I've ever had a girlfriend or anything, but I had anticipated that, when I got married – or even just had a bloody relationship – I would have some say in it!"

"Maybe he thought you would never have any prospects." Hugh laughed. "He's helping you out."

I took off my left shoe and pegged it at him. He threw up his hands to protect his face, pointlessly, as the shoe landed in the centre of his stomach. I listened to his loud groan with satisfaction.

"Maybe it's some sort of code!" I spluttered, a wave of genius crashing over me.

"What?" Hugh hissed. "You've completely lost it."

"No. Hear me out. He's always running around the globe, getting himself into who knows what kind of trouble. What if he's been captured by gunrunners or tomb raiders and they're holding him at ransom? Maybe somehow, he got a letter to me, but it had to be in code." I pulled the letter out of my pocket and scanned the words. "The word gift could mean, I don't know, clue, or something!"

Hugh stared at me long enough to make me squirm. Slowly he stood up, walked over to me, and bent down. "Alfie, I want you to know that what I do now is for your own good." With that, he drew back his hand and slapped me hard, right across the cheek.

I recoiled in pain as Aslan screeched from atop her pen, ever my protector. I held my palm over my throbbing cheek and nodded. "Thanks," I said. "You're right. I needed that."

"Look, it's probably just a joke." Hugh sat back down on the couch in front of me. I heard the crunch of the crisp packet as he landed on it. "You know him – he's bizarre. A little… a little quirky." Hugh exercised his considerably jazzy jazz hands, framing his face in a 'Just Jack' kind of way. "This is probably just his way of making you writhe. He'll be at your parent's place on your birthday, and you'll both have a good chuckle. Him probably a touch more so than you."

"Of course." I sighed in relief. "You are absolutely right."

"I always am," Hugh sighed, as if he were a man long burdened.

I watched him lift his left cheek off the couch and tug the crisp packet out. He inspected the contents before shrugging and upending it into his mouth. Fragments of salt and vinegar potato rained down on him, only half of it making its way to its intended destination.

Four

Hugh was right. It was probably all just a joke. What reason would he possibly have to get me a mail order bride? It would be the most ridiculous idea he had ever had. He would not do it. I would be seeing him tomorrow. Of course, I would.

I typed the last sentence of my essay and stood up from the computer, cracking my knuckles and yawning. I had been forced to get up at six this morning to finish it, because I had to be on the road by ten. I looked to the clock hanging on the kitchen wall. It was nine forty-nine.

I had had every intention of packing last night, but being overwhelmed by Uncle Oswald's cruel joke, I had decided to continue my Doctor Who marathon until three in the morning, wallowing in self-pity until I was lost in a Sci-fi induced comatose state. I was currently running on three cups of coffee and three hours sleep. I walked into my room and picked up my rucksack from the ground. Stuffing a few shirts and an extra pair of jeans in there, I zipped up the bag and walked to the front door, throwing it at the handle. It thudded and fell.

Aslan scuttled along the floor behind me and grabbed hold of my leg, mid stride, swiftly making her way to my shoulder. She tugged at a strand of my hair and I yelped.

"I know, I know. I need a haircut." I reached up and scratched the top of her head. I looked at the clock again. It was nearly ten. My mother was free spirited and, well, strange. She had a lax opinion about most things but there was one thing she was a stickler about. Timing. She had only once been late in her entire life and even then, it was only by a few minutes.

She was due to be born September 9th, and she was born September 10th at 12:02am.

I suspected she had never forgiven herself. She made up for her apparently unacceptable tardiness by being punctual to the point of ridiculousness. On the first day of school, every year until I graduated, I had been twenty minutes early. Never nineteen. Never twenty-one. Exactly twenty.

I had finally given in to her pestering me as to what time I would be leaving Wandsworth and I was positive that by now she had worked out the precise amount of time it would take me to get to our family home in Doddinghurst. She would open the door on the very minute I was due and stay there until I arrived. The unfortunate thing about Mum's issue with punctuality was that she expected the very same punctuality from everyone else.

I grabbed Aslan's cage and she hopped in obediently. Making my way to the door, I picked up my bag and grabbed the handle, swinging the door out wide.

A woman, appearing to be somewhere between twenty and twenty-three years of age, stood at the door, her hand raised in a closed fist, as if about to knock. She had deep dark eyes and russet hair. I returned her stare, open mouthed and ridiculous, for a lot longer than decorum would allow.

"Oh, I'm sorry. Hi. Can I help you?" I asked, slightly breathless.

"I am Dominika Zolnerowich. I believe you are expecting me." Her accent was heavy, and she seemed to struggle through the sentence.

I racked my brain for a reason I would be expecting her. Did I know her? I let the name run circles around my mind, over and over, trying to place her, but to no avail.

"Do you go to my University?" I asked.

She shook her head, confused.

"Are you looking for Hugh?" I questioned, though as soon as I said it I knew the answer to be no. If Hugh had a friend that looked like that I would definitely know about it. He would have told me. Multiple times.

"I'm sorry, I'm not sure that I know you."

Dominika smiled a coy little smile then looked down to her toes. "No, you do not. Not yet. But we have time to change this."

Oh.

My stomach dropped.

Three words slam dunked themselves into the hoop of my mind.

Mail.

Order.

Bride.

I stood, entirely immobile, as the girl named Dominika Zolnerowich looked from me to Aslan, then back to me again. Her expression of slight confusion at the monkey in my hands was quickly replaced by what looked like a mixture between sadness and shame as she took in my horrified stare.

"Do I not please you?" she asked.

I remained completely incapable of speech.

"I am not pretty enough." She spoke the words as more of a statement than a question.

Despite my shock induced state of synaptic failure, I was still a red-blooded English man, and could immediately reassure her that she was inexorably mistaken. "No, no. You are definitely pretty enough." My cheeks burned with the strange compliment that flitted out of my mouth.

She smiled. It was a gorgeous, shocking smile that caused me to choke awkwardly on my own spit. I gasped for air and coughed violently, waving her away with my hand as she tried to aid me. I attempted to smile, between raking in breaths, to gather some composure and salvage my dignity, but from her countenance, I presumed my face had contorted into a mask of terror.

I wiped my watering eyes when finally, the coughing ceased and I could breathe without looking like I was missing a few brain cells. It was too late by the time I realised that I had simply returned to staring at her like she was a lost Monet that had found its way to the Louvre, as she stood in front of my doorway.

"Will you not invite me in?" she asked.

"Oh!" I spluttered. "Right. Right. Yeah." I stepped out of the way and let her in the house.

"Oi!" I heard Hugh call. "Who was at the bloody door at bloody ten in the bloody morning on a bloody Saturday?"

Chagrined, I held up my forefinger to Dominika, the international sign of one moment please, and walked through the living room, leaving Aslan at her feet. The moment I was out of her sight, I started to run, awkwardly as I was trying to keep quiet. I burst into Hugh's room to find him sprawled out naked on his bed, his sizeable backside facing the roof.

"Bloody hell!" I shrieked, and slammed the door again, hiding from the unhallowed sight. "Put some pants on, you wanker!"

"No need to shout," Hugh protested from behind the door. I heard him shuffling around, before he added. "Righto. I'm decent."

I walked back into the room, tentatively this time. "Sorry." I said, clasping my hands in front of me. "You know, for the, uh, for the intrusion."

"Never mind that. What could be so bloody important you'd bloody barge into my room this bloody early on a bloody Saturday morning?"

Bloody was literally the only swearword I had ever heard Hugh say. When he was tired, mad, excited, or basically feeling any emotion at all, he used it more often than he'd stop to breathe. He came from a strict Catholic family that disagreed with words that held a negative connotation and it seemed bloody was the only word that didn't wreak havoc on his conscience, though not much else from his upbringing seemed to have stuck.

I sat down on the end of his bed.

"Getting kinda cosy are we?" Hugh said. "I always suspected something. Mate – you're not my type." When he received no response from his playful dig, he sat up from his previous almost horizontal position. "What is it? You look like someone just stole your last teabag."

"She's here," was all I could say.

"Who's here?"

"The woman."

Hugh sighed. "Alfie, I'm gonna need some more information. It's practically dawn."

"The girl!" I shouted. I looked to the door in fear, half expecting the stranger to burst on in. I turned back to Hugh and hissed, "The woman! The mail order bride! From Uncle Oswald!"

Hugh shot up from the bed but got tangled in his sheets in the process. He fell, face first, onto the ground with a loud bang. I watched him roll over and squirm out of the sheets, kicking his tied-up legs wildly, before getting to his feet and slapping a thick hand over his mouth.

"Thank you for that somewhat energetic response." I muttered, joining him on my feet.

"She's here? As in…" Hugh pointed aggressively at his closed door, over and over. "As in outside?"

"Yes. In the living room!"

"Bloody hell!" Hugh's mouth was open in the shape of a capital 'o'. "The old man actually did it! He actually bought you a wife!"

"Yes!" I hissed.

Hugh huffed out a chuckle, then put his hands on his hips. "Crazy, innit?"

"Crazy?" I snapped. "Crazy is not the word I would use! Utterly insane! Completely horrifying! These are the words I would use."

"Hey," Hugh said, patting me on the shoulder. "Calm down, eh? Let's not overreact."

"Overreact? I have a woman waiting to marry me in the living room!"

Hugh grinned. "Pretty cool, innit?"

I dropped my arms by my side, exasperated. Without another word, I left the room and walked back into the living room. Unfortunately, it seems that men have an internal radar that alerts them to the presence of attractive women, and therefore my unwelcome guests from last night were no longer sleeping on my floor, and were now peacocking in front of my would-be fiancé.

I shoved myself in front of them and ushered her away, but to no avail. The men were everywhere.

"Hello, lovely lady," a sultry voice echoed.

I turned around and saw Hugh leaning against the wall, his hair freshly combed and an – almost – clean shirt on. He smiled and winked at her as she looked up at him.

"Hello." She stood up and walked towards him. "I am Dominika Zolnerowich." She looked confusedly from me to Hugh, then smiled a small, apologetic smile. "Which one is Alfie Alvey?"

The way she said my name was adorable. But that was of absolutely no consequence.

"I am." I waved a hand gawkily, then quickly put it down by my side. "Me. Alfie." My eye caught the time on the way, and I slapped my forehead and sighed. "I'm late."

"Oh, no." Hugh started to laugh. "Your Mum is gonna belt you."

"I'm not ten. She hasn't belted me in years. But she might just upgrade to first degree murder."

I ran to the door and picked up my bag again. I paused and turned back to the people standing in my living room.

"Do you like Age of Empires?" Dark Lord asked in a voice that didn't sound his own.

"I don't know what that is," Dominika replied.

Hugh was winking at her again, running his fingers through his beard as if he thought that girls actually liked that. She stood there uncomfortably. Quietly, she looked back to me, as if expecting that I, who had been thrust into the unexpected position of doting fiancé, would save her.

I couldn't leave her with Hugh, Wizard and Dark Lord for the weekend, but I absolutely had to get on the road. I groaned. "Dominika," I said. "Come with me, will you? I'm late."

Dominika dutifully followed, picking up her two old-style suitcases. Hugh shot me a disappointed glance, before he bowed to her and said, "My lady." As he kissed his hand and blew her a kiss, with Dark Lord and Wizard clambering to get a better view of her from behind, I quickly closed the door before they could do anything worse.

"I'm very sorry you had to see that." I started down the path towards my little car, parked on the curb. "Actually, I'm just sorry about them in general." Aslan squawked in her cage as if in complete agreement.

Dominika smiled politely and followed me to the car. I had an ordeal before me to get the bags into the trunk of a car that made the Gee Wiz look oversized. When finally, we were in, I took off, seventeen minutes after ten. My mother was going to be standing at the door for seventeen minutes waiting for me.

It struck me, however, that I had a greater problem ahead of me. I was going to arrive at my parent's house with a girl. An actual girl. What was I going to tell them? I couldn't tell them the truth – that Uncle Oswald had thought so little of me that he deemed it necessary to purchase a woman to pretend to love me for the rest of my life.

I looked across to her and racked my brain for something to say. I felt tension rise inside me until I thought I was going to burst. The silence was too heavy. I spat out the first words that came to me. "So… Dominika."

Profound.

"Nika," she said.

"I'm sorry? What?"

"You call me Nika. My name is too long."

"Okay. Nika. Nika. Nika."

Stop saying her name, you moron!

I cleared my throat. Honesty was the best policy. That's what everyone always said, wasn't it? I would just tell her the truth. Simple. Raw. Sophisticated. It was a good plan.

It turned out I wasn't brave enough to tell her the truth until we were halfway through our journey. There was nothing to be heard but road noise and the deafening thud of an awkward silence for approximately 40 minutes. Finally, it was too much to bear. "Look, Nika," I began. I waited another thirty seconds before I spoke again, just repeating the same half-witted sentence. "Look, Nika…"

"Yes?" she encouraged.

"Yes. Right. I'm sorry about all this. There's been a big misunderstanding. I didn't order you."

"Order me?" she gasped.

"No, I don't mean order you, like…like… like order, order. You're not chips. Or an ale. You're a person. But I just, it's just that I-I didn't ask for you. I don't want you."

I subconsciously punched myself in my gentleman sausage for that statement. It could never be said that I knew all that much about women, but I did know that you should never tell one that you don't want her. Not unless you wanted to be strangled in your sleep with piano wire, or have your soup poisoned.

"You don't want me?" she whispered.

"No. No, no, no, no, no. Not like that. I don't not want you. I just don't want you. To get married. Me. Married. Myself." I stopped and took a breath, gathering my words.

Nika sat beside me, fuming. I could almost see steam pouring out of her ears.

"Okay, my Uncle, he wrote me a letter that said that for my birthday, he had ordered – not ordered, I'm sorry – but bought, or asked for, a bride. I had no idea about you until yesterday. I don't want to get married. This is all just a big misunderstanding. I thought he was joking or kidnapped by murderers or something. Currently, I'm wishing it were the latter." I let out a small chuckle.

"You think I am joke?" she asked, indignant.

"No!" I said, too quickly. "No. Not at all. You are not a joke. I just didn't believe that he had actually done this, without my permission. I mean, I'm six months from finishing my law degree. I can't get married!"

"What are you going to do with me?"

I was confused. "I'm sorry, what am I going to do with you?"

"Yes. I come here, all that way, for you. To be yours. What are you going to do with me if you don't want me?"

"I…I don't know." I paused, tapping the steering wheel nervously. "Can't you just go home?"

"Home?" she spat. "Home? I don't have home! That is why I am bride. I have nowhere to go!"

Several colourful words rippled through my mind.

"Stop the car!" she screeched.

"What?" I asked, dumbfounded.

"Stop the car right now!"

Expecting some sort of emergency was underway, I dutifully pulled the car over safely on the side of the road.

Nika promptly opened her door and stormed out of the car.

I looked up to see Nika walking away, heading down the road.

I hurried out of the car and followed her. "Nika!" I called. She didn't stop. "Nika! Come back!"

She was completely ignoring me whilst maintaining what I noticed to be an extremely sassy walk. I lunged forward and gripped her arm, and she spun around angrily, ripping her appendage out from my grip.

"Get away from me!" she hissed.

"It's not safe," I protested, almost amused by her idea to waltz off down the road. "I can't just leave you here. You'll probably be murdered or turned into a pair of boots by a vicious, yet somewhat talented, psychopath."

Nika stared at me blankly, either because I was stupid or because her English was not quite good enough to comprehend me. I blinked rapidly. "Do you…do you want to be a pair of boots?"

Her lips curled. "You are stupid."

I supposed that answered that question.

My mouth popped open. "You don't even know me! I…I'm studying to be a solicitor! I am not stupid."

"So? You and your big words and your big universities! You look down on me like I am underneath you."

"Underneath you?" I was lost for a moment, but quickly found my way back. "Oh. Beneath me. Yes. You're beneath me."

Nika hissed in a sharp breath, alerting me as to what I had just said. I tried to backtrack. "Oh, no, no, no, no. You're not beneath me. I just meant that I understood what you were saying. I'm sor-"

Before I could finish my sentence, a hard hand slapped across my face. I had never been slapped before. I had seen it been done in the movies, and more than a few times in person, inevitable as it was living with Hugh, but I had never considered what I would do if it actually happened to me.

Unprepared as I was, I let out the most pitiful of squeaks, and raised a pale hand to cover my reddening cheek.

Nika looked almost shocked for a moment, comprehending my abhorrence at having been assaulted by a flighty Czech creature of whom I had never had the displeasure of encountering before today. Her face, however, quickly hardened to a scary mask of fury that seemed much more familiar. I tried to recover some aspect of control over the situation, clawing at my fraying dignity. I dropped my hand by my side and huffed out a breath.

"Now, see here," I said firmly. "You can slap me all you like but there is one thing that is simply not happening on my watch today. Believe what you like about me, but my mother raised not only a scholar, but a gentleman too, and I will not leave you stranded on the side of the road. It is out of the question. Now, you can either take yourself willingly back to my car, or I shall simply hike you over my shoulder and drag you. Which shall it be? I leave the choice in your apparently very capable hands."

Nika's mouthed popped open in surprise as I stared back at her unflinchingly. On the outside I looked calm and forceful – or so I hoped – but on the inside, my heart was pounding against my ribcage to the beat of Flight of the Bumblebee. I had never spoken to anyone, let alone a woman, like that, and I was both impressed and frightened by the split personality that had reared its head. The moments seemed to pass agonisingly slow and, just as I was about to crumble and apologise profusely, Nika stepped up close to me, until her face was just an inch away from mine.

"Fine," she whispered. The feeling of her hot breath on my face made my lips tingle. "I will go with you. But just know," she pointed a finger in my face, causing me to flinch, "I am not happy about it."

As she stormed towards the car, I felt an overwhelming need to have the final say, so I blurted out a useless sentence. "Well, neither am I!"

With such a witty comment hanging in the air, I let my head droop low and followed Nika to the car.

Five

I was, it turned out, forty-seven minutes late.

After returning to the car, Nika and I spent the entire trip in frosty silence. As I pulled up to the driveway, I looked over the garden and saw my mother standing, with a cup of tea in her hands, at the open door. I sighed internally, and turned to Nika, prepared, yet slightly hesitant, to break the silence.

"This is my family. Please, try to be nice to them. Assuming, of course, that you are, in fact, capable of that."

Nika smiled coyly. "I'm the nicest person you'll ever meet, Alfred. You just can't see that through your boorish stupidity."

"Boorish? Well, well, aren't we grasping English well?" As I turned to get out of the car, I paused and looked back at her. "And it's Alfie. Never Alfred."

Despite the icy air, I was grateful to be out of the frosty car. I was sweating under my collar, but I supposed this had more to do with the debilitating anxiety teeming around my body. To introduce my family to a woman who was ordered for me, because I couldn't get my own girlfriend, was too humiliating a concept to entertain. But, to inform them that this was a girl I was dating, let alone a girl I was going to marry, seemed too ludicrous to say out loud.

"Hi, Mum," I called from the centre of the driveway.

"Hello, darling," she said rather flatly. "Forty-seven minutes late, hmm? And you brought that creature."

"That creature is my beloved pet, and you know this," I retorted, placing

Aslan down inside. "And, I know, I know. I'm sorry. I got held up. But you do know you don't have to stand here and wait for me. You bring this on yourself." My mother didn't seem to register that I was speaking. Instead, she thrust her empty teacup into my hands and began the ascent up the driveway towards a waifish looking girl who padded her way towards the house, lugging her bag with exaggerated effort.

"Who, darling, is this?" Mum called over her shoulder, though the question was directed more at Nika than at me.

"Hello," Nika said softly. "You must be Mrs Alvey?" she said, in an accent that seemed much thicker than the one I had heard only moments ago. "My name Nika."

My name Nika? Just a few seconds ago, this woman had called me boorish, in a voice that seemed to lack none of the confidence she appeared to go without as she spoke to my mother.

"Nika! Well, how wonderful. What a pleasure!" I watched my Mum clasp her hands over her chest before she sucked in a cross breath. "Alfie! Get this woman's bags, will you? Look at the poor girl, struggling with the weight of it. Honestly. Where are your manners? I raised you better than this."

Nika wiped a droplet of fictitious sweat from her brow as I reluctantly stepped up to take her bag from her hand. "Sorry, Nika," I said coolly. "My mistake."

We followed Mum inside and stopped in the living room for her inspection. "So," she smiled, holding her hands out in front of her expectantly.

I waited for her to say something more, but when seconds turned into a minute, I realised it was she who was waiting for me. She flicked her honey blonde plait off her shoulder impatiently.

"So, Mum. Yes. Right." I dropped the bag and awkwardly put my arm around Nika's shoulders. "This is Nika."

"Yes, dear, I know that much. What, uh, what exactly is the nature of your relationship together?"

Nika let out a little soft giggle and looked away as if shyness had overcome her.

I felt my cheeks burn as my brain struggled to come up with a suitable response. "Uh. Well. Nika, she is… Nika is my…"

"I am his fiancé!" Nika blurted happily. She bounced up and down on the spot and clapped her hands together as though she had won the lottery.

I turned my head slowly towards her, my mouth open in pure horror.

"Your fiancé?" I heard my mother shriek with excitement. "But, Alfie, we didn't even know you were seeing someone!"

I whipped my head back to Mum and tried to smile. "Um, we, uh, w-w-we wanted it to be a surprise. And isn't it!" I chuckled weakly as Mum threw her arms around me in delight. "Isn't it a surprise? A big…big…surprise." My teeth were pressed together as I realised that the person who was most surprised at today's news was me. How could Nika do that? She just threw out into the nether-nether that she was my fiancé. All I could do was play along. I felt rage bubble inside me, as Mum let go of me and grabbed Nika, who hugged her back enthusiastically.

"This is such wonderful news! Alfie, it's your birthday, but it's us to whom you are giving the gift!" Mum raised a hand to her eye and wiped away a glistening tear.

I felt my stomach roll. This wasn't right. She was so happy about something that was never going to happen. Guilt wound its way up my throat until I thought I was going to blow chunks. "Mum, I had no idea that this was so important to you."

"Of course it is, sweet pea. My only son is getting married. I'm the happiest I have ever been. Let me get your father. George. George! George!"

Mum disappeared out of the room, in search of my father, who was, no doubt, nestled somewhere deep in his office or pottering out in the garden. As soon as Mum was out of sight, I turned to Nika.

"Why the hell would you say that?" I hissed.

Nika looked at me innocently. "Say what?"

"Say that we are engaged! To my Mum! She's a real person you know, with feelings. You can't just say whatever you want to people."

"No," Nika said coldly. "You can't."

I flinched, knowing that she was talking about me now. "So," I said, gritting my teeth. "This is how it's gonna be, then?"

"Yeah," Nika said, crossing her arms. "This is how it's going to be…honey."

Mum walked in and grinned broadly, a somewhat bewildered looking man following behind her. I had long since realised that my Dad was more interested in his garden and his books than he was in my private life and he was, in fact, the only one from whom I felt no pressure within my family. If I had remained single until the day I departed this earth it would not have bothered him at all.

"Hey, Dad," I said, as he shuffled to a halt in front of us.

I watched him adjust the glasses on his nose before he brushed his muddy hands on his favourite garden shirt. "Alfie," he smiled, "Good to see you, son."

"George, you're completely missing the new addition to our family. Don't be rude!" Mum smacked him lightly across his chest with the back of her hand, before turning back to Nika and smiling. "Sorry, dear. He's just on his own playing field sometimes."

Nika looked confused, but smiled politely. "Hello, Mr Alvey."

Dad reached a hand forward to shake hers. "It's a pleasure, uh…"

"Nika," Mum said quickly, filling in the gap. "Her name is Nika. Isn't that just a darling name? Simply splendid. It really is."

"Petal," Dad whispered, trying to settle her down.

"Sorry, dear."

"Nika, I hear that you and my son have quite the news." Dad tried to look interested.

Nika giggled. Giggled. Like a bouncy teenage girl, with pig tails and a strawberries and cream flavoured lollipop in her mouth.

"Uh, yeah," I began. "About that, we-"

"Are getting married!" Nika squealed, interrupting me.

Dad nodded gravely. "Well. This is quite the bit of news, isn't it? Congratulations, Alfie."

I felt my face begin to burn. "Look, Mum, Dad, about this whole getting married thing. Nika and I aren't-"

Once again I was interrupted by the suddenly vivacious Nika, who had taken it upon herself to spill every ounce of fabricated information her evil mind could conjure. "We aren't looking at long engagement. We are to wed in just a few weeks."

"Months!" I shouted. "Months." I tried to chuckle, as I grabbed Nika around her shoulders and tugged her closely to me. I squeezed her shoulder in fury, while maintaining what I hoped to be a convincing smile. "She, ha, she means months. Her English," I started to whisper while leaning close to my parents, "it's not so great."

I coughed as Nika drove her pointy elbow into my delicate, yet still manly, ribcage. "Is this pleasing to you?" she asked, looking mainly at my mother, who was already wrapped around her little finger like a member of Cirque du Soleil.

"Well, yes, of course! The quicker the better!" Mum stepped forward and looped her arm through Nika's, dragging her towards the backyard, where there was a tea table waiting. "You and I have a lot to talk about."

Their absence, of course, left Dad and me standing rather awkwardly.

"So," I said.

"So," he countered.

"Yeah."

"Marriage?"

I sighed internally. "Apparently."

"Pretty."

"Nika? Yeah."

"Russian?"

"Czech, actually."

"Nice?"

"Sometimes."

"You happy?"

The last question caused me to pause. The look in his eyes threw me. He was my father, and lying to him felt truly horrid. But would telling him the truth, that this was all some sort of ridiculous joke, be any better? In that moment, I wanted nothing more than for him to continue in the fairy tale for just a little longer, because, even if it made me miserable, it might make him proud. Before I answered, I plotted several different ways I could kill Nika. "Yeah, Dad. I'm happy."

"Good. Coffee?"

"Intravenously, please."

Six

I dumped our bags in my old bedroom, unsure where Nika would be sleeping. I always felt a strange sense of nostalgia whenever I came home. The first few seconds after walking into my room, I felt like a kid again. But then the Hackers movie poster on my wall, and the bad hair days reminded me that my childhood was not something I wanted to relive.

As I did my usual scan of the room, I noticed a large school photo of me on the wall. I was rocking long, orange hair, braces and glasses that were entirely too big for my face. I was smiling hugely, grinning at what I remembered to be a very attractive photographer's assistant. My thirteen year old brain thought it was love at first overbite.

I rushed to the wall and removed the picture, hastily throwing it into the back of my closet. If Nika got her hands on that she would, no doubt, hold it over me for the rest of my life. Or at least until the moment I would be rid of her.

I turned from the room and squealed like a girl when I noticed my sister standing in my doorway.

"Queenie. Hi. When, uh, when d-did you get home?" I straightened my hair in an effort to regain my composure.

"Just in time, it would seem. Hiding your embarrassing photos from your fiancé?"

I turned back to the incriminating closet and quickly closed the door behind me. "Oh, that?" I chuckled half-heartedly. "No, no. Nothing to hide. Just…moving things around. Making room. Getting my Fang Shay on."

"It's feng shui," Queenie corrected.

"Of course. Feng shui. Harmonization. Becoming Zen." I swirled my hands in front of my face in what I hoped was similar to Tai-chi moves, and thus informing my sister I wasn't entirely ignorant.

"Ri-i-i-ght." Queenie's amused face quickly transformed into a grin as she slapped my shoulder. "Good work, eh?" she whispered conspiratorially. "Definitely batting above your average."

I smiled and ruffled her dark hair. Somehow, out of a parentage consisting solely of peculiar creatures, who managed to produce red headed, geeky spawn, success was somehow achieved with my sister. She was strangely normal, which made me believe that perhaps she was adopted, or, when I was a child, that she had come from outer space and was sent here to study our ways. I once asked her what it was like on her home planet. When she stared at me blankly, I realised that she wouldn't remember anything even if she was an alien. She would have been programmed to believe she was human – the aliens most likely had a system where she reported information without evening knowing it. I liked her even more from that day onward, though I became strangely territorial over my breakfast crumpets.

Now, however, as a grown up, an adult, an almost solicitor, I considered that being slightly more normal than the rest of us was, in all likelihood, a small act of rebellion, like the gothic parents who have a blonde haired, bubble-gum popping, choir singer for a child. Or vice versa.

"How's school?" I asked.

"Boring, as usual. I actually had to explain who Leo Tolstoy was to my English teacher."

"Ah, well, not long until you can embrace college education and embarrass your professors instead." We headed back down the stairs, to the living room, where Nika and Mum were sitting with matching cups of tea in their hands.

"There you are darling." Mum cooed. "We've been having such a lovely chat without you. It's so nice to have a girl around the house."

"Hi, Mum. Here's a girl." I extended my hands like a game show host to display that my sister was actually standing in the room, complete with a pair of ovaries and two X chromosomes.

"Oh, don't be silly, Alfie. You know what I mean. A girly girl."

"Oh, right," Queenie said dramatically. "Someone who likes braids and lipstick and eye liner."

"Darling, don't be rude," Mum scolded. "You would do well to welcome Nika into our home, thank you."

Queenie sat down on the couch and sighed. "I do welcome her, Mum. You are welcome Nika. It's very lovely to meet you."

I tried to breathe through my frustration.

"Thank you," Nika sighed wistfully. "Such a wonderful family you have Alfie. They are not crazy. I do not know what you mean when you say this on the drive here."

My stomach dropped.

Mum turned to me with the same look she used to give me when I was being a tiny misbehaving little twerp. "Is that so?" she said, cocking her head to the side. "Crazy?" She turned to Nika. "He used that word?"

Nika nodded innocently.

"No!" I yelped. "No, no, no, no. I didn't say crazy. I said amazing. Her English." I sighed and shook my head. "To her, they sound the same. Crazy. Ama-zing. See?" I let out a weak, not quite believable chuckle.

Mum smiled a tight smile. "Right. Of course."

This was too much to bear. "Honey, uh, would you mind?" I waved Nika over. "Just come with me for a quick moment?"

Nika dutifully stood and walked over to me, as Mum and Queenie watched us curiously. "It's been like an hour since I've hugged her. That's what we do!" I patted her shoulder rigidly. "So full of love. Just… just can't keep our hands off each other."

I spun her around and shoved her down the hall towards the first available room, which happened to be the bathroom.

I closed the door quietly behind us and turned to see Nika's smug face smiling back at me. "Are you enjoying yourself?" I hissed.

"Actually," she shrugged. "Yes. I am."

"Yeah, well, your fun and games is messing with my family. They are real people, and I actually happen to care about them, so if you could not say that we are getting married in a few weeks that would be swell."

"What's wrong, pumpkin? Am I upsetting you?"

"Yes!" I snapped, a little too loudly. I put my hand over my mouth to silence myself, before lowering it to speak again in a more even tone. "Nika, please. Don't do this. I want to play nice now. I do. But telling my family I said they were crazy? They have feelings, Nika!"

"I know they do!" she growled. "Just like I do!"

"I get it, okay? I know I hurt you and I'm really sorry. I'll do whatever you want me to do so that I can make it up to you. Just stop. Please."

Nika deliberated for a while, before folding her arms and sighing. "Okay, Alfie."

"Okay?" I clarified.

"Okay."

I sighed in relief. It had always been a simple fact – it's what the law was based on – that reasoning with people gets you everywhere. I had upset her, and all I had to do was properly apologise and then this madness would end.

I opened the door to the bathroom and let her walk out first. I followed her into the living room and stopped once again in front of my family.

"Sorry," Nika said in her thick Czech accent. "He wanted kiss me. Too much tongue, he uses," she whispered, leaning towards Mum and Queenie. "Just between us girls."

As Mum looked at me in horror and Queenie spluttered out laughter, I leaned my head against the wall and sighed.

Clearly, it was still game on.

Seven

"I'm sorry, Mum," I paused for a moment to gather my scattered thoughts, "you invited how many people?"

"Just a few, darling. Just the neighbours, and the people from town, and your Dad's gardening crew, and," she added under her breath, "all their daughters."

"Daughters, hey? No sons?" I scoffed.

"Well," Mum waved her hands in my direction to shoo me away, "if you were interested in the sons, darling, you should have said so. But, of course, all those concerns were kicked out the window when you brought home a fiancé." I watched as Mum shoved the meatloaf in the oven, before returning to chop vegetables fresh from Dad's garden.

"No, Mum, I don't mean I wanted the sons, I meant it's bloody suspicious you only invited the daughters. Oh, jeez, never mind." I took a tea towel in my hands and grabbed the wet bowls from the sink. "You can't invite a bunch of girls here, specifically for the purpose of meeting me, when I have a fiancé. What's she going to think?"

"Well, how was I to know that you had a fiancé!" Mum spluttered. "You weren't even seeing anyone five minutes ago, and now you're getting married!"

"I thought you were happy about it," I said quietly.

"I am, darling," she said, putting down the knife. "I am so very happy and so very proud. All I'm saying is that you shouldn't blame me that a bunch of pretty girls are going to come here for your birthday party!"

"Birthday dinner. I stopped saying birthday party when I turned ten." I

49

put the tea towel down, sulkily.

"I'm sorry. Birthday dinner."

I chuckled at the face she pulled while trying to give way to my freedom of thought that so brusquely clashed with hers.

"So," she continued, "speaking of your fiancé, how long have you two been seeing each other?"

I swallowed hard. "Not long. Practically feels like it all just started this morning."

"And why didn't you tell us about her? Don't you think that we are approachable? We try so hard, you know. I know we don't understand all the things that you're into; the shows and the movies and the games and that physician that travels around seeing patients in that blue thingy. But, darling, we do try. And we aren't crazy. I know that that whole amazing/crazy thing was utter rubbish. You did say we're crazy and it's not quite fair. We are normal. Well, mostly, anyway."

"Mum, Mum, stop. Relax. Don't be silly. Nika was just having a lend of you. I didn't tell you because," I paused, looking into her eyes, as the guilt ate me alive, "because I wanted it to be a surprise, all right? I know what you all think of me, that it's impossible for me to find a girlfriend and that I'll always be alone, lost in my own little world, and, I don't know, maybe I just wanted to prove you wrong." I held her eyes for what seemed like a while, surprised at the truth dripping from my tongue and how it blended so believably with the lies.

"Oh, how utterly ridiculous." Mum said suddenly, waving her hand in the air dismissively.

"Smells so good."

I turned towards the overly accentuated Czech accent and saw Nika standing in a short summer dress and cardigan in the entry way to the kitchen. I hadn't known she had changed from the somewhat plainer clothes she was wearing earlier, and, seeing her standing there, with long legs disappearing up into her floral dress, I couldn't help but start at her feet and work my way up, entirely defenceless against her weapon of choice. Her hair, which I now noticed had strong touches of red, sat in loose curls past her shoulders. It framed her round face in a way that made me lose all train of thought.

"Nika," Mum said in a besotted voice, "don't you just look utterly darling in that dress."

Nika smiled coyly, then her gaze fell to me. "What do you think, Alfie?"

Her voice sounded innocent, but I knew there was evil intent behind her red lipstick and batting eyelids. Even so - what did I have in my arsenal to come up against that?

"Alfie?" she asked again.

"Huh? What? No. Yes, I mean no." I stopped to take a breath and gather my thoughts. "I mean you look lovely, Nika."

Her face literally shone as she smiled at me. If I didn't know better, I would have thought that she actually cared about my opinion.

Good thing I did know better.

"Except for the lipstick," I added, as if an afterthought. "Yeah. The lipstick is kind of slutty."

"Alfie!" Mum exploded.

Nika's eyes narrowed as Mum slapped my shoulder in surprise.

"Does he always speak to you like this, Nika?"

Seeing an opportunity, she looked down at her feet and let her head hang low. "It is okay," she said, sniffing. "I deserve it."

I took an involuntary step back when Mum looked at me as if I had insulted her weekly Wednesday aquatic aerobics class. I suddenly felt very small, as her face changed to a remarkable shade of puce.

"You deserve no such thing!" Mum squeaked. "I thought I raised a better son than that, but no, I see I've raised a…a… an emotional invalid!"

"No," Nika said, shaking her head. "He tells me I am not good fiancé. So I must do better."

Mum slammed her hand down on the kitchen bench. "He said what?"

It was about the time that Mum's voice reached a volume that could out-screech Aslan that I knew I was in real trouble.

51

"Mum," I said, shaking my head. "That's not true. I never said that. Ever."

"That's just something you would say when you've been caught out!"

I stood there in shock as Mum lead Nika out of the room, one loving, maternal arm wrapped around her shoulder. I was dumbfounded as to how I had managed to become the bad guy in a situation that had completely spun out of my control.

Eight

Sitting outside in the garden, perched on the aging park bench, I watched Aslan play around on the ground. I had dumped her cage in with our bags in our rooms, having been entirely side-swept by the events of the day and had promptly forgot I had brought her.

It was when I felt the extreme need for a hug after my mother practically disowned me and smuggled my fake fiancé out of the room, that I remembered I had treated her like a common piece of luggage. I had quickly retrieved her, woken her from her boredom induced sleep and carried her outside.

The sun was wallowing about the loss of the moon, high up in the sky, but I felt cold. I was many things, but a good liar was most definitely not one of them. This very fact had been pointed out to me numerous times, along with the tagline of 'How are you going to make a good solicitor if you can't lie?'

Despite the fact that, being old-fashioned, I considered the law to actually be about truth, I was a constant conundrum to my family, thus the reason they had no reason to question my sudden engagement.

I had no idea how I was going to pull this off. The way I saw it was that I had two choices. Firstly, I could carry on with the lie, marry the woman and animate the rest of my life as a miserable old cod, living vicariously through romantic comedies and the convicted murderers I would be face to face with every day.

Secondly, I could come out with the truth and tell my family that Uncle Oswald had finally and truly lost his mind and it was all one big lie. This would, of course, lead to me confessing that I really was as pathetic as everyone thought, and I would die alone and be found by burglars who would steal my belongings and set my decaying body ablaze.

I dropped my head into my hands and sighed until my lips made the sound of a trumpet.

I felt Aslan grab hold of my jeans and pull herself up until she sat triumphantly atop my head.

"Thanks, buddy," I said, reaching up to pet her.

"I still think it's weird."

I recognised my sister's voice, yet felt no desire to lift my head. "What's weird?" I asked. "This is my life you're talking about. I'm afraid I'm going to have to ask you to be a tad more specific."

"You and that monkey."

I gripped Aslan and plopped her on my lap, covering her ears and giving my sister an expression of mock horror. "Don't say the 'M' word around her. She doesn't know yet."

"That she's a-"

I held up a finger to silence her.

"Monkey?" she whispered.

"Well, I tried to tell her, but look at those eyes. However could I tell her that she's adopted?" Aslan dropped onto the ground and resumed playing amongst the flowers.

"No. Right. My mistake because that would be cruel." Queenie sat down and joined me in staring at my monkey. "I can't believe that you're getting married."

I let out a deep sigh and cleared my throat.

"Sore topic?" she asked.

"No," I said quickly. "No, no. I just, um, you know. Wedding stuff."

"Ah," she nodded knowingly. "You're being a typical guy, hey?"

"So it would seem."

"Just don't be one of those guys."

"And who exactly are those guys?"

"The guys who make their fiancé feel like she's silly and girly for wanting everything that she wants. Don't leave it all up to her, or be disinterested. And more than anything, don't look at this like it's just temporary. Cause one day she'll be old, and probably hunched and wrinkly, yeah, but so will you. Just remember that."

When my sister began one of her speeches, I usually started to picture her in a large library, puffing a pipe, sitting on a high backed French chair. She was wiser than her years, and more often than not, this irritated me. However, today it just made me sad.

I was worse than the men she described.

"I will," I said, coughing to clear my throat and cover the sound of another lie.

A hard hand slapped my back. "Anyway, come on, weakling," Queenie said, standing up. "They're here."

"Who?" I questioned. "Who's here?"

"Our worst bloody nightmare."

As Queenie disappeared beyond a path of my father's floral escapades, my face went numb.

There were only two people in this world of whom Queenie referred as our worst bloody nightmare. It was a phrase I knew well, from their multiple visits throughout our childhood. Their presence promoted fear and concern, furrowed brows, and clammy palms. We were to prepare for long, sweaty hugs, sloppy kisses that leave clumps of saliva on our cheeks just a wee bit too close to our mouths, and a near constant barrage of questions; an interrogation that would last their entire stay. I cringed and stood up, Aslan crawling up my trouser leg until she reached my shoulder. Slowly, I headed for the house to visit the two people whose manifestation I felt entirely unprepared for.

My Grandparents.

Nine

The back door had a creak that, when opened too quickly, reverberated throughout the house in an altruistic groan, alerting everyone to your entrance. It was, therefore, the very last option used during my youth, as a means of entrance when arriving home past a curfew. However, since my mother and father were not entirely oblivious to this fact, it was the only door in the house they left unlocked.

It was, hence, imperative to discover the equation, consisting of the exact amount of leverage coupled with the perfect speed, which would lead to the door's muffled silence.

Many years of practicing this process had made both myself and Queenie somewhat of an expert, however, we were no match for our Grandmother's Vulcan hearing.

"Is that my darling grandchildren?" she shrieked, as we entered as silently as possible.

I let out a weak sigh, as Queenie gave me a stern look meant to bolster my spirits as we prepared for battle.

"Yes, it's us Grandma," Queenie called back.

"Come here to me this instant so I can have a look at you," she beckoned.

Dutifully, Queenie and I rounded the corner and put on broad smiles for the two elderly people awaiting us.

My smile quickly turned to a frown. Nika sat on the arm of the lounge chair that was encasing my nimble old grandfather. He was looking at her lovingly, a pipe wedged between his teeth. He looked exactly as one would expect an old man, stiffly upper-lipped and bent on his grandchildren living out the dull routine of a life already lived, to look. He was tall, long nosed and had a permanent look of frustration on his face. Except for now, where he seemed to have taken on the qualities of a school boy - giddy and ridiculous.

I watched Grandma squeeze Queenie out of the corner of my eye and braced myself for my turn. But it never came.

I waited there awkwardly for a hug I didn't want, yet, at its absence, I felt somewhat rejected.

Grandma turned around and stroked Mum's arm. "Darling, you're looking skinny. Don't you eat your dinner?"

"Of course I do, Mother." Mum blushed and turned for the kitchen. "Tea, anyone?"

She didn't wait for a response before disappearing out of the room.

"And George. You look… the same." Grandma forced a smile, baring her little teeth. She had never really approved of my Dad and felt some inane desire to remind him of it every time she saw him.

"Well, it was only four weeks ago I saw you," Dad replied, adjusting his glasses.

The feeling was quite mutual.

As they continued to speak, both of my Grandparents completely ignoring my presence, I began to feel flustered. "Um, excuse me," I said, even waving a hand in the air to further announce my presence. "Grandma?"

Slowly she turned to me and pressed her hands to her hips. She was a tiny woman, stout and stern. Usually she was like an enormous bowl of cake mix, peppered with chocolate chips. Except, instead of chocolate chips, there were little tiny bombs that would explode in your face until all you could see was thick puffs of angry sweet smoke, to the point where you couldn't tell if she was being nice, cruel, a bit of both, or being cruel by way of being nice. Today, however, she was all chocolate chips, and no cake mix. I could tell by the expression on her face.

"Um, how are you?" I asked, clasping my hands in front of me. "It's nice

57

to see you."

"Well, I wish that I could say the same," she snapped. "However, it appears you don't care about me at all."

"What?" I croaked.

"I walk in the door to celebrate my grandson's birthday, and what do I find out? I find out he has been hiding the fact that he has a wife!"

"F-f-fiancé," I stutter.

"The very same thing, they are!" she yelled. "Wife, fiancé. No matter at all, it's the same principle. You had a woman that has decided to spend her life with you and you didn't even have the heart to tell us! Your grandparents, who love you! Unforgivable. Simply unforgiveable."

I watched in utter horror as she began to cry, right in front of me. Tears ran down her face, slowly at first, then suddenly faster, until she was blubbering, her head in her hands, right there in the living room.

Grandpa quickly rose to his feet and placed a protective arm on her shoulder, shaking her slightly and glaring at me. "You should be ashamed, boy."

"Now, there's no need for that," Dad stepped in, in my defence.

"I-I-I'm sorry," I stammered, hands held up in surrender. "You don't understand. I didn't, I mean, we aren't, she isn't…"

Nika brushed past Grandpa with a small smile and stepped in between us. "Mrs Montgomery, please, do not cry."

Grandma looked up into Nika's imploring face. "Do not be sad. Alfie did not tell anyone about me. Perhaps he was ashamed."

"Great," I sighed, throwing my hands up in defeat. "Just great."

"You're ashamed of her?" Grandpa asked.

"No!" I shouted. "No, I'm not. We…we…we just wanted to keep it a surprise." I felt my stomach lurch.

"Well it bloody is a surprise!" Grandma cried.

"Lulu, your language." Grandpa petted her shoulders calmingly.

"Well, I'm sorry dear, it's just that I feel utterly horrible. I do."

I looked down at my feet, ashamed, then up to Nika, who stared at me with a peculiar expression.

"Mrs Montgomery," she said, turning from me. "I am sorry, it is my English. I was making joke. Alfie did not tell anyone - not even you - about me because I ask him not to. Not because he is ashamed of me. I was nervous. It was wrong of me, I see. I am sorry."

I looked at Nika in surprise. She was saving me.

"Alfie is protecting me when he said it was for surprise. It was because I was afraid. To meet all of you. To have a real family. In the Czech Republic, I was orphan. I had no family. So, I was scared."

Grandma wiped her eyes, as I stood there, open mouthed.

"Oh, my dear," Grandma said, taking Nika in her arms and dragging her down for a tight hug. "You have nothing to be afraid of. Come sit by me."

Grandma tugged her over to the couch and sat down. "I have such a good grandson," she said, patting Nika's knee. "He will always protect you. I always said he would make someone a wonderful husband. You'll see, you will."

I breathed out a sigh as Mum came back from the kitchen with a tray of teas. "Oh," she grinned. "Everyone's getting along so well. How lovely."

Ten

I stared at my plate. It was the only place to look that didn't either have me fuming with anger or racked with guilt. Nika sat beside me, laughing dutifully on cue whenever someone said something even remotely humorous.

I tried to focus on the unique shape I was making with my peas and the peculiar texture of the roast beef to entertain my wandering mind. I was almost able to entirely block out the inane, Nika-focused chatter around me, which is why I didn't hear my name being called until it was far too late. Queenie's foot came down hard on mine, and I yelped, yanking my foot out of the way, only to bash my knee on the table.

"What did you do that for?" I snapped.

"Ah," Grandpa said, "it speaks."

"Sorry?" I rubbed my knee like a puppy licking its wounds.

"We've been trying to get your attention for who knows how long, dear," Grandma said. "You've been positively ignoring us!"

"No, no, no. I wasn't ignoring you. I just have a lot on my mind. I'm very sorry. What was it that you were saying?"

"We were saying that you two make a lovely couple," Mum said, taking another bite of her roast.

"Oh, right." I nodded. "Thanks."

"She's very pretty," Grandpa said.

I had the misfortune of looking at my Grandfather just in time to see him wink at Nika, who then smiled demurely and shuffled her mashed potato around her plate. I cringed.

"And what a charming accent," Grandma continued.

"She's positively radiant." Grandpa was beaming.

"Perhaps it's you lot that should marry her then, eh?" I muttered a little too loudly. When I realised the entire table heard what I had absentmindedly said, I tried to laugh to accentuate that I was, of course, joking.

Six pairs of eyes stared back at me in abject horror.

"No need to be rude, there, son," Grandpa said gruffly.

"I was just joking," I choked.

"Why in the world did you say yes to this man, when he asked you to marry him?" Grandma hissed across the table at Nika. "I know he's somewhat pleasant looking, in that endearing…odd way, but, honestly, it's those manners I can never get over. I told you, Petal, your son needs to be reined in. No more of those video games, and television shows. They're rotting his mind. And his mouth, it would seem. Utterly distasteful."

"I agree wholeheartedly." Grandpa slapped his fingers on the table pointedly. "Look at him. Sitting there all evening, not saying a single word to his grandparents whom he hasn't seen in an age, let alone the rest of his family or his fiancé. It's your fault, George."

"Yes," Grandma added. "Indeed."

"You've let him get away with too much. You haven't raised him the proper way. You should have sent him to Eton, like I told you to. You would have a different son sitting here at this very table if you had."

There was nothing I could do but sit there and be barraged. I felt sick to my stomach, as my cheeks flamed red with a compelling mixture of shame and fury. I covered my brow with my hands, trying to disappear.

"See here, Hubert," my father piped in. "That is nonsense and I won't have you speaking that way to my son."

I watched as Grandpa's eyes went wide and his lips parted. He threw himself up from the table, shoving back his chair. "Why, I never!"

"Daddy," Mum said weakly, "do please sit down. Let us all just have a nice…quiet…family dinner. Hmm? What do you say?"

Grandpa was ever the victim of his daughter, unable to stand up against her, particularly when she called him Daddy. I watched as he slowly sat down at the table, and picked up his knife and fork, prepared to resume his evening meal.

The table was eerily silent for some time before I could bear it no longer.

I stood up slowly from the table, my head pounding. "I am very sorry to have caused offence," I began, my voice quiet. I kept my eyes away from Nika, whose expression I could not read. "It was never my intention to be such a disappointment to you all. I will do better in the future."

With that, I pushed my chair under the table and disappeared behind the nearest wall, desperate to be out of sight as soon as possible.

I leaned my head back and tried to take slow deep breaths.

It was Queenie who was first to speak after my departure. I let myself sigh as I heard her say, "So Nika. Welcome to the family."

Eleven

"I put fresh sheets on the bed, for you darling," Mum said as she stopped by my bedroom door. After one of the most uncomfortable family dinners on record, it was finally time to sleep. I would be alone, mercifully. I would be able to think of how to get myself out of this mess.

"Thanks, Mum," I said, kissing her cheek. "Where is Nika sleeping?"

She laughed. She actually laughed at me.

"What?" I asked. "What's funny?"

"Oh, darling, of course she'll sleep in here with you. I may be getting older, but I'm not so sheltered that I don't know you two… you know…"

I swallowed. "Uh, Mum, no that's not necessary. Really."

"Well, darling, I'm sorry, but there is nowhere else for her to sleep. Queenie gave up her room to your grandparents and she's sleeping on the couch, and unless you've miscounted, that means we are all out of bedrooms." She patted my cheek. "I respect that you're trying to pretend though, dear. For my sake. It's very sweet. Keeping your mother in the dark. I appreciate it. But you're twenty-five now. I'm not naïve."

With that, she turned around and tottered down the hall to her bedroom. I flinched as she closed the door, the thud like the banging of a judge's gavel.

I turned around and saw Nika standing behind me, horror in her eyes.

"So," I said, raising my eyebrows. "I guess you heard that, huh?"

"No," she said, shaking her head. "No way."

I grinned at her discomfort and stepped inside my room. "Coming?"

Nika glared at me furiously, and slowly stepped inside.

I closed the door behind us and paused, in a minor state of panic.

"What?" she asked, seeing my sudden uneasiness.

"Nothing," I said, too quickly. "It's, um, you know… this is just the first time I've ever had a… girl in my room."

I expected her to laugh and I wasn't disappointed. I sighed and made my way over to the bed, sitting down and yanking my shoes off. Aslan was already asleep in her cage, and I planned to be snoring as quickly as possible. I stood again, wanting to change into my pyjamas, but Nika's presence caused me to pause.

"Nervous?" she asked.

"No," I lied. "I'm just comfortable like this. I'll sleep in these clothes. What about you?"

She looked down at her body, already clothed in pyjamas, then back to me with an expression that told me that the level of my stupidity was, to her, always a constant surprise.

I cleared my throat and turned around, tugging the covers back on my single bed. "Look, I wanted to thank you for stepping in like that. With my grandparents. Earlier. Before dinner. They can be a little…well… horrible, actually. As you saw."

"What are you doing?" she hissed at me.

I looked down at the bed I was preparing. "Getting ready for bed," I said.

"You mean, getting my bed ready for me?"

My jaw dropped open. "Uh, no."

"You are not going to take the bed! Where am I supposed to sleep?" She walked over and sat on the bed, folding her arms like an indignant child.

"You know, I do hear that the floor is quite comfy."

The horrified look on her face shouldn't have made me feel all warm on the inside, but it did. Nika was making my life miserable, whether she stepped in for me with my grandparents or not. "I flew on a plane today. I am exhausted. Do you really think I am going to sleep on floor?"

"The floor."

"I know. Sometimes I slip," she snapped.

"To answer your question, I do expect you to sleep on the floor. That, or," I felt a rush of adrenalin as I egged her on, as this was by far the edgiest thing I had done in as long as I could remember. "You could share the bed with me."

The threat, I expected, would be more than enough to silence her and end the conversation. This was my bedroom, this was my family, this was my life. She couldn't just walk into all of it, sit down with some tea and biscuits, and take it all away from me with one bat of her bloody eyelashes. There was nothing I could do about the damage that had already been done, but dominion of the bed was something I still had control over.

"Fine," she said, with a carefree shrug of her shoulders.

Oh, bother.

"Excuse me?" I asked, blinking rather too rapidly.

"I said fine. You want to share the bed, we share the bed. I am not sleeping on the floor." She walked up to me and held a pointy finger to my face. "If you lay a hand on me, I will break your thumbs. I grew up in an orphanage with ninety-four boys and only six girls. I know how to do a lot more damage than that."

I didn't doubt it. I took advantage of her closeness and observed her. She was rather short, in actuality. Definitely pretty. Even when she scowled. She had deep brown eyes, that were so dark they nearly perfectly matched her pupils, save for the flecks of light fawn that penetrated the darkness. Her hair sat in loose waves, sitting just above her sizeable…chest. Her face was round, accentuated with plump lips and a button nose. She was quite captivating.

For a she-devil.

"Menacing as you are right now, your warning is entirely unnecessary. I have no desire to touch you," I lied, ever so believably. I was, after all, a guy.

Nika let her hand fall and squinted her almond eyes at me. "Good."

I watched her crawl into bed, and had a sudden urge to flee. This was not exactly how I imagined having a girl - an actual girl - in my bed for the first time. I had, in the countless fabricated scenarios that my over-romanticised brain had conjured, imagined something a little more intimate than reluctantly sharing a bed with a short, angry Czech woman, whom I had just met, with apparent issues with pathological lying and thumb breaking. Nevertheless, I couldn't back down now. Not after I had goaded her into it. I would look the fool.

Slow and steady I lowered myself onto the bed and squeezed in beside her.

"You're touching me," she snapped.

"I can't help it, can I? It's a bloody single bed." I found myself resentful of the wall that the bed was pressed up against. This way the only person who could potentially fall out of the bed was me.

I rolled onto my side and tried to get comfortable, as Nika squirmed around me, making every effort not to touch my apparently toxic skin.

"Ow!" I complained as she kneed me in the shin accidentally.

"Be quiet," she retorted. "You are the one who wouldn't give up his bed to a woman, like a gentleman would."

"I guess it must be because I'm not a gentleman, then, eh?"

She suddenly shrieked and sat up, clawing at the wall.

"What is it?" I asked, searching the bed for a dead mouse or a severed horse's head.

"I said not to lay a finger on me!" she hissed.

"I didn't!" I held my hands up in surrender.

"Not that kind of finger!"

It didn't take me long to realise what she was getting at. "Well, sorry!" I growled angrily. Now I was apologising for being a male. What was next? Apologising for breathing?

I rolled over, huffed out a breath, and folded my arms across my chest. In relation to any scenario I had imagined about sharing a bed with a girl for the first time, I expected that actually liking me, and not being afraid of parts of my anatomy, would kind of be part of the deal.

Twelve

I stood in the shower for longer than was necessary. So far, it had been the only place I could get some peace and quiet. After possibly the longest night of my life, I woke up with a sore neck, a bruise on my shin and Nika's drool on my shoulder.

If I wasn't developing a keen hatred for her very being, the first thing I saw this morning when I opened my eyes would have been cute. Adorable, even. She was lying on my shoulder, eyes peacefully closed, mouth open and smooshed against my arm. Her hair flew in every which way, and a river of drool trickled down from her plump red lips. But I did hate her, and therefore the view was a disturbing representation of what evil looks like in the morning.

I had slipped out from her beastly grasp as smoothly and quietly as possible, unwilling to wake the sleeping leviathan from her much needed beauty sleep.

How could she possibly be so hateful?

I recognised my mistakes in the first few moments after we met. And I had apologised, but she refused to let it go. I had tried to be nice, tried to help, but she had insisted on becoming my mortal enemy. A cruel little tyrant wrapped in the body of an ever so slightly attractive Czech maniac.

I had to form some sort of plan of attack. I had to figure out some way to survive this weekend. A dull ache hit my stomach when I recalled the fact that my birthday dinner was today. I was twenty-five. The idea of turning twenty-five used to seem like an achievement, some milestone that I was on a head-on collision with. But now, on the morning I was officially one year older than I was at this exact time last year, I felt nothing but the hot water on my back as I stared at my twenty-five year old feet and patted them in the water, popping bubbles that had formed from run-off soap.

A fist bashed on the door. "There are other people who need to shower, too, you know, darling."

I sighed at Mum's interruption and turned off the tap. Stepping out of the shower, I wiped the fog from the mirror and stared back at my reflection with resolve. I was going to take control today. And if Nika wanted a war, she was going to get one. I could take her. I knew about war.

I had played over three hundred hours of Call of Duty.

Thirteen

I walked into the kitchen and kissed Mum on the cheek. She turned and patted my cheek before shoving a bowl of pancake batter in my hands. "You don't mind finishing up, do you? Grandma and I just have to run into town to finish some last minute errands."

I looked down at the batter then back up to Mum. "You want me to make everyone pancakes on my own birthday?" I clarified.

"Oh, don't be so melodramatic." She paused, then grinned. "But, essentially, yes."

"As long as we have that straight, then." I took the bowl and set it down on the counter, then checked the heat of the pan. "What have you got to do in town?"

"Oh, you know, this and that. Bits here, bits there." She waved her hand effervescently. "For the party, you understand."

"Of course." I took a whisk to the batter, unsatisfied with its texture.

"Darling, do you think that Nika would like to come? Nika. Such a darling name. Odd though."

"Well, it's Dominika. And it's not that weird." I wasn't really sure why I was defending her. "And I don't know. Why don't you ask her?" I stopped, then realised my error. In front of me was a golden opportunity to spend the morning without her. How could I pass this up? But on the other hand, was it dangerous to leave Nika alone with my Mum and Grandmother? She would use the chance to defame my character at every turn, even more so than she already had. She simply could not go. "Actually, Mum, she probably wouldn't-"

"Good idea, darling. I'll go ask her right now."

Frantic, I sputtered, "I think she's asleep."

I should have known better. Mum pursed her lips and shook her head. "Well, I had better help get her up. It's eight thirty in the morning! Who would still be sleeping at this hour?"

"Normal people," I muttered.

Mum didn't believe in sleeping in.

"Mum!" I called after her uselessly. She had already broken out into song, trilling Nika's name as she trotted down the hall.

I poured the batter onto the pan and tried to imagine I was somewhere else, until I felt Aslan's little fingers tug at my trouser leg. I looked down at her and she stared up at me with a sorrowful expression.

"Come on," I said, beckoning her up onto my shoulder.

I took a berry from the punnet and handed it to her.

"Get that filthy animal away from breakfast!"

I didn't need to turn to know it was Grandpa who chastised me.

"That creature needs to be put down. Killed! Thrown out with yesterday's garbage! It's disease ridden!"

I turned, ready to unleash a verbal vomit of rage, when Queenie walked in.

"Aslan is very tame, Grandpa," she said, sweetly.

As if on cue, Aslan dropped from my shoulder and crawled over to Queenie, who scooped her up and petted her head lovingly. "She's not disease ridden. She's family."

Grandpa huffed, and muttered something under his breath, before stepping forward with an empty plate. "I'll take the first pancake."

I didn't say anything as I flipped it onto his plate. Whenever Grandpa and I were in the same room, I couldn't help but wonder how the man had fathered someone as extraordinary as Uncle Oswald. It seemed to me that they had nothing in common whatsoever.

"Grandpa, don't you think Alfie should get the first pancake?" Queenie asked.

"Why?" he croaked.

"Well, today is his birthday, after all."

"Oh," Grandpa looked at me twice, suspiciously, as if he had forgotten that the sole purpose of his visit was to attend a family birthday gathering for me. "Right. Happy birthday."

He turned with his pancake and headed for the table. Queenie snorted a laugh as she walked up to me and slapped a hand on my back. "Happy birthday, big brother."

"Thanks."

"You want me to take over here?" she asked.

"It's fine. I have it."

"She's coming!" Mum sang, as she walked back into the room. "Oh, I'm so excited. I simply must get to know her better."

My stomach sank as I removed another pancake from the pan. "Just… go easy on her. She just got here." What was I saying? "And don't listen to virtually anything that she says. She'll probably be joking, and you won't know, because of her English. You know, she's a bit slow."

"Am I?"

I gulped at the sound of Nika's voice. "Nika," I said, spinning quickly to face her. My sleeve caught on the handle of the pan and it fell to the floor. I bent to retrieve it, and burned my hand on the hot iron. Straightening I let out a heavy breath. "I didn't, uh, I didn't see you there." I attempted to thwart the pain in my hand by shaking it wildly by my side.

Nika watched me with disdain. "I can see that."

I pulled the tea towel from the counter and carefully picked the pan up off the floor, leaving a squashed pancake on the ground; Aslan wasted no time in scurrying over to clean up my mess.

"See, Grandpa?" I started. "She's pretty useful to have around."

He looked over his shoulder at Aslan and shrugged.

Mum was all too familiar with my break-outs of insanity. She petted my shoulder lovingly, before turning to Nika. "Come on, dear, time to go! Grandma is getting impatient."

Nika held my stare as Mum scuttled her out of the room.

Sighing, I slapped a batter covered hand against my forehead, leaving behind a thick, creamy hand-shaped globule.

<h1 style="text-align:center">Fourteen</h1>

I spent the hour and a half that they were gone impatiently pacing around the house looking for something to do. Normally, I would have no problem entertaining myself for a weekend back at home, but something about knowing that Nika was out with my mother –and worse, my grandmother – caused me to have an odd, bubbly feeling in my stomach. What was she saying? What was she doing?

I entered the kitchen and looked at the perfectly clean sink. Turning abruptly, I went to the living room and sat down on the settee. I flicked through a couple of channels, before turning the television off and walking into my bedroom. I made the bed, double fluffed the pillows, then stopped when I realised that I was going to have to hand in one of my Man Cards if I cleaned or spruced or rearranged one more thing.

"Darling!" Mum tweeted. "We're home. Come here."

I straightened and sighed with relief. Before I could stop myself, I ran, I actually ran, out to meet her in the kitchen, where she stood surrounded by shopping bags.

"Mum. Hey. How are you? How was it? What did you get up to?"

"Darling, why are you breathless?" she asked, looking at me the way she often did – like I was the strange one. Though, right now, I could hardly argue with any diagnosis she came up with.

"No reason. Been, uh, jogging." I started to jog up and down on the spot, as if to emphasise my point. When Nika walked in front of me, with her own little bag of goodies, and looked at me in much the same way my mother was, I came to an immediate halt. "On the spot. On the uh, on the spot jogging. I hear cardio is good for the heart." I tapped my chest like Tarzan, then squeezed my eyes shut in humiliation.

You are an utter pillock.

"That is why I do martial arts," Nika said, leaning up against the kitchen bench. Her stocking covered legs popped out from underneath a short denim skirt.

Of course she did martial arts. "Oh, really?" My words croaked a little when I thought of all the physical pain she could inflict upon me. I didn't know how to fight. I barely knew how to clench my fist for a punch. The most threatening thing I could do was run away, with my arms flailing.

"Really," she confirmed. "Black belt."

"Right. That's…that's interesting. Is that the, the, uh, the darkest belt you can get?"

Nika's brows furrowed, confused as she was at my question.

"Darling, everything is sorted now for the party. People will start arriving in the next half hour or so. Are you all ready?"

"Yeah, ready." I tried to neaten my hair to look more presentable. I wasn't really one for big family gatherings, and truthfully, I was more than a little cut that Uncle Oswald wasn't coming. In the back of my mind, I still held hope that this was all some big joke and Uncle Oswald would burst through the doors and make everything right again.

Perhaps it was like that show in America. Punks. Or Punking. Maybe there were television cameras all around and my every move was being recorded and the whole nation would be laughing at me when my story went to air.

I shook my head to gather myself. "Do you need any help?"

"Oh, no. Of course not. You're the birthday boy. You should be relaxing. Oh, wait! We haven't done our birthday tradition."

My stomach dropped and Nika's lips spread into a wide grin, sensing embarrassment wasn't far away. "Um, no, Mum, I don't think it's necessary anymore. I'm twenty-five, now."

"Nonsense." She shook her head and waved a single finger in the air.

"You'll always be my little boy. I'll get the pencil. You take off your shoes."

As Mum hurriedly left the room, Nika slowly walked up to me and touched a fingertip to my belly button. "You know," she said, beginning a slow walk up my stomach with her fingers. "I love your family. They are such a good source of information about you. I did not know that you wore nappies until you were four. That's a little old, don't you think?" Her fingers paused around my neck. She traced my throat smoothly, causing disconcerting little chills down my back. "I cannot wait to find out what the pencil is for."

My eyes started to flutter against my will, as I was becoming more and more tantalised with her touch. Goose pimples appeared on my forearms as she leaned towards me until her face was close to mine.

Her voice was a whisper against my cheeks. "This is going to be so… much…fun."

Quickly, she drew back, grinned, and walked away.

Snapping out of my reverie, I rubbed my throat to take away the lingering tingle from her touch and stared after her. "I hate her. I absolutely bloody hate her."

Fifteen

I stood against the door frame to my parent's bedroom, with my eyes closed to try to minimise some of my mortification. Mum was standing on a small step stool, as my height had long since overtaken hers. She reached up and leaned forward. Since my eyes were closed, I couldn't dodge the incoming attack of her considerable assets. I gasped, buried in her chest and turned my head to the left as quickly as I could. "Mum!" I shouted.

"Sorry, darling," she whispered, petting me on the head. "Just a few more seconds." She drew a line at the top of my head to measure my height. It joined dozens of other lines, drawn on the day of my birthday each year since I could stand.

She stepped down and shoved me out of the way to view her handiwork. "There," she sighed nostalgically. "Look at how you've grown."

"Mum, the line is nearly exactly where it was last year."

"No, it's not. Not really. Every little bit matters. When you were a child you used to wish so hard to be tall. You'd even walk around the house in my high heeled shoes just to-"

"Okay, okay. That's enough."

I watched Nika snicker out of the corner of my eye.

"It's nothing to be ashamed of, Alfie. You wanted to be taller, and they were such an excellent way to help you steal baked goods off the kitchen bench." Mum laughed and petted my cheek as a knock on the door rang out.

"Oop. Someone's here!"

I leaned back against the wall and sighed. "And so it begins."

Sixteen

To my horror, there was not one person at the door, but a dozen. Mum welcomed them in with open arms, grabbing each of them for a quick and cheerful embrace. I watched from the hallway as the cacophony of greetings filled my ears with unintelligible words.

Queenie appeared at my side and chuckled. "Looks like you're popular."

I gulped. "I thought it was just family. And some of the neighbours."

Queenie snorted. "Where do you think Mum went today?"

"For errands," I replied. "She said so."

"Oh, Alfie," Queenie sighed. "I love your innocence. She went to spill the exciting news."

"What exciting news?"

"Wedding bells, you plank. She's been holding onto it since yesterday when you arrived with a mysterious Russian."

"She's Czech," I said, absentmindedly.

"You really thought Mum wasn't going to go out and tell the entire town that her precious baby boy has snagged himself a pretty brunette to have and to hold? Speaking of, punching a bit above your weight aren't you?"

"Hey," I cried, wounded. "What's that supposed to mean?"

"Come on. She's gorgeous. Look at her."

I turned from Queenie back to the entrance way, where Mum was shuffling Nika ahead of her, so that every man and his dog could get a peek at the newest fruit on the gossip tree. My eyes roamed from her toes to her head and for a second I almost got lost at the curve of her lips and the shape of her eyes. I quickly looked away so as not to be captured by her nefarious and evil ways.

"Yeah, sure," I shrugged. "She's pretty."

"Do me a favour. Try and reign in all that lovey-dovey stuff, hey? It's really too much."

I could practically feel the sarcasm oozing from her. Maybe she was right. I had to put on more of a show. At least for this weekend. The last thing I wanted was to come out as a fraud to my family in front of the entire town. Mum lived and breathed this place. I couldn't do that to her. I somehow had to make them all believe that I was head over heels in love with this evil Goblin Queen.

No matter how difficult it would be.

My Mum's future happiness depended on it.

"I'm sorry. I guess I'm just nervous," I said. "Having her around everyone is quite intimidating."

"Well, it wouldn't be so bad if we had met her before, with less pressure. Like when you were just dating. You've been keeping her to yourself all this time."

"Something like that," I mumbled.

"Alfie, come over here!" Mum shouted.

The sound of my name made me squirm uncomfortably. "Time to go to war," I said quietly.

Queenie elbowed me in the ribs. "To the frontlines, soldier."

I began my march to the battle cry of my mother's beckoning. I was going to have to change the game. Turn the tables in my direction. I simply had to so that I could protect my family. And beat Nika at her own game. I swallowed hard.

"Hurry up, darling," Mum cooed. "You're not a tortoise. Your guests are waiting."

My guests?

I garnered my courage and closed the gap between us quickly. Coming up behind Nika, I wrapped my arms around her and bent my head down to kiss her neck. The feeling of her warm skin against my lips made my stomach flip around inside me. The crowd in front of us released a coo of awww's.

"Hi, everyone," I said, rather too joyfully. "Thanks so much for coming."

Nika stiffened in my arms, clearly confused. I moved to the side of her and placed an arm around her waist. "This," I said proudly, "is my beautiful fiancé, Dominika Zolnerowich."

"What a beautiful name," my Uncle Neal said. Neal was a tall, academic type. He knew, or at least claimed to know, everything about everything. My father had always been close with his brother, as the two shared similar interests. "It's Russian, is it not?"

"She's Czech," I said, almost impatiently. Why did I care, exactly?

"No," Nika said, smiling a small smile, "you are right. It is Russian. I am from the Czech Republic, but my father was Russian, and my mother Czech. My father named me."

"I see," Uncle Neal replied thoughtfully. "And what is your father's name?"

"Sasha," she replied. "But, I believe in English, you say Alexander."

"And your mother?" he pestered.

"Uncle Neal, no need to interrogate her," I interrupted.

"It is okay, Alfie. My mother's name was Anezka."

"And are your parents coming to the wedding?" he pressed.

My face went cold. Uh-oh. "Uncle Neal," I chastised.

Nika looked down at her feet, before gaining the courage to look up. "No. My parents passed away. I grew up as an orphan from the age of four."

A silence fell over the enthusiastic crowd.

Nika stood, looking small and fragile, in the middle of a dozen bodies. I squeezed her tighter. Not to confuse her, or keep up the ruse. She was hurting, drowning in a pain that haunted her like a ghost.

I wanted her to know I was here. Even if, to her, it made no difference. I wasn't entirely cold hearted. I couldn't imagine what it was like growing up without a family, alone and afraid in a world that was far too big for you to find your way in.

In that moment, I felt I understood her a little better. Of course, none of it was an excuse for what she had done, but how must it have felt to her, to arrive on my doorstep, heart in her hands? What had it been like to grow up in a cold orphanage, without the warmth of a mother's hug, or the direction from a father's wisdom?

I saw my Mum, surrounded by her friends, her face alight with joy, and wondered how my life would have been different without her. Sure, she was nothing if not a little unhinged, but I loved her.

I felt my heart race a little faster in my chest as I was overcome with a strange and foreign affection for Nika, desperate to somehow bandage the wounds she carried.

Another knock on the door infiltrated the dark silence.

"More guests!" Mum sang, loosening the crowd. They each walked further into the house to make room for the new attendees, dispersing into clumps of carefree chatter, happy to be away from the awkward situation that had arisen.

I stayed still with Nika, my arm holding her close to me, for, apparently, too long. She yanked herself out of my grasp and glared at me with a look that immediately eradicated the warm feelings that had overtaken me.

Shocked, I couldn't say anything in response, before another wave of people greeted us, shaking my shoulders and Nika's hand.

I watched her plaster another smile on her face and wondered why she didn't just leave now. She was only in this to torture me. She didn't have to stay and put on a brave face for my random relatives and nosey neighbours. She could just leave and save herself from it all.

But then, maybe torturing me was just that important to her. I felt a cool anger bubble up under my pale skin as I regarded this monstrous creature of mythic proportions. My overactive imagination had me picturing her with three heads, snakes for hair and the body of a dragon.

I could see her traipsing through cities, gobbling up innocent people and trampling anything in her path.

I shook my head to clear the image and focused on putting on a good show.

The only way I was going to beat her, was to become her.

Seventeen

It turned out my mother had the biggest mouth this side of London. Thirty-seven people showed up for my small family celebration. Hugh, my only backup in this ridiculous charade, was, of course, late. By over an hour. When I saw his cranky old car arrive, I practically ran to the door to greet him. I opened the door before he even had the chance to knock.

"Hey," I said. In my excitement for his arrival, I nearly missed the fact that he was not only wearing a clean shirt, but a suit jacket as well, over an almost stain-free pair of jeans.

"What the actual hell has happened to you?" he asked bluntly.

I blinked. "What?"

"You're eyes. They're all…squinty. And shifty. Yeah, shifty. Dartin' from the left to the right like you're absolutely bloody mental."

"Well," I said, tugging him inside by the lapels, "it's been an interesting weekend so far."

"Yeah?" Hugh attempted to look past me, his eyes scanning his surroundings. "Where's the, uh, where's the bride-to-be?"

"Snacking on small children," I guessed. "Or stealing from the homeless."

"What are you talking about?"

"She's evil!" I hissed, taking two fists of his shirt in my hands.

"Okay," Hugh said, taking hold of my hands and attempting to pry himself free from my grip. "Okay. Now, you spat on me a little bit then, but I'm gonna let that slide because, well, you're scaring me. Okay, there we go. Let go. Good boy. That's it."

My hands fell by my side, and I turned quickly to check behind me, to ensure I wasn't being watched. "Hugh, you are the only one who knows that this isn't real. Her and me. You are the only one who knows that we aren't actually together."

"Well, what does everyone else think?"

"That we are engaged!"

"Bleedin' hell. You told them that?" Hugh laughed.

"No! Of course not! She did. Before I could say anything, she stepped in and told everyone that we are getting married in a few weeks. She's made them believe we are the real deal. She said she's going to have fun with this. Like she's going to destroy me."

"Ooh," Hugh grinned. "She's a feisty one then is she?"

"Yeah, if you could try not to sound so impressed, that would be a real help."

"I can't help it. She is impressive. A lot more impressive than you. Look at you. You're sweating."

"No, I'm not."

"Are you gonna let me further into the house, or are we just gonna spend the rest of the day here, by the umbrella stand?"

"Why exactly are we friends?" I asked, turning and heading towards the backyard, where everyone was scattered.

Dad was on the barbeque, talking to Uncle Neal and Mum's younger brother, Harry. Harry had four boys, all of whom were married with children. They were all here, standing with their wives, beers in hand, while their children ran around their legs, hyped up on sugar.

Mum was sitting with her friends, pointing over at Nika. Mum was no doubt filling them in on random information about Nika's life, claiming that though they hadn't known each other for long, they were the best of friends, and she would, of course, be involved in all of their wedding plans – she was the mother-in-law to be, after all.

Nika was standing with Queenie. She was genuinely smiling, laughing even, at whatever Queenie was saying. She looked almost normal, chatting and giggling.

"That's her there then, I see," Hugh said, not requiring that I point her out. "She looks different."

"Well, it's amazing what a strategically planned outfit can do for one-self."

"She's fit, isn't she?" Hugh adjusted his jacket.

I backhanded his arm. "Whose side are you on?"

"Oh. Hers," he said wistfully. "Definitely hers."

"Hugh!"

"What?"

"Focus."

"Right," he said, wriggling his shoulders and kicking out his legs as if getting ready for a tennis match. "Game face on. What's the plan?"

I placed an arm around his shoulders and pulled him in. I pointed at her subtly. "The plan," I began, "is revenge."

"Nice," Hugh said. "I like it. Good. Now, I don't mean to put a damp-ener on anything, but how exactly do we plan to exact said revenge on the beautiful foreign girl who, for some unknown reason, you don't want to marry."

"Be serious, Hugh."

"I am being serious," he countered. "Very serious. What are we gonna do?"

"We," I said slowly, "are going to…we are gonna… I don't know yet. I've been waiting for you. I thought you'd have a plan."

Hugh shook his head and sighed. "How exactly do you survive without me?"

I rolled my eyes. "It's difficult."

"Right," Hugh said, shrugging out of my grasp. "I propose total annihi-lation."

I nodded in agreement, scowling in her direction. "I like the sound of that."

"We are going to ruin her reputation in this family, bruise her ego, and bring her back to earth. She has no right to do what she has done to you. She just walked into your life and now she's tramplin' all over it. She thinks you're weak." Hugh shoved a finger against my chest. "She barely thinks of you as a man."

I was shaking my head in fury, egged on by his encouragement.

"We're gonna take your life back."

"Yeah," I said ferociously.

"We're gonna put you back on the map."

"Yeah."

"We are gonna squish her like a bug."

"Yes!"

"Then I'm gonna swoop in, be the hero, and have my way with her."

"Yes! Wait, what? No! Hugh! Focus, remember?"

"Right. Right. My apologies. I got a little carried away with myself."

"I can see that. So how do we start?"

"We start with what that famous old Chinaman said – Sun Choo."

"Sun Tzu," I corrected.

Hugh carried on, undeterred, "Keep your friends close and your enemies closer."

"Yes! Brilliant. That's what I thought too. I've started, but she's cold. She's tough. She's…vicious."

"Alfie. You can do this. Gather your manhood and realise that your whole life has been leading up to this moment."

"It has?" I questioned.

"It has."

"Why?"

"Because you are Alfie Alvey. Serial bachelor. You have been waiting your whole life to turn the tables. You can do this."

It all made sense now. "You're right. I can."

"Yes, you can. Now, go over there and show her how much you love her."

Hugh shoved me forwards. Slowly I made my way across the back yard.

Upon reaching Nika, I grabbed her waist, spun her towards me and did something I had, embarrassingly, never done before.

I kissed her.

Eighteen

I had often imagined what it would feel like to kiss a woman, but nothing quite prepared me for the soft feeling of Nika's plump lips against mine. They were like pillows. Juicy pillows, made from the dew of heaven. Juicy pillows, made from the dew of heaven, that, I had to remember, belonged to an evil, tyrannical orc.

After what felt like a considerable amount of time, I pulled back from her face, to regard her stunned expression.

There was silence for an age as we stared at each other. She was probably wondering what the hell I was doing, while I was trying to remember that I hated her, because feelings of fondness were pulsating through me in a way I could not control.

"Gross."

Queenie's voice penetrated my brain.

"Thanks for that display of mushiness."

I turned and smiled at her. I had to keep myself under control. "I can't help it. I just can't keep my hands off her."

"Well, I guess that's a good thing," Queenie conceded. "Seeing as how you're getting married and all."

I grinned toothily. "Exactly."

"Do you have a date set?" she asked.

I paused for a moment too long. I didn't know what to say. Unfortunately, this gave Nika enough time to step in for me.

"We were thinking a quick wedding. As soon as possible. Less than one month."

I choked a little on my own spit.

"Wow," Queenie said, letting out a whistle. "That's quick. Shotgun wedding?"

Nika looked at her curiously. "Shotgun? No. There will be no shotguns. I do not like guns."

Queenie laughed. "No, shotgun wedding means a quick wedding, like for instance, because you're pregnant."

I choked again. A build-up of saliva was forming in my mouth. I was surprised I wasn't drooling. "Whoa. No. No one is pregnant!"

I realised a moment too late that I had all but shouted.

The humdrum of chatting ceased and every eye turned to me. I looked to Hugh for support, but he was hiding behind a paper plate, laughing at my enormous cock up.

"Just in case," I said loudly. "Just in case anyone was wondering. She's not…she's not pregnant. She's just eaten a lot today. We're just…" I grabbed Nika and petted her head. "We're just in love. So…so in love."

I once again faced Nika and Queenie, my shame written all over my face in the form of deeply red cheeks.

"Well," Queenie said, hiding a chuckle. "I'm glad we all know, then. Nika just has a hardy appetite."

"Yeah. Glad we cleared that up," I sighed.

Nika's face was red. I tried to recover, but was floundering. Gratefully, Queenie stepped in.

"So, a wedding in less than a month. How in the world are you going to make that work?"

"I am sure," Nika said quietly, "that you and your mother will be full of good ideas."

Queenie smiled. "I get to help?"

"If you would like to."

"Absolutely," Queenie said, thrilled.

"And, I do not know very many people in England. So, maybe you be my maid of honour?"

My stomach dropped as Queenie's eyes widened. "Really?"

"Please?"

I stood there dumbfounded as the two girls embarked on a colourful discussion about my lifelong imprisonment to a girl who hated me. I felt the somewhat childish urge to run home and bury myself in a blanket fort.

I had to do something. Fast.

Nika was in control – again. She was dragging my family down the rabbit hole into her twisted little world, and I had to stop her. I had to pull out all the stops. It was time to go in for the kill.

I abruptly turned and headed to the veranda. Stepping up onto the old wood, I faced the crowd of people and cleared my throat. When no one paid me heed, I waved my hands as if I was hailing a Taxi in New York. "E-excuse me. Everybody, excuse me. If I could just get your attention – just for one moment – that would be great."

Slowly people silenced themselves and gave me their attention. I had had a plan, but suddenly I was nervous. I had never been great at public speaking, and, even though I was among family – and a few dozen assorted strangers and neighbours – my hands were quivering.

"Right then," I began. "I just wanted to take the stage for a moment to thank you all for coming…uh…for coming out here today to celebrate with me." I looked across the crowd and tried to think of ways to calm myself, when I remembered something that I had once been told in high school. If you imagined the crowd naked it supposedly made it easier to speak. I set my imagination to work and allowed embarrassing underpants to fill my vision. When my eyes fell on the girls my mother said she had invited before she knew about Nika, I had to quickly look away. They looked at me with eager eyes and I did, for a moment, feel guilty that my mum had gotten their hopes up and then dashed them. I forced my eyes to carry on as I continued to speak. "There is something, though, that I wanted to tell you all. Something that I wanted to say about someone…someone…." My eyes finally landed on Nika.

It was easier than it should have been to imagine Nika in her underpants, and my brain betrayed me by failing to make her underpants embarrassing, as was, I presumed, the way the little trick was supposed to work. I imagined her legs, reaching all the way up to her stomach. Her chest lightly cupped in a red lace... I stared down at my feet quickly, trying to gather my thoughts. "What was I saying? Right, yes. I wanted to say something about someone special." I looked up and abandoned my underwear game. "That someone is Nika. By now I am sure that you have all heard that we are in fact...uh... we are in fact engaged. To be married. Together. Us. Married. But what you don't know is that..."

I watched Nika suddenly go pale. She stepped forward and her jaw clenched. She looked, for an instant, neither mad nor evil, but terrified.

"What you don't know," I continued, my eyes never straying from hers, "is that she is, to me, the most perfect person to have ever walked the earth. She has the most beautiful smile I have ever seen. The most spectacular mind. I couldn't imagine a single day without her by my side, and so I want to make her my wife. I want to hold her in my arms every night when we go to sleep, and wake up next to her every morning. I want to face the trials and joys of life with her. She is truly, and completely, my perfect match in every way. And I love her. Madly."

Nika no longer looked terrified. I couldn't read her face. She held my stare, her mouth open in a small 'o'. Realising that I was required to either leave the veranda or continue speaking, I opted to do one last thing. I stepped off the veranda and quickly walked to Nika, trying not to lose my nerve. I took her face in mine and kissed a girl for the second time in my life.

There was something different about this kiss than the first one. Still her pillowy lips sent a shiver down my spine, but there was something more honest, more real, about this kiss. She gave in to me, relaxing her body against me. Her lips moved with mine, creating a sensation I never quite thought possible. I felt her place her hands on my waist. Her touch was gentle, yet firm.

Reluctantly, I pulled away slowly, aware of the dozens of eyes taking in the spectacle we were creating.

We stared at each other until the clapping, which I hadn't realised had begun, ceased.

I had to remember that it was all part of the rouse.

She didn't really want to kiss me. She meant nothing by her touch on my waist, or her pressing against me. She hated me.

I had to remember that she hated me.

Quickly, Nika smiled and turned to the approving audience. She rubbed my back with her hand and giggled, as if on cue.

Hugh caught my eye. He was shaking two thumbs up at me, vigorously. I had, apparently, succeeded in our plan, but I couldn't help but feel both a pang of guilt and a wave of confusion. The biggest thing weighing on my mind was the effect that all of this would have on my family. How would I explain it all to them? How would I recover from this? Would they ever forgive me?

It also didn't feel right to toy with her emotions, even if she was doing everything she could to ruin my life. But even more than that, everything I said came so easily. Was it just wishful thinking? Were my romantic tendances spilling out of me in the form of verbal diarrhoea?

I had, no doubt, wanted a girlfriend for many years now. To no avail, of course. Though I had little or no luck in regards to women, I had always imagined that I would, in fact, make an excellent partner. I would be kind and loving, and always encouraging to her. I would treasure her as my one and only. I was a romantic at heart, and I wanted very much to share all of that with someone. It just built up inside me over the years, with no one to give it to. I was suffering from too much romanticism, to the point where I became, quite possibly, too intense for any of the girls I met. I had never even so much as been on a date. I was that guy. That lonely, geeky guy who watched Doctor Who and Firefly to the point of being able to memorise almost every line. I was, in so many ways a…a nerd. Not that kind that you see on your Facebook feed, of some gorgeous blonde who had to get a pair of spectacles, so she takes a picture of herself and captions it, 'I'm such a nerd'. No, I was the actual definition of nerd. Right down to the pair of The Flash underpants I had in my closet. So, should I have been happy, as Hugh had suggested, that a beautiful stranger showed up at my door to marry me? Should I have seen this as my chance to avoid the inevitability of a solitary existence? But how could I? How could I be happy knowing that she didn't really love me and that I was never good enough for someone to truly love, out of their own free will?

Nika was more than someone who was trying to ruin me. She represented everything I hated about myself, everything I believed I lacked. She represented my eternal loneliness.

My cousins Julian and Howard walked up to us in congratulations, snapping me out of my whirlwind of thoughts.

"How do you put up with him?" Howard asked, laughing and nudging his brother.

"It is very hard," Nika began, seriously. "He cannot cook. He does not help around the house. And he has a very small-"

"She's joking!" I shouted, reaching a hand up to cover her mouth before she could ridicule my manhood. Of which she knew nothing. I was perfectly in proportion, thank you very much.

"Yeah, right, mate!" Julian chuckled. "I'll trust her over you."

I had never been close to Julian and Howard. They were two of Harry's kids. Today's encounter with them didn't exactly inspire me to change that.

"Sweetheart," I said through gritted teeth. "Would you like to get some food with me?"

Nika smiled bashfully. "Sure," she obliged.

Nineteen

The table was filled with assorted barbeque goods, like salads and sausages, potatoes and steaks. In the left hand corner, though, was my favourite dish. Chicken curry. Mum had made it especially for me, and I made a beeline for it.

"Why did you say all of those things?" Nika asked as I ladled the curry onto my little paper plate.

"What do you mean?" I was buying myself time. I knew exactly what she meant.

"Everything you said on stage. Why did you say it? In front of everyone."

 I watched her scoop enormous amounts of mashed potato onto her plate, along with four sausages. "How can you possibly eat this much?"

"Don't change the subject."

I sighed. "Why did you say that we were getting married in less than a month?"

Nika was silent, now pouring herself a glass of punch.

I felt smug. "Exactly."

Nika adjusted herself to face me. I held my breath, as if it would somehow help me keep my cool, as she neared me. She brought her face close to mine and whispered in my ear. "Don't ever kiss me again."

With that, she withdrew, smiled and walked away. Somewhat frazzled, I turned from the table and began to walk towards Hugh, who was, no doubt, awaiting a status report. I was nearly by his side when Howard stopped me and pointed at the front of my trousers.

"Alfie peed himself!" he shouted. "Aren't you a little old for that?" His uproarious laughter caught everyone's attention. Their eyes all travelled down to my crotch. Hesitantly, I looked down and saw the contents of Nika's cup had been poured onto the front of my trousers, making it appear as if I had, indeed, wet myself.

I found Nika in the crowd and glared at her, as she grinned and raised her empty cup at me.

Twenty

I stood in front of my bed in my room, staring at my punch covered trousers, which I had laid out on the bed. Aslan screeched in her cage. With the influx of people into our house today, I had had to keep her in her cage all day. The afternoon was wearing on, the sun beginning its slow decent. I just wanted everyone to leave. This had been, beyond a doubt, the worst birthday of my life.

As I was about to shove my leg into a new pair of trousers, my door opened. I spun around and slipped in my socks on the smooth floor and stumbled backwards, landing on the bed.

It was Nika.

Again.

This woman was going to drive me insane.

"What the bloody hell are you doing?" I asked, covering myself as best I could with my trousers.

"I want to talk to you." She closed the door behind her and began approaching me.

"You could knock, you know."

"Knock? On my fiancé's door?" She feigned horror.

Something wasn't right. What was she doing? She seemed…playful.

"I'm not really your fiancé, remember?"

She pursed her lips and halted directly in front of me. I could smell her perfume.

"Look, I'm in my underpants. Could you at least give me a chance to properly dress?"

"Why?"

"Because you're a girl. And I'm a boy. And I...I...I would just like to be dressed."

Nika laughed. No, giggled. "But it makes it easier if you aren't wearing any pants."

"Makes what easier?" I was getting worried.

"This." Forcefully – rather too forcefully – she threw me back against the bed, until I was staring at the ceiling. Then she straddled me. She sat on top of me, while I was in my underpants. I held on very tightly to thoughts of droughts, famine, the murder of innocent puppies. Anything I could really, except for the beautiful girl on top of me.

"What are you doing?" I asked. "Get off."

"Get off?" she pouted, pretending to be wounded. "Why?"

I began to wonder if she was suffering from some unfortunate mental disorder. Schizophrenia, perhaps? "Because I'm not dressed, and we hate each other, and I'm in my parent's house, and a myriad of other reasons."

I tried to get up, but her martial arts belt made it rather difficult. She shoved me back down and pinned my hands above my head. I started to feel like I was going to be the star in one of those films where the girl turns out to be some terrifying vampire or something, with teeth between her legs.

I stopped struggling and tried another tactic. "Please," I said quietly. "Please will you get off me?"

Without responding, Nika began kissing my cheeks, my neck, my ears. She traced her tongue over my lips, and as she did so I began to wonder how on earth I had managed to go from my first kiss to my third in one day. It was about the time of my pondering that my mind began to literally stop functioning. It all became some kind of a blur. My body grew hot and cold at the same time, and all thoughts of dead puppies and starving people went right out the window of my brain. All I could feel was her body against mine and everything that it was doing to me.

Suddenly, to my dismay, the kisses stopped and were replaced with a

96

cold, hard slap to the cheek. I blinked rapidly. "Ow!"

Nika was standing upright, a furious glare on her face. "How does it feel?" she snapped.

"Painful," I answered. "You slapped me."

"No, how does it feel to be taken advantage of. For me to come in here and not give you any choice. To straddle you without permission."

I tilted my head to the side, not overly unimpressed with how I had spent the last five minutes. "Well…"

"Oh, shut up!" she hissed. "I do something so personal, then I stop. How does it feel?"

"I'm really not following." I shook my head in confusion.

"When you kissed me! You took advantage of me. You violated me. You stole something."

"Wait, I stole something. What?"

"Nothing," she hissed. "Forget it. Don't touch me again."

She slammed the door with a reverberating clang and left me to gather my dignity. After a few breathless seconds, my equilibrium had levelled and I could pull up my trousers. A knock on my door made me nervous. If it was Nika, I couldn't be held responsible if I ran from the room screaming like my hair was on fire.

"Come in," I said tentatively.

To my relief, it was Hugh. I covered my face with my hands and moaned.

"What happened?" Hugh asked. "I saw Nika come into your room."

"Hugh," I said, dropping my hands down against my thighs. "We need to step up the game plan, here. She's insane on a whole other level. She just came here and straddled me like some deranged cowgirl from a bad film."

Hugh snorted in disbelief. "She… her? That gorgeous girl out there came in here and threw herself at your feet and you rejected her?"

"No," I groaned. "I wouldn't exactly say that."

"Then, what happened?"

"She went bloody mental! She started kissing me all over, then slapped me! Then she started screaming about how I violated her and stole something from her. I mean, she's gone off the reservation."

"Have you thought about just calling for a truce?"

"I tried, Hugh. I tried to apologise, but she doesn't want to hear it."

"Then come clean."

"To my family? I can't. Mum's invited everyone she cares about. If I come out and say that it's all one big lie, they're not going to see my side, and I'll be forever known as the pathetic, lying, spinster son who betrayed his family."

"But if you just try to explain."

"Explain what? That when I got up there tonight and said that big speech I was just lying to everyone, spitting into the wind. That I don't really love her the way I claimed to, that I don't adore that smile, and that mind?" I ran my fingers through my orange hair and rubbed my face vigorously.

"Oh. My. Giddy. Aunt." Hugh spoke slowly and deliberately. I looked up in confusion.

"What?"

"You like her!" he accused.

"No, I don't!" I stood up from the edge of my bed in abject horror.

"Yes, you bloody do!"

"Hugh, don't be ridiculous. She's a she-devil. She's a banshee. She's… she's…"

"Your dream girl?"

"Hugh, be serious," I moaned. "My whole life is crumbling into ruins. This woman is tearing everything up, piece by piece."

Hugh was silent for a while, digesting. "Right then," he said. "We need to go to the next level. We have to step it up. We have to obliterate her."

I grinned. "That's exactly what I was thinking."

Twenty-One

"Darling!" Mum clucked. "Where are you?"

"In here," I called, getting up from the bed and stepping out into the hall. "What is it?"

"It's time for cake, Alfie." Her voice was almost reprimanding. "You know, all of your guests are out there. You should be spending time with them. Not hiding out in here with Hugh."

"Sorry, Mrs Alvey," Hugh said quietly.

"I had a little wardrobe malfunction," I said, defending myself for some unknown reason.

"Well, come on then. Hurry, please."

Dutifully I followed Mum outside again, where a chocolate cake was waiting for me on the small table in the centre of the garden. Nika and Dad stood beside it, Nika holding the cutting knife. A thrill of fear trickled across my skin. Nika with a knife. Nothing good could come of this.

"Happy Birthday…sweetheart," Nika said, holding out the knife, blade first.

I cringed. "Thank you." I took the knife carefully and bent down to kiss her cheek. She stiffened. I turned to face the crowd of onlookers who waited for me to dig the knife into the cake and slice the first piece. Mum stopped me before I could dig the blade in.

"Stop dear, we have to sing you Happy Birthday! You're turning twenty-five, after all."

Counting everyone in, Mum lead a rusty, squeaky rendition of Happy Birthday. I noticed even Nika sung a few lines quietly. To keep up appearances, no doubt.

"Thanks. Really. Thanks." I said, nodding my appreciation to the guests. "Also, I would like to thank Nika, for her constant support and love." I turned to her and smiled. "May this be the beginning of a brand new and beautiful chapter in our relationship, where we go from strength to strength. Fighting hard every day." I reached out and touched her arm. "For each other, of course."

Her eyes narrowed as I smiled and turned towards the cake. I dug the knife in and sliced the first piece.

"You touched the bottom, dear. You know what that means!" Mum nudged me in the ribs.

"Of course." I turned to Nika. "It's a tradition in our family. You touch the bottom, you have to kiss the nearest girl." I winked. "That would be you."

I planted another kiss on her lips and, as I did so, I felt her knee rise quickly, hitting me between the legs, without anyone seeing. I bent over, trying not to alert the onlookers that I had just been sack whacked for kissing my faux fiancé.

I coughed, holding my stomach and breathing deeply.

Mum looked at me strangely, but I waved away her concerns. "Just hungry. Hunger cramps. Let's eat."

I stepped aside and let Dad take over the cutting of the cake so that I could concentrate on one day being able to father my own little ginger children. Nika put a hand on my back and dug her nails into my skin. I let out a pitiful squawk and tried not to react any further. I had always believed that resorting to physical violence was the sign of a weaker man. But enough was enough.

Two could play at this game.

I slowly lifted my foot and dropped my heel down on her toes. I felt satisfaction ripple through me as she whimpered. My satisfaction was, however, short-lived, as Nika leaned in close, smiled and slammed a scissor-like hand into my ribs. I gasped for air and clutched at my torso. She was using her belt on me. In front of everyone, she was trying to beat me up. Like as if I was some sort of pipsqueak. My brows furrowed together in proper British rage. Unwilling to lower my standards so far as to further attack a woman, I instead opted for something that would upset her far more. I lifted my hand from my side and cupped her right buttocks cheek in my hand. For added effect, I gave it a little squeeze.

Apparently, that was enough to cause her fury to bubble like blazing fire. She tore herself away from me, bared her teeth at me like some werewolf out of a story from the Grimm brothers, and wrapped her hands around my throat.

I stumbled backwards as she lunged at me, roaring like a banshee. Taking her hands from my throat, she started bashing her fists against my chest, pushing me further and further back until I fell into the table.

The cake table, to be exact.

The chocolate cake was handmade by Mum. It was a two layered, frosted construction, with the numbers two and five piped onto the face in melted white chocolate. Inside were layers of cream and chocolate chips. It looked positively marvellous. However, when I was finished with it, it resembled more the mud pies that I used to make in the garden as a child. As Nika shoved me back, I had tripped on my own feet and fallen like a bowling pin. I knocked the table, pushing Dad to the ground. I landed solidly on the grass, as cake flew in every which way. Nika crashed against my chest, no longer roaring in fury, but yelping in fear. In a matter of seconds, Nika had managed to destroy my birthday. A day I would never get back. As I lay there, covered in cake with a furious Czech woman on my chest, and as my father stared up from his backside wondering what in the world had just happened, I plotted at least seven different ways I could kill her. Two of which involved removing her horrid little head from her horrid little shoulders with nothing sharper than a spoon.

I looked over tentatively at my mother's face. It was, as predicated, a mask of pure, unadulterated horror. If I had stripped naked, adorned my head with a soiled pair of underpants and danced around to Lily Allen's

Hard Out Here, I could not have seen a more disappointed face than the one she currently wore. I sat up slowly to speak to her, groaning in pain as I did so.

"Mum," I began.

"Alfie Ignatius Alvey!" My mother screeched.

I stood up and slipped on smudged frosting. I managed not to fall to the ground again by supporting myself on the upturned table. I straightened and clasped my hands in front of me. A piece of cake fell from my hair to my lip, giving the appearance of a bulbous wound. I blew out a breath and watched it shoot off my lip and onto the grass. "Mum, I'm so sorry."

Mum held up a hand to her mouth and closed her eyes, on the verge of tears. I swallowed hard. If there was one thing I couldn't deal with in life, it was my mother crying. How was I supposed to deal with the woman who birthed me into this world spilling salty little balls of devastation down her cheeks? Knowing I was the cause was even worse.

She abruptly turned and headed into the house.

"Give me a hand, Alfie."

Dad's quiet voice sounded loud to my ears. I took his hand and lifted him up, then turned to Nika. She was still sitting on the ground, bits of cake all over the front of her shirt. I stared at her with as much venom in my eyes as possible. She held out a hand for my assistance. I ignored it and followed my Mum, as the murmur of chatting guests picked up again.

I found her in the kitchen, standing over a mixing bowl, cracking eggs.

"Mum, I'm so sorry. I didn't mean to let that happen. Nika and I, we're just…" I paused. "Mum, what are you doing?" I watched her curiously as she threw cups of flour at the bowl. The white powder was puffing up in big clouds. Her blue and white dress was peppered, the bench was covered and very little was making it into the bowl.

"I'm starting again!" she snapped.

"What?"

"The cake! It's ruined, so I'm bloody starting again!" She raised a hand to wipe away a tear, smudging flour over her face.

"Mum, stop. That's really not necessary."

"No, it's all ruined. I have to make a new one!"

I grabbed her hands and held her still. "Mum, I don't need a cake, okay? It's all right. It's my fault. I'm sorry."

Mum looked down, slowly took her hands out of mine, and rested them on the bench. She sniffled. "I've just been planning this for so long and you and Nika, you both…you both…"

"I know. We're fighting. We're…it's just the pressure of her coming here and meeting everyone. It's making her crazy. And I'm pretty sure it's…" I pursed my lips. "I'm pretty sure it's that time of the month."

Mum looked at me crossly. "Just because a woman is upset with a man does not mean that she is menstruating!"

"I know," I said, pulling her away from the bowl. "I'm just trying to lighten the mood. Why don't you come back outside and talk to everyone? It will make you feel better. Just tell them she's crazy. She won't mind. I'm sure she feels awful. I'll have a chat to her."

"Okay," Mum whimpered, pressing her head against my chest.

I petted her back and kissed her head. "There we go. It's all okay."

I closed my eyes and let out a deep sigh as my Mum clung tightly to me. It was getting personal now. She made my Mum cry.

Nika was going down.

Twenty-Two

I closed the door to my bedroom, grateful the day had finally ended. Nika was sitting in my bed, her legs up against her chest. I didn't say a word to her as I sat down, comfortable in pyjamas this time.

"Is your Mum okay?" Nika asked.

I chose not to respond. Before changing into my pyjamas in the privacy of the bathroom, I had again been with Mum making sure she was okay. The guests had all left within the hour after the cake was destroyed. We had spent the rest of the evening cleaning up and doing dishes in unhappy silence. We would be the talk of Doddinghurst for the next month, at least. And not in a good way. Mum was already planning another party – to which we had not yet been invited – to replace the bitter memories of her guests with happier ones.

"Alfie," Nika snapped. "I am asking about your Mother. You could answer me."

I sighed. "She's upset. You ruined the party. The whole town was here; she's embarrassed."

"I ruined the party?" Nika hissed.

"Yes." I spun around and faced her. "You ruined it. You pushed me into the cake. I know it might not make sense to you, but my Mum loves parties – she loves to host people, and cook and bake and have a bunch of random people come into her home and trample through everything. It might not be your idea of a good time, and it might not be mine, but that is not the point. Tonight, she was excited to show you off to the town and instead you embarrassed her in front of all of her friends."

"It was your fault!" Nika shouted. "I told you not to touch me again, but you couldn't help it, you…you… you pervert!"

"You were physically assaulting me! What was I supposed to do? Hit you back?"

"Why not?"

I scoffed, continually amazed by her ability to surprise me. "Oh, I don't know. Maybe because I'm not a monster! I don't believe in hitting women! For goodness sake."

"You trampled my foot!"

"Oh, barely. It's not the same as punching you in your face, now is it?"

"I'm not weak!" she cried.

"No," I shook my head. "Of course not. Wouldn't want to show any vulnerabilities. Wouldn't want to remind people that you're human."

We stared at each other, until my breathing had returned to normal. I lay down and brought the duvet up to my ears, ending our conversation.

"You are a pig," she spat, fulfilling her need to have the last word.

"If I'm such a pig," I said, reaching up to flick off the light, "why don't you just go back home?"

We dwelled in silence, surrounded by darkness, for some time before she responded. "Because," she whispered, "I don't have a home."

Twenty-Three

I bit into my toast, with Aslan perched on my lap, frequently stealing crumbs off my plate. With a nice hot cup of tea in front of me, I watched Mum potter about in the kitchen. She was in a better mood this morning, with plans for her next party well underway. Apparently it was going to be themed. I hoped she was still hesitant about my presence at future parties. Dressing up for a themed party on a Sunday afternoon with Mum's friends didn't exactly seem like a thrilling time.

Nika sat opposite me, her plate already empty. She held her own tea, both hands wrapped around the warm cup. She held it just under her nose, appearing blissfully lost in the aroma.

Dad walked in and dropped two sure hands down on my shoulders. "Morning, son."

"Hey, Dad. How's the garden doing?"

He sighed that funny sigh he always did when he wistfully thought of his garden. "Oh, she's doing all right. She's always a little worse for wear after a party. Particularly when there's cake involved." He chuckled, but I knew that the large chocolaty smudge we had hosed down yesterday had messed up his watering routine, upsetting the delicate balance of Dad's water-to-sun ratio. Next to Mum, and possibly – but not yet confirmed – Queenie and me, Dad's garden was the most important thing to him.

"Sorry, Dad. Again."

"Oh, it's really no problem. Just a good story to tell later." He smiled and readjusted his glasses.

He was the most forgiving man I knew. Which would come in handy later.

I loved my family, despite their elevated levels of strangeness. Odd things were deeply important to them – like parties and gardens and Doddinghurst. The way they functioned was, in many ways, rather peculiar. But I was, also in many ways, quite the same.

"Heading off today, then, are we?" Mum was whipping up a batch of muffins, and I couldn't quite tell if she was asking or telling me.

"Uh, yes. After breakfast actually. I have a bit to do before class tomorrow." It was a small lie. I had no study to do before tomorrow, but I wanted to get Nika away from my family as soon as possible.

"Shame." Her voice sounded a little too jovial for her choice of words.

I chuckled. "Admit it, you're happy to get us out of your hair after last night."

Mum looked at me, eyes wide. "No, not at all darling. I just have to make a trip to the shops. The party is going to be in two weeks."

"Sounds like you have your hands full."

Queenie came up behind me and wrapped her arms around my neck. "Morning, Alfie."

I petted her arms. "Morning, Queenie."

"Rocking party last night." She reached over my shoulder and plucked my last piece of toast off the plate.

"Queenie!" Mum chastised. "Alfie needs a good solid breakfast. Make your own toast."

"It's fine, Mum," I said, standing up from the table. She had always been obsessed with ensuring that both Queenie and I ate a hearty breakfast. "I'm full anyway. I'm going to go pack the car."

Aslan followed me to the car with my bags. I was desperate to get home. Nika could do less damage there than she could here. Once I was away from my family and I no longer had to keep up any pretence I could figure out what to do.

I let out a rather feminine squeal when I turned around to head back into the house, after stacking the boot with our bags. Nika was standing in front of me, having appeared out of nowhere like a member of the undead. I smiled when I realised the title undead seemed to suit her.

"We've taken to skulking around now, have we?" I chuckled, then abruptly stopped when I saw Aslan abandoning her clutch on my trouser leg, and instead scampering up into Nika's arms.

Nika laughed, utterly delighted, as she cradled my little Judas in her arms. My eyes narrowed at her spectacular level of malevolence.

"Are you ready to leave?" I asked.

"Why so early?" she asked quietly.

"Do you really have to ask?"

"I told you – last night was not my fault!"

I sighed. "Let's go say goodbye to my parents. Try not to knock anything over, or destroy anything." I looked down at Aslan, comfortable in the arms of my arch enemy, and huffed, before brushing past her. It was going to be a long drive home.

Twenty-Four

It would take a single flick of the steering wheel to run my car off the road and into the line of trees that marked my way back to London, ending it all in some fiery, if not somewhat dramatic, blaze.

Sitting in an enclosed space with Nika made me think of these kinds of things.

We had been in the car for mere moments before she began to torture me with her incessant nattering. Apparently I was to blame for everything from the extinction of the dinosaurs to the inevitable future apocalypse.

I tried, I honestly tried, to let it go, to ignore what she was saying and let it slide out of the corners of my mind. But there is only so much a man can take.

"It is your fault that I am here, and not back in the Czech Republic! You lied to me! You took me away from everything I know and forced me into your ridiculous life. You took me from my home."

"You didn't have a home, remember?" With the windows up, my voice reverberated around the car, stunning her into complete silence. I immediately regretted what I had said. I glanced over at her and took in her brutalised expression. I groaned and waited until I could trust myself to speak at an acceptable volume. "Look, I'm sorry I said that. But I did not bring you here, Nika, and I did not lie to you. My uncle organised this, without speaking a single word to me. Now, you have sufficiently ruined my birthday, made me lie to my parents and embarrassed me in front of everyone in my home town. Where you get off blaming me for all of this, I shall never know. Once we get home, we can figure out what our next step is. But for now, just for now, will you please, please, stop talking?"

It was about then that the very worst thing that could have happened in that moment, unfolded right in front of my eyes. Just when I braced myself for her to rip my head off, she raised her open palms to her face and covered her eyes, bursting into tears.

"No, no, Nika, please don't cry," I moaned, reaching a hand from the steering wheel to tap her shoulder. "I'm sorry. We'll be home soon. Everything will be all right. You'll see."

Nika looked up at me, her eyes brimming with tears. Had I helped her to stop crying, somehow?

"Everything will be all right?" she sniffed.

"Yes," I said, in what I hoped to be a comforting tone, "yes, of course it will be."

"No!" she cried. "No, it won't!"

She threw her face into her palms again and sobbed with ever more fervency.

I screwed up my face in abject terror. This was not good. "Oh, bollocks."

The rest of the drive home was spent in either silence or blubbering sniffles. Aslan let out a weak little screech every time Nika started crying again. When I finally pulled up in front of my house, the relief I felt was so intense that I almost burst out laughing. I opened the door to the house before returning to the car for our bags. Nika slowly emerged from the passenger's seat and took hold of Aslan's cage. She walked directly into the house, head low.

Once all the bags were inside, I found Nika on the lounge, Hugh sitting opposite her. He appeared to be doing a very good impression of someone who believed he was rather suave, but fell quite short of the mark.

"Do you," I paused and clutched at my fingers. "Do you want me to show you around?"

Nika simply stood without speaking.

"Right. This way then."

She followed me around the house as I led her through the kitchen and pointed out our bedrooms. As a two bedroom flat, we were, unfortunately, unable to supply Nika with her own bedroom, unexpected as her arrival was. I was, however, willing to share my bedroom with her. I had a spare mattress under my bed that she was more than welcome to use, though I had the feeling that when the time came it would be me sleeping on the floor, not my feisty, if not suddenly emotionally overloaded, Czech friend.

As I turned to carry on with my tour, I got halfway down the hall, blabbing about the architectural soundness of the building, before I realised she wasn't following me. I headed back down the hall just in time to see her walk back into my bedroom, only this time with her suitcase. I leaned on the doorframe as she started making herself at home, pulling my clothes out of the drawers, dumping them on the ground, and situating her own clothes neatly inside.

"Do you mind?" I asked.

"Not at all," she replied.

"You are going to pick those up, aren't you?"

"I didn't plan to, no."

I sighed angrily and thumped across the floor, bending down to pick up my clothes. Irritated, I shoved them back into the drawer, only to have them immediately thrown back out again.

"Stop that," I hissed.

"You stop it!" she retorted.

I bunched up my clothes and pushed them back in, as Nika, once again, threw them out.

Enough was enough.

Instead of picking up my clothes again, and reliving the same infuriating instant over and over again, I opted to give her a taste of her own medicine. I took hold of a pile of her clothes and threw them over my head, grinning with satisfaction as they slapped against the wall.

Nika paused and stared at me, completely horrified. "How dare you?" she spat.

111

"How dare I?" I scoffed. I opted for her suitcase next, which, to my considerable advantage, had her underpants still inside. I took hold of her unmentionables and flung them across the room.

She screeched at my behaviour and started throwing my clothes in a dozen different directions. When she ran out of ammunition, while I still had her entire wardrobe remaining, she started hitting me, wildly slapping her hands against my chest. It was beginning to become a trend with her. Perhaps I should have told her that Queen and Country frown at domestic violence.

I flailed majestically in a rather pointless attempt to grab her wrists and stop her cat-like assault of my face. I fell back against the bed, Nika falling on top of me. I rolled her over, in a surprisingly impressive display of man-liness, and pinned her down.

"Stop attacking me!" I shouted.

Nika struggled in my grip, shrieking madly. I wondered if she hadn't gone completely mental.

"What the bloody hell are you doing?" Hugh shouted, brazenly walking into my room.

I tried to shout over Nika's inane blabbering. "She was hitting me!"

"So you tackled her?" Hugh snapped.

"No! She tackled me. I just rolled her."

"Get him off me!" Nika shouted. "He's attacking me!"

"Get off her!" Hugh wrapped his arms around my waist and started yanking me.

"I didn't do anything!" I yelled, as Hugh picked me up, my legs kicking out into the air. As I tried to get out of his Herculean grip, my feet gesticulating insanely, my right foot connected hard with something. Something that made an oof sound upon contact.

I immediately stopped thrashing.

Hugh froze.

"What was that?" I asked, still dangling in the air, my back bent uncomfortably over Hugh's girth.

"Oh. Bloody. Norah." Hugh's voice was hollow, as he put me down on the ground.

My eyes fell immediately on Nika, who lay entirely unconscious on my bed, bent into a peculiar position against the wall, a blushing red mark forming across her cheek.

"Oh," I whimpered. "Oh, no."

I had unintentionally knocked Nika out. I had kicked her in the face with my foot, hard enough to actually send her into unconsciousness.

"What the hell did you do?" Hugh gasped.

"Me? You were the one holding me up in the air! I didn't mean to!"

"Look at her!"

I covered my face with my hands. "What are we gonna do?"

"We?" Hugh scoffed. "No, I have somewhere to go. I have to go...do some laundry."

Hugh started to walk out of the room, but I grabbed his collar and tugged him back. "Oh, no. No way. You haven't done a load of laundry since you started university. You're not beginning now. You did this. What are we going to do?"

"Check her pulse," Hugh blurted.

"Her pulse?" I spat. "She's not dead! How could she be d-" I stopped. Abruptly, I stepped forward and reached for her neck. My heart was racing. Had I killed her? What was I going to do if she was...if she was...dead? I couldn't go to prison! I was a weedy ginger! They would eat me alive! I would be someone's toy-boy by morning tea. I placed my hand gently on her warm neck and waited with bated breath. "I can't feel a pulse!" I screeched.

"You killed her!" Hugh cried.

"How?" I shouted. "I couldn't have!"

"Check again!" he shouted. "Make sure you have the right spot."

I swallowed back a bit of vomit. Taking two fingers, I pressed them against her neck, under her jaw. I closed my eyes and tried to concentrate. She had to be alive. She had to be. A bleak future danced in front of me as

I imagined what I would do if she was no longer alive and I had, in fact, ended her life. How would I dispose of the body? Or would I even? Perhaps the guilt would simply be too much and I would have to hand myself over to Scotland Yard. Would Hugh be able to keep his mouth shut if I did try to hide her body? The more likely scenario was that he would bend over and tell the police everything they wanted to know. What countries had no extradition with England?

I tried to silence my mind. I concentrated, trying to feel her pulse. "I feel it!" I shouted, elated. "She's alive! She's alive!"

"Ha!" Hugh erupted. "Ha! She lives! We're not going to prison!"

I sprang up from the bed and hugged Hugh. We jumped up and down like teenage girls who had each just had their first snog.

Our elated dance was soon put to a halt when we realised that if Nika was alive, she was going to wake up at some point. And when she did, she was going to be furious.

We exchanged glances, each keenly aware of what the other was thinking. Together, we slowly backed away from the room and closed the door, dreading the moment when the beast would awaken.

Twenty-Five

It was an entire hour of peace.

No angry woman shouting at me.

No lie to uphold.

No cakes being toppled over.

It was, however, not to last. I heard a door slam and both Hugh and I jumped in unison. We looked up from our episode of Sherlock, towards the hall she would no doubt be walking down. The footsteps were faint at first, before growing steadily more ominous and louder. Hugh and I stole a fearful peek at each other, panic and guilt building to a crescendo in our bloodstreams.

She appeared in our vision as terrifying as Lady Galadriel in The Fellowship of the Ring, at the point in the film where she grows green and frightening, with glowing eyes and flying hair. We both stood up, clasping our hands in front of us, like we were naughty children about to get reprimanded by our cranky Headmistress.

I thought it would be best to start by saying something. But when I opened my mouth to speak, nothing happened. I stared at her, open-mouthed, petrified into some sort of comatose state.

Folding her arms across her chest, Nika took slow and deliberate steps towards me, until she stood directly in front of us. We dropped down onto the couch. She seemed taller, somehow.

"H-hello, Nika," I stuttered.

"You look lovely," Hugh said. "Really. Beautiful. That glow of your face – do you use a special moisturiser or?"

Nika held up a single finger to silence us. We both flinched unconsciously.

"Do you," she began, breathing slowly to keep herself steady. "I mean, I…" She placed her hands determinedly on her hips. "I remember you on top of me, Alfie. I remember you attacking me. I remember you kicking me in face. In face! Since I woke up with a headache, in an empty room, my instincts tell me that I was knocked unconscious!"

"Nika-" I began.

"No!" she shouted. "I am not finished. What is wrong with you? I should go to the police."

"There's no need for that," Hugh said, standing up, with an outstretched hand, as if trying to approach a wild lion.

"Sit. Down," she spat.

Hugh dropped slowly to the couch, placing his hands daintily in his lap.

"It was an accident, Nika," I said firmly. "I'm sorry. But you attacked me. Then Hugh grabbed me, and I was just trying to get free. You got in the way. It was all just one big accident. It's funny really, if you look at it that way."

Hugh hissed in a breath, warning me.

I realised in that moment, as Nika's eyes grew wide and dark, that I had said something wrong.

"Funny?" she snarled. "Funny?"

I blinked, silent.

Nika laughed. Not a happy-go-lucky, everything's all right, kind of laugh. It was more Jack Nicholson, less Mary Poppins.

"Funny," she said, waving her hands in the air.

I started to feel like I had crossed the Godfather and was going to wake up tomorrow with a horse's head in my bed. Or perhaps my head would be in a horse's bed.

Abruptly, Nika stopped laughing. She leaned close, her lips beside my ears. "We will see how funny you think it is soon. We…will…see."

She rolled to the side and sat down on the couch beside me. "So, honey," she said, "what are we watching?"

"Um, Sherlock," I muttered. "It's about these two-"

"Oh, I love Benedict Cumberbatch. Is this the new season?"

Hugh and I exchanged confused glances. "Yeah. It is."

"Well, press play."

I tried to sit at ease on the couch, and raised the remote for the most uncomfortable episode of Sherlock yet.

Twenty-Six

Staring up at the pock-marked ceiling, I wondered how I had allowed myself to be relegated to the living room. With my legs hanging over the arm of the lounge chair, I was forced to wriggle my toes to keep blood moving.

What was I going to do? Just…live with her for the rest of my life?

She was going to make my life a waking nightmare. I was living in Fatal Attraction.

I sat up and rubbed my face. I just had to think rationally. Consider my options, and move forward in a logical, unemotional way. In mere months, I was to officially become a solicitor. I could handle this situation. I had a squatter. A life-squatter. I just had to get rid of her.

It was then that the idea hit me like a bolt of lightning. It sent a tingle down my spine, all the way to my blood-reduced feet. The idea took root, right in the pit of my stomach, and sprouted green tufts in record time. My idea was simple. Legal, even.

I could have her deported.

Yes. So simple. All I had to do was contact the appropriate authorities, and mention that a mail-order-bride had been thrust upon me – an unwilling accomplice. I would assure them I had no plans whatsoever to actually marry the newt, and they would send her packing back to the Czech Republic on the next flight out.

I would be free.

She would be gone. Forever.

Then I would decide if I was ever going to speak to Oswald again.

There was something else sprouting in the pit of my stomach, right next to my blossoming idea. I couldn't quite put my finger on it.

I tried to shake it away, but it was most definitely there.

I lay back down and closed my eyes, attempting to push away the intrusive feeling with sleep, but it appeared sleep was not such a willing participant in my denial. That's when I realised what this uneasy, uncertain feeling was.

Guilt.

I scoffed out loud, rolling over to face the back of the lounge. Guilt! Whatever would I need to feel guilty for? This woman had done nothing but attempt to ruin my life since she entered it! Surely it wasn't wrong to send her back home, to the place she was born and raised.

True, she said she had no family, and didn't have what one would classify as a home, but was that my problem? I submit that it was not.

I was going to have her deported and end this hideous affair.

Twenty-Seven

Does anyone really stop to enjoy a sunrise anymore? I mean, a stunning, unique painting, is splashed across the sky every morning. New and glorious, each day.

Birds tweet their merry little tunes as the clouds turn into puffy pink piles of candyfloss. Golden rays stretch their long fingers up towards the heavens, as if the sun is heaving itself out of bed.

Today's sunrise was beautiful. I knew this because I saw it through the living room window. I saw it through the living room window because I was unable to get even a wink of sleep.

I threw my legs over the side of the lounge and sat up. I was the human equivalent of porridge that had been sitting on the bench all day. Nika walked in, towel drying her hair, looking refreshed and well-rested.

"Good morning," she said curtly.

"Morning," I groaned. "I trust you slept well." I added under my breath, "In my bed."

"I did, actually. Very comfortable."

She walked into the kitchen and prepared herself a glass of water and a piece of toast. I watched her move around my kitchen like she belonged here, and I wanted to peel my own skin off with a potato peeler.

She flicked the kettle on, found the stash of teas – a wide and varied selection I was quite proud of – and made herself a tea. Of course, everyone knows proper etiquette is to ask if the person in the same room as you would like a cup of tea also, but I was beginning to understand that Nika was the sort of person from whom I could expect little more than a proper burial after she proved to be the death of me.

I marched over to the kitchen and began the assembly of my own tea, hoping that each aggressive movement was getting my subliminal message across to her subconscious.

I took sweet satisfaction in knowing that today I would be notifying the proper authorities of her unwanted presence in my life and my apartment, and I would be enjoying the sweet relief from her invasion shortly. I smirked to myself, like a happy pig who had just had a bowl of delicious slop plopped down in front of him. Fat with joy.

"What is happening to your face?" Nika's voice pierced my reverie.

"What? Nothing. What's wrong with my face?"

"Something weird is happening to your lips."

She began to poke holes in my air, and I shooed her hand away.

"I assure you my face is as God made it."

She nodded, a knowing expression coming over her face. "Ah. That must be the problem then."

I resisted the urge to commit a major crime in my kitchen.

She smiled sweetly, lifted her tea to her mouth and inhaled the sweet aroma. She was so pretty when she didn't open her mouth.

Hugh thudded his way into the kitchen, barely classifying as a human before nine in the morning. Unfortunately, a lot of his classes started at eight.

He groaned something unintelligible, and I passed him the tea I had just made myself. He took it gratefully and sat down at the table, moaning.

Our little morning routine, which had been largely uninterrupted throughout the time we had lived together, was now impeded by Nika's presence. I wanted to discuss my plans with Hugh to eradicate her from my life for good, but to do so was impossible with her standing right there.

I would have to wait for the opportune moment, like Captain Jack Sparrow would.

Twenty-Eight

The opportune moment, it seemed, would be hard to come by. Everywhere I turned, Nika was there. Hugh, her ever-doting follower, was never far from her side, swooning over her like she was an Amazonian queen.

I took the only chance I could get, and scurried into the bathroom, while he was showering. Mercifully, there was a curtain to separate us, but he was nonetheless displeased to learn I was in there with him.

"Hugh!" I hissed. "Hugh!"

"Is that you, God?" Hugh asked, with genuine earnestness.

"It's me, Alfie."

Hugh stuck his head outside the curtain, to behold me with his own eyes.

"What the bloody hell are you doing in here?" he hissed.

"I need to talk to you," I whispered.

Hugh wiped soap suds off his face. "Then make me a cuppa and sit down on the lounge with me like a normal person."

"Away from Nika. I have to talk to you away from Nika."

He sighed, resigned to the fact that I was not going to leave until I had my say. "What is it?"

I leaned in as close as the limited decorum between us would allow and whispered, "I've figured out how to get rid of her."

The rolling of Hugh's eyes was my first indication that he was uninterested in the direction this conversation was taking. "I still don't understand why you're so desperate to be free of her. Our standing is higher than ever at class, you know. Everyone I've told thinks we're total studs now."

"You've told people?"

Hugh looked at me as if I were a simpleton. "Of course, I've told people. Why would I miss this opportunity? This sort of thing doesn't happen to everyone, you know."

I threw up my hands, exasperated. "I see."

"What's your plan, then?" he asked.

"I'm going to report her."

"What do you mean?"

"I'm going to report her to the authorities. She's on a fiancé visa, I presume. If there's no fiancé, she can't stay."

Hugh stared blankly at me. The hissing of the shower was the only sound. I started to fidget uncomfortably, until he finally spoke, his disapproval palpable. "Right. So, by report you mean deport?"

"I guess," I admitted, sheepishly.

"Wow. Cold."

It was the first time I could ever recall Hugh looking at me like that. Like someone he didn't even recognise.

"Cold? It's not cold! This woman has come out of nowhere and is ruining my life. What do you think was going to happen here? Did you think I was actually going to marry her?"

"I guess," he shrugged.

"Are you insane?"

"I thought you made a cute couple. I'd marry her, if it was me."

"Well, let's trade then."

"Alfie, I freely admit that I am not a genius when it comes to women. I know this. I accept this. But even I know they don't like to be traded like playing cards."

"That's not what I meant," I sighed.

"You can't deport her, Alfie. It's stone cold evil."

"Actually, it's completely lawful," I said, swallowing the lump rising in my throat. The guilt in my stomach was gnawing at my innards like a hyena chomping on the rotting remains of a gazelle carcass. "I would be upholding British law and all things good and upright. A true hero of the Commonwealth."

Hugh clicked his tongue and shook his head sadly. "I can't let you do it, mate."

"What's that supposed to mean?" I asked.

"It means, as soon as I'm out of this shower and decent once more, I will stop you from doing this."

I scoffed. "You can't stop me."

"Uh, I believe I can."

"I'd like to see you try," I challenged.

"And try I shall. If you ever leave this bloody room, where I am currently soapy and naked, a position I never planned to be in with you."

I nodded. "Fair." I turned around and walked out. As I closed the door behind me, I shook my head in disgust. This woman was now turning friend against friend.

She had to go.

Twenty-Nine

The first thing I was going to do was discuss this with my professor. He was wise and knowledgeable and he would know exactly what steps I would have to take to get Nika out of here prontissimo.

But now the race was on. If I knew one thing about Hugh it was that he was a bulldog. When he was determined to do something, he would see it through, no matter what. If he said he was going to stop me from reporting Nika, he meant it.

I needed to get out of the house quickly.

I heard the shower turn off. Panic grew in my chest.

I ran to my room and threw on my jumper. In my haste, I half strangled myself in the sleeves, but after a painful alien-birth like situation, I managed to squeeze my awkward frame into my jumper and reach for my bag. I stuffed my belongings inside it and threw it over my shoulder. It was when I arrived at the front door that I realised I wasn't wearing any shoes.

I sprinted back to my room in time to hear the door to the bathroom open.

"You can run all you like, Alfie." Hugh's voice echoed down the hall. "But like the great Liam Neeson, I will find you."

I stuffed my feet into my shoes, and ran out of my room, tripping over the blanket strewn haphazardly on the floor.

Blast it, my mother was right. I should always make my bed.

I slammed down on the floor, landing with impressive intensity on my right shoulder. I didn't have time to marinate in my pain. I had to get out of here.

Up on my feet once more, I made my way down the stairs as quickly as I could. The door was within reach. I could taste freedom.

Then, like a siren appearing to a tired, wounded sailor at his most vulnerable moment, Nika appeared in front of me. Her eyes were narrow, suspicious.

I screeched like a little girl, recoiling from her presence.

"Where are you going?" she asked. "Why do you look so scared?"

"I'm not scared," I said, a little breathlessly. "I'm just… uh… late. I'm late for class."

"Oh," Nika said, seemingly somewhat deflated.

Her reaction took me by surprise. Was she… disappointed?

"What's wrong?" I asked.

"Nothing," she said, a little too quickly. "I just thought you might show me around London today. I've always wanted to see Big Ben."

"Oh," I said weakly.

"It's fine. There's plenty of time. I live here now." She smiled a little. "I guess I'm a Londoner, now. Go to class." Nika turned away and headed for the kitchen.

The stab of guilt in my stomach was almost enough to kill me.

Almost.

I heard Hugh thudding down the hall. He would be at the top of the stairs any moment.

I threw myself out the door and into the street.

I waved my hand frantically, hoping for a cab. I heard the door behind me open.

"I see you, Alfie," Hugh crowed.

I started to trot down the street, flailing my hand like I was batting away a swarm of bees.

Hugh slowly descended our front steps and began to follow me.

Finally, a cab pulled up beside me. Before it had come to a complete stop, I was inside it, ushering the driver on.

I checked behind me to see Hugh standing in the street, arms folded across his chest. I laughed maniacally, bloated with my success, until I saw him pull his phone out of his pocket.

I abruptly stopped laughing.

I knew exactly what he was doing.

He was calling for reinforcements.

Thirty

Despite his eccentricities, Hugh was one of those people everybody loved. He attracted good friends. Not the kind of friends that are good for a laugh, or good to go to the pub with. But real friends. Ride or die friends, as Dominic Torretto would say.

I put it down to his general nature. He was kind. One of the kindest, biggest-hearted people I had ever known. His family was wealthy – ludicrously so – but he never took a pound from them, because he wanted to make his own way. That's why he was living in a crappy apartment with me in Wandsworth, instead of a city-centre flat overlooking Hyde Park.

He was always the first to introduce himself to new people, not because he was ostentatious, but because he knew what it felt like to be the new, lonely kid in school. He was goofy and lovable, and kind of ridiculous, but in the best way. He attracted the best people, quite simply because he was the best person.

Unfortunately for me, in this particular situation, it meant that he would be calling people who would run to his aide immediately, no matter what they were doing. I didn't have to think hard to know who it would be that Hugh was calling for backup in his pursuit of me.

Dark Lord and Wizard.

Of course those two Vitamin D deficient ding-dongs would be the ones he called upon to stop me from doing the only logical thing I could do in my predicament. After it was done, Hugh would understand. I couldn't marry Nika. Surely Hugh could see that. We would recover from this.

Wouldn't we?

I sat back into the seat and wiped sweat off my brow.

The truth was that telling my professor was a copout. Once I told him, I knew that stuffed-shirt would be biologically incapable of allowing me to fail on following through with reporting Nika. If I didn't do it, he would do it for me.

Maybe that's what I was hoping for.

I could only imagine what I would say – or possibly even do – to Uncle Oswald if he was here. How could he do this to me? How could he upend my life like this?

I found myself thinking altogether ungodly things. I wanted to hurt him the way he had hurt me. Perhaps I should sell all of the items he had given me. They were worth a fortune. Until now, it had never even crossed my mind to sell them, because they were special. They were hunted down, discovered, dug out of the earth, and then given to me. Selling them was never an option, but now, sitting in the back of a cab that smelled like moth balls and old socks, with a driver who kept humming show tunes, I felt the need to strip my home of everything Oswald had ever touched. My best friend on the planet was chasing me down, Cruella De Vil had taken up residency in my bedroom, and my entire family was under the impression I was getting married in a matter of weeks.

Maybe the special bond I thought we had was nothing but a joke to him.

I had never felt like I really belonged anywhere. I felt like somewhat of a fool in my family. Throughout my horrible teen years, Oswald's frequent gifts and visits to me had always been a reminder that I belonged. That someone thought I mattered.

Now, I felt nothing but cold.

Until we came to a dead stop in the middle of the street, and then I felt intense anxiety.

"Excuse me," I said to the driver, "can we go a different way?"

"Nothing to be done about it now, lad," the cabbie answered in his thick, northern accent. "There's another protest. All the streets are bloody jammed."

I groaned, wondering what my next step would be. If this was a movie, and I was Tom Cruise, or Tom Hardy, or some other equally dashing actor named Tom, I would get out of the car and run.

But this was not a movie, and I was no athlete.

So, I waited.

We moved almost five hundred feet in twenty minutes. By London protest standards, that was pretty good.

I used the time to attempt to meditate and calm myself down. I had never meditated before, and when I emerged from my attempt feeling more frustrated than ever, I decided I wouldn't ever mediate again.

As I opened my eyes, I looked around to see when we might be able to move freely again. Unfortunately, my eyes fell on Hugh, Dark Lord and Wizard traipsing down the street, looking like members of a 90's grunge band out on a photoshoot.

My eyes met Hugh's through the back windshield.

My stomach rolled.

I pulled out my wallet, handed the cabbie his due, and stumbled out the door.

I had never considered myself athletic, but I was going to give running a good go, anyway. Hugh, Dark Lord and Wizard took off after me. I only hoped that my limited skills in long (or short) distance running would be slightly better than theirs.

Of course, about two minutes in I was bent over in pain, gasping for air.

Hugh and the vampires were close. I straightened and hobbled on. I could hear Hugh wheezing behind me. To anyone watching, we must have looked like the saddest of all morons.

But I was ahead of them, and that was what mattered. I just had to make it to the professor's office before them.

But Hugh was nothing if not a master, and my cavalier attitude of waiting in the car for so long had come back to haunt me. Hugh didn't need to catch up to me first. Nika appeared in front of me, instead.

The perfect road block.

"There you are," she said brightly.

"N-Nika?" I stuttered.

"Hugh told me to meet you here."

"He did?" I said lamely.

"He said you'd changed your mind about showing me around London today."

"He did?" I repeated.

"He did," Hugh answered, somewhat breathlessly, arriving beside me and slapping my back jovially.

Dark Lord and Wizard, catching their breath, nodded their agreement.

Superstar athletes, the lot of us.

"Oh," I chuckled weakly. "Of course. Yes. London." Nika was looking at me with such hopeful expectancy that there was little else for me to do than say, "Let's go, shall we?"

Nika smiled, and for a moment I was struck deaf and dumb, because, objectively speaking, she was the most beautiful monster in the world.

She clapped her hands together and looped her arms between mind and Hugh's. The look on his face said it all. He was hers, completely. Between cake and Nika, he would choose Nika, no contest.

That was saying something.

Hugh really liked cake.

I looked over Nika's head to Hugh. His self-satisfied grin was odorous to me.

He had won this battle.

Thirty-One

I had never really looked at London through a tourist's eyes, but watching Nika's lips stretch into a grin every time she saw something new and exciting had me acting every bit the newbie.

Big Ben was our first stop, and as she looked up at the famous clock-tower, I was tasked with capturing the moment on my phone. From there, we hopscotched around, wandering through the Strand, strolling down cobblestone streets, and enjoying the National Gallery. Dark Lord and Wizard were quite fascinated with the collection of Van Gogh's, and it surprised me that somehow, I had actually never stepped foot inside the gallery.

There was something about walking around next to enormous canvasses, painted hundreds of years ago, that made me feel like a little part of something bigger. Nika was quiet, wandering past the art that seemed to speak to her somehow. There was a chance that it was the fact that Nika barely spoke a word the entire time that made the National Gallery such a joyful experience. I liked to watch her. Not in a creepy, murder-y way (although, there had been times I had considered removing her head from her body), but in a peaceful, comfortable way. She was nice to look at. She had a calm face, when she wasn't screeching at me, and she moved with a ballerina-like grace, like she was floating, instead of walking. When she was deep in thought, her lips pursed a little, crumpling at the sides, creating dimples in her cheeks.

It was all very pleasant until we got kicked out.

Wizard had been desperate for a photo next to a Van Gogh, and when I offered to be the one who took the photo, I didn't realise he meant right next to a Van Gogh. He even touched it, and that's when a very angry looking security guard marched over and escorted us all out of the building.

We stood there, silently, on the steps of the Gallery, as the security guard walked back inside. Like chastised children, lined up for a spanking, we waited until he was behind closed doors until we erupted in laughter. Nika laughed so hard she could barely breathe, and I thought in that moment, there was very little I wouldn't give to hear that sound again.

While walking along the River Thames, there was a small part of me that was quite happy that Hugh had stopped me from seeing my professor today. I hadn't had a day to just be in as long as I could remember. I had been focusing so hard on finishing my degree, that I hadn't spared any thought for a day off, or fun, or living.

I made a mental note to remember that fun was a good thing.

It was at the gates of Buckingham palace that I saw Nika wipe her eye. She walked away from us, and as Hugh, Wizard and Dark Lord offered their photography services to a very large group of Japanese school students, I followed Nika.

"Is everything all right?" I asked, confused. She seemed upset. I thought she was happy.

"I'm fine," she answered, sniffing.

"What is it, Nika?" I asked quietly.

"I just… never thought I would be standing here."

"What do you mean?" I asked.

"If you knew where I had come from, you would understand how unlikely it is for me to be standing in London, looking at Buckingham Palace right now. I never thought I would escape."

"What did you escape from?" I asked.

Nika wiped her eyes and forced a smile. She looked over my shoulder at Hugh, who was suddenly standing between all the Japanese students, pulling superhero poses. She laughed and walked over to him, and just like that the moment of realness was gone.

Piccadilly Circus was alive and bustling, as we sat at a table by the window, overlooking the busy street.

Dark Lord was talking, and Nika and the others were laughing, so whatever he was saying must have been funny, but I couldn't think about anything other than Nika's face outside Buckingham Palace.

There was something I didn't know. Something she may never tell me. But one thing was for sure, I could never send her back there.

I felt sick at how close I had come to sending her back to whatever nightmare she had left. Honestly, I also felt a little sick at the lack of options it left me.

I was lying to my family. My parents were daydreaming about my impending wedding, and even my sister – who I had never lied to before – was preparing to be maid of honour. I couldn't keep up the charade, but ending it would prove disastrous to Nika. She couldn't apply to switch her visa to something that didn't require wedding bells, while residing within the UK. She would have to go home, and who knew how long the visa application would take? And even then, how was she going to live here on her own?

Hugh leaned over to me, his voice low. "This is nice, innit?"

If I could get out of my own head, maybe it would be nice. Wandering around London with Nika and the guys had been fun, I had to admit, but now I was feeling all kinds of low.

Our food arrived, saving me from having to commit to an answer.

There had to be something I could do. Something to help her and save me.

I lifted a sauce-drenched chip to my mouth, and watched as Hugh spilled an enormous globule of tomato sauce on his shirt. Nika laughed and took a serviette and cleaned it up for him. Dark Lord and Wizard munched into their burgers. If every day was like this, maybe having Nika around wouldn't be so bad.

I stuffed another chip in my mouth and sighed, knowing I wouldn't send her away. Until I figured out what to do, she would stay with me.

Thirty-Two

I waited a preposterously long time for Nika to be done in the bathroom, and when she finally emerged, I waded into the room, thick with steam, and stripped in preparation to shower the day away.

I wiped the fog off the bathroom mirror and pulled only three different poses in the mirror before establishing for certain that nothing had changed, and I was still a weedy git.

Unfortunately, it was during my third pose, which involved my leg up on the counter and my best supermodel face, that the door swung wide open and Nika walked in.

Upon seeing me, she screamed.

Upon seeing her, I screamed.

I was unable to determine who, at that moment, had the more girlish scream, but my money was on me. The embarrassment of being caught completely naked, posing in front of the mirror, my gentleman sausage swaying in the breeze, was more than I could bear.

If a piano had fallen through my ceiling and crushed me at that very moment, I would have been grateful.

But life is a cruel thing, and it did not see fit for my embarrassment to end there.

Hugh, convinced there must have been a knife-wielding maniac in our home, or at least a sizeable spider, came running down the hall and into the bathroom, where he was taken quite by surprise at my nakedness.

"Bloody hell!" he shouted, covering Nika's horrified eyes. "Cover your pork sword, Alfie!"

Hugh, Nika's gallant rescuer, dragged her out of the bathroom and slammed the door. I rushed to the doorknob and locked it.

Breathless, my heart racing in my chest, I closed my eyes and tried to pretend that it had all been a terrible dream, but the fact that my man bits had literally just recoiled back into my body was indicative of the fact that the horror that had just occurred was going to live on in my memories forever.

I crawled into the shower, sat beneath the spout, my arms wrapped around my knees, and prayed for the apocalypse.

I snuck out of the bathroom, after looking both ways down the hall to ensure Nika and Hugh were nowhere to be found. I ran as quietly and quickly as I could, into the living room and threw myself under the blanket on the lounge I was to call my new bed.

Why had she come back into the bathroom?

Why had I not locked the door?

How was I going to face her – or Hugh, for that matter – ever again?

Perhaps I could change my name and get plastic surgery to change my face. There was no other way, surely. I couldn't live with what had just happened. I had to run far away. Surgery, however, was expensive. And painful. Maybe I could just move to another country. England was out of the question. News of my shame would spread far and wide. I had to go somewhere much further. Bali, perhaps. That was about as far away as I could get.

I heard footsteps and immediately closed my eyes, pretending to be asleep.

"Do you think he's awake?" Nika whispered.

Hugh's hoarse whisper replied, "If he is, he's probably thinking about moving overseas to escape his total mortification. Or changing his face."

It scared me how well that man knew me.

Footsteps entered the living room. I did my best to look either dead or asleep.

"He's asleep," Nika said quietly.

"Or he's faking it because he's embarrassed enough to die."

I needed to get new friends.

"I hope he doesn't feel like that," Nika said sympathetically.

"Oh. He does. Trust me. See, Alfie is a tender-hearted creature. He's proper, and innocent and, well, childlike. He must be handled delicately."

Or kill the friend I had.

"Oh," Nika replied. "No wonder he hates me."

"He doesn't hate you."

Nika scoffed. "Yes, he does."

"Maybe just a little bit."

"Well, the feeling is mutual," she snapped.

It was remarkable how much that hurt.

"He's a good guy, Nika," Hugh said. "Bit odd? Sure. Total geek? Absolutely. Friend to all animals, weird and smelly? Always. But still good. Possibly the best."

"Maybe," Nika whispered. "If you say so."

As Nika and Hugh walked away, I opened my eyes and stared at the ceiling. My cheeks were burning, like a hot poker had just jabbed me in the face.

Thirty-Three

Monday involved back-to-back classes from the beginning of the day to four in the afternoon. I arrived home at around five, after a relatively peaceful day of complicated lectures and bad food. Perhaps during any other week, I would have rather loathed the day, boring as it was, but I was happy to float through it, unconcerned, because it meant I was not with Nika. I was alone. Blissfully alone.

Upon arriving home, however, I discovered that Nika's state of singularity had not been quite as enjoyable for her. I found her standing at the backdoor, staring at a spider's web, complete with a little Daddy Long Legs.

"What are you doing?" I asked.

Nika wiped her hand across her face, and I realised, quite taken aback, that she was crying.

"What's wrong?" I asked.

"Look at him," she moaned.

I looked down at the small spider, pottering happily along his web. "Right. Okay." I tried desperately to determine what she wanted from me. "Do you…do you want me to kill it?"

Nika gasped, horrified. "Why would you say something like that?"

"Well, I'm sorry, it's just that you're staring at a spider in tears, and usually, in my experience, with my Mum at least, that means you want it, uh, you want it…dead."

Nika clasped a hand to her chest. "I never kill spiders."

"Never? Not even the really poisonous ones?" I screwed up my face in confusion.

"No!"

I raised my hands in defeat. "Okay, okay. Well, what do you want me to do?"

"Nothing," she sniffed.

"Then why are you crying?"

"Because…because…because…"

I waited, expectant. Surely something horrible had happened. Had she been bitten? But then, I didn't think that Daddy Long Legs had fangs quite long enough to bite people. Or was that just a myth? Should I take her to the hospital? Was she going to die? "Nika?"

She sniffed and her lips quivered as she spoke. "He's just so alone."

My brows furrowed.

The spider was…alone?

"Uh, is he?" I asked. "I personally think he looks quite happy, sitting there in his little web."

"Sitting there alone! How could he be happy when he is always by himself? Look at him! He looks so sad."

I tilted my head to the side and looked back down at the oblivious spider. I wasn't sure how the tiny little pinprick of a body, the eyes of which were simply not visible, could possibly look sad. I tipped my head to the other side to get a better vantage point, but it was to no avail.

"I'm sorry, I just, I don't see it." I leaned forward and squinted a little.

"Oh, forget it," she sighed.

"Why are you so upset about the spider?" I asked.

"Because we are kindred spirits!"

"Kindred spirits?" I repeated. "You and the spider are kindred spirits?"

That explained a lot.

"Yes!"

"How exactly is that?"

Apart from the obvious shared trait of lethal venom stored somewhere inside the mouth.

"Because I have been cooped up in here for days!" she yelled.

139

"Oh."

"I have no life! What am I supposed to do, just wait around for you to come home, so I can cook you dinner as if I am going to be your wife when I am not?"

"Firstly, I never asked you to cook. Secondly, you have never cooked for me. Thirdly, what do you want from me?" I asked. "I have to go to class. That's how one graduates."

"I want to know why."

"Why what?"

"I want to know why your uncle did this to me. I was promised a home. A life. And if you do not want me, then I must go to him." She jutted out her chin, determination on her face. "I cannot stay here. I am not allowed!"

"What do you mean, go to him?"

"If you will not have me, we must find your Uncle and he must take me."

"You want to find my uncle?"

Nika nodded. "Yes."

"He's overseas. Who knows where? How do you suppose we get to him?"

"The same way I got here. We fly."

I laughed. "With what money?"

Nika shrugged and screwed up her face as if the answer was obvious. "Yours. Of course."

"M-mine? My money? I…I…I mean that would take up all of my savings. Every penny!"

Nika's jaw set and her eyes went hard. "It's that or I make your life a living nightmare."

I tried to scoff. I tried to wave my hand fervently to dismiss her. I tried to shake my head. But I ended up just sort of blowing little spit bubbles out of the corners of my mouth.

"You know, I spoke to the neighbours today. They were very interested to hear that we were getting married. They thought I was so kind."

"You? Kind?" I stuttered.

"Yes, seeing as how I was marrying you to keep your secret from your family."

"What secret?"

"Oh. You and Hugh. Your love affair, I told them, is a truly romantic thing. Your parents don't understand though, and so I, your loyal friend, chose to marry you so that your secret could remain hidden from your parents."

I ground my teeth together in fury.

"Your neighbours promised to keep your secret. They said they always suspected it. You two make a lovely couple, they said."

"You told the neighbours I am in…in…love with Hugh? With Hugh?" I hissed. "Don't you think if I was that way inclined, I would go for someone who changed his shirt more than once a week?"

"Well, the heart wants what the heart wants." Nika smiled sweetly. "I plan to meet the neighbours on other side tomorrow. Unless, of course, we have other plans."

"The other side."

"What?"

"It's the other side. Not other side."

Nika sucked in an angry breath. "I know! Only sometimes I slip up. I try. English is a stupid language."

"And yet it's the most widely spoken language in the world. Funny that."

"Shut up, pig."

"Why are you doing this to me?" I moaned.

"Put yourself in my shoes! What would you do? Wouldn't you go crazy?"

"So, you want me to spend all of my money to return you to Uncle Oswald so that you no longer set about ruining my life. Well, that feels like a win, win situation, doesn't it?"

Nika's eyes had become narrow. I suddenly felt rather small.

"What have I done now?" I asked.

"Return me?" she snarled. "Like a pair of jeans, or a faulty television?"

"Now, that's not what I meant."

"You have no regard for me at all."

"That's not true."

"Am I not even human to you?"

"Nika," I groaned. "Please."

"We are going to find him."

"I don't even know where to begin, Nika."

She smiled suddenly and relaxed. "I do. I called your Mum today. He's in India."

"India? I can't afford to go to India!"

"Of course, you can. Besides, I stole your credit card before you left this morning. We leave tomorrow at ten." She grinned at me and walked away. "I'm going to go pack."

I watched her, my hand clutched at a sudden stabbing pain in my chest.

"I really like her."

I hadn't noticed Hugh had been listening to our conversation, though I presumed that to remain incognito was his intention all along. He slapped me on the shoulder, in a weak attempt at support.

"Is this what it feels like to have a heart attack?" I wheezed.

"Nope," Hugh grinned. "This is what it feels like to have a fiancé."

Thirty-Four

"What do you mean the tickets are non-refundable?" I asked in a state of shock. "I told you, I didn't actually order these tickets! Someone else used my card."

"I understand that, sir," the woman on the end of the phone crooned in her most soothing voice. "But unfortunately, it's an issue you will have to take up with your bank. We cannot refund this ticket within 24 hours of the flight."

"But I do not want to fly to India tomorrow. I don't want to fly to India ever. I am one of those live-in-London-die-in-London people."

"I see," she said, sympathetically.

"Haven't you heard that famous quote by Samuel Johnson?"

"No, sir, I'm afraid I haven't."

I scoffed. "Well, allow me to introduce you to a statement I live by. "Sir, when a man is tired of London, he is tired of life; for there is in London all that life can afford."

"I would like to take this opportunity to inform you I am in fact a woman," she said a little tersely.

"Not sir, you sir. Sir, the quote, sir."

"I'm afraid you're losing me, Mr Alvey."

"Look," I sighed, ready to rip my hair out and start eating it. "I need to cancel the tickets. Someone took my card and bought two tickets to India. I do not want to go to India. So please refund me."

"As I've already mentioned, I cannot refund the tickets with less than 24 hours until the flight. The system will not allow me. I suggest you call your bank and open an official investigation."

"An investigation?"

"Yes. To prosecute whoever stole your details and bought the tickets."

I sat down on the edge of the lounge. "But I already know who did it."

"Then you might want to call the bank and the police, and have the situation handled by the proper authorities."

Foolishly, the thought that Nika had in fact committed a crime hadn't really entered my mind. Perhaps the what's mine is yours part of marriage had already taken a hold of my malleable brain. "The police? But that would mean she'd be arrested," I said, stating the obvious.

"Yes, sir. Is that something you would like to pursue?"

The thought of having Nika arrested landed solidly on my amygdala and lingered there. That would solve all my problems. One little phone call, and away she goes. A little tingle ran up my spine as the image of Nika in a black and white striped suit with a ball and chain tied to her foot rippled across my mind.

"Sir?" the voice on the phone prompted.

"Yes?"

"Is that something you would like to pursue?"

I rubbed my face with enough force to mutilate my expression, dragging the skin of my eyes so far down there was a chance they would pop right out of their sockets.

"No," I said through gritted teeth, "I don't want her arrested."

"Then you'll be happy to know your flight is confirmed for tomorrow morning. Please arrive at the airport at least two hours early. Have a wonderful evening, Mr. Alvey."

I hung up the phone and resisted the urge to throw it across the room. Aslan, sensing my displeasure, scuttled across the floor, and sat in my lap. She began searching my hair for foreign objects. I petted her back, appreciating her gesture of love.

Looks like I was going to India, whether I wanted to or not.

India. Whatever was I supposed to do in India? How were we going to find Oswald? I had never flown further than Ireland before, where we spent summers when I was a child. Now I was supposed to fly all the way to India?

Tomorrow.

Nika walked into the living room and dropped her bags, stuffed to the brim. She was full of self-satisfaction. Oh, how I loathed her.

"Happy?" I asked acidly.

"As close as I can come," she answered.

"You know you've committed a crime, right? I could have you arrested."

"Do it," she snapped. "At least I'd be welcome in prison."

"You can't seriously think that living with me is worse than living in prison," I gasped.

"I've spent my entire life not being wanted, Alfie. I have no desire to spend the rest of it the same way."

Hugh walked in and slapped his hands together, gleefully. "Right. The lads are coming round tonight for a last hurrah before you two head off."

My eyes bugged wide. "You knew about this?"

"Of course. I think it's a great idea. It was very generous of you to pay for the flights, Alfie."

"Ah. Nika told you that?"

Nika quickly interjected. "I told him you didn't want me to feel lonely anymore, and that you said Oswald would know what to do. You bought the tickets before I could stop you."

"That does sound so much like me," I rumbled.

"I told her you'd come through in the end," Hugh said happily. "The Wiz and the Lord are on their way and we shall eat pizza and play games and eat more pizza."

Hands on his hips, Hugh protruded his stomach into the living room, rocking back and forth on his toes. He grinned, oblivious to the growing tension between Nika and I.

When the thought, I wish I could be more like Hugh crossed my mind, I realised I had entered a dark place.

145

Thirty-Five

Dark Lord and Wizard arrived together, each sporting boxes of pizza. I was relieved to see them. Nika seemed to like them, and their presence would hopefully put an end to the ice forest I was suddenly living in.

I excused myself to head upstairs and pack, while they got started setting up board games.

I carefully packed shirts and trousers into a suitcase, then added a couple of extra pairs into my carry-on. I retrieved my passport from my top drawer and tried not to blubber like an infant as I packed it into my carry-on rucksack.

My phone buzzed in my pocket. It was Queenie. I hesitated for a moment, not sure if I could handle the possibility of lying to her again if she brought up Nika. But there was always the chance my plane was going to crash land in Azerbaijan or Romania or something, and I knew that as the plane was plummeting down, wings on fire and engines stalled, that I would regret not answering her call.

"Hey, Queenie," I said, trying to sound cool and calm.

"Mum is going completely mental about your wedding, you know," she began. "I'm the one left here, dealing with it. She wants to invite everyone we've ever met. She's talking about hiring court jesters to entertain people during the reception. It's getting ridiculous."

"Why is Mum planning the wedding at all?" I asked.

"Because she's Mum. She's biologically incapable of not interfering. She's asked me to call you and find out who Nika is planning on having there. She wants to know if there's any family or close friends she needs to meet before the big day."

"Not that I know of. As you know, her parents aren't alive anymore, and as far as I'm aware, she doesn't have anyone else."

"Not even any friends? Bit sad." Queenie had always been empathetic. "No wonder she asked me to be the maid of honour."

"Queenie…" I started, before realising telling her the truth would be placing an enormous burden on her shoulders.

"What is it, Alfie?"

"Uh, have you heard from Oswald lately?" I plopped down on the end of the bed, feeling like a cockroach caught on one of those sticky bug pads that end up ripping their little legs off.

"Not for a while. He's been mysteriously MIA lately. I mean, more so than normal. He missed your birthday this year. That's a first. I was expecting to see him, but Mum said he's really busy at the moment. Apparently he's getting calls nearly every day requesting he go to this country or that country. You know, I was really surprised when you decided to go to law school."

"What?" I asked, taken aback by the direction the conversation had taken. "What do you mean?"

"I always thought you'd follow in Oswald's footsteps. Sometimes I think you only studied law to make sure you were always the one we could rely on."

"Oh," I breathed.

"Mum's a verifiable nut job, Dad's a garden-recluse and I know you've always thought you had to take care of me."

"Well, that's… you know, I…" I stuttered my way through a hopeless sentence, unsure if I felt exposed that I had been discovered, or surprised to learn that these had been my motives all along.

"I just want you to be happy. I don't want you to do something you don't really care about out of some sense of obligation. I don't know where I'm going to be or what I'm going to do, but I know that I'm going to be all right. Even if Mum ends up in a nuthouse and Dad spends more time talking to his poinsettias than he does to any human being."

"We don't say nuthouse, Queenie," I scolded quietly.

"You know what I'm saying," she pressed.

"Yes. I do. Thank you."

"Well, anyway. I'm gonna go. I've got homework to do."

As Queenie hung up the phone, I continued to hold it to my ear, frozen in some sort of cryostasis. What had just happened? Had Queenie just excavated my soul? Was she right? Had I chosen law simply to be a solid, reliable member of our family? Had I chosen to be a wig-wearing, dust-covered member of the bar simply because I thought Queenie might need me to be?

Why hadn't I chosen to follow in Oswald's footsteps? I was closer to him than anyone else in our family, and if anyone was going to go into the business of archaeology, wouldn't the most expected person be me? Oswald would have opened every door I needed, would have prepared the path completely. Why had I chosen law instead?

I couldn't remember anymore.

I shook myself out of my state of confusion and fumbled down the stairs and into the living room, where Settlers of Catan was set up and waiting.

"Finally. What took you so long? Pizza's going cold," Hugh grumbled.

I sunk into the chair and opened a pizza box. "Oh, you know, just rethinking my entire existence."

"I do that every day," Wizard said wistfully.

"Somehow that doesn't surprise me," I said.

"What's wrong?" Hugh asked.

"Can you remember why I wanted to be a solicitor?" I asked.

Hugh's lips crumpled together, his brows furrowed, and his eyes drifted away; his thinking face. We waited at least an entire minute before he shook his head.

"Nope." He shrugged. "Why?"

Nika grabbed a slice of pizza and took a bite. Through her mouthful she

148

mumbled, "If you don't want to do law, just do something else."

"It's not that simple," I protested.

"It really is," she said, after she swallowed. "Look where you are. You're in London, with a good family and good friends. You have nothing to lose. The world is at your feet. Don't be so ungrateful."

"I'm not being ungrateful," I argued. "I'm trying not to throw away the last few years of my life."

"Then don't." Nika took another bit.

"I'm getting whiplash here, Nika."

"Look," she said, cheesy pizza visible between her gnashing teeth, "you can do whatever you want. Finish your degree, don't finish your degree. Make up your mind and stop complaining. There are a lot of people out there with much less options than you."

"So, because there are people less fortunate, I can't have any problems?"

"That's not what I am saying. Look, I know what it is to have no options. I don't have a family, and lots of opportunities. It's why I am here. A lot of people in the Czech Republic have wonderful, beautiful lives. Not me. I was sold into a bridal program when I was fourteen, when the orphanage couldn't take care of me anymore. I lived in a small apartment with twelve other girls, and we were all competing for a different life. There was only one option for me, and look how well that turned out. So, stop acting like a spoiled little girl and make your choices and be grateful for what you have got."

Wizard and Dark Lord sat as still as statues, unsure what to say or do. Hugh looked from Nika to me, then back to Nika again. I reached into the pizza box, took out a slice and said, "Let's play, shall we?"

Thirty-Six

I was a nervous flyer, but I had to admit I did feel slightly more relaxed in premium economy. The seats were bigger and more comfortable and my blanket, which I had draped delicately over my legs, was soft and fluffy. The benefits, however, did not outweigh the monetary inconvenience Nika had exposed me to. Not only had she stolen my credit card and purchased two tickets to New Delhi, India, but she had also upgraded the tickets, adding a further expense.

I had a sneaking suspicion that accommodation, food, and other expenses would also, no doubt, be coming out of my credit card. Nika sat comfortably beside me, nestled into her seat, overflowing with satisfaction. I had had to take off a week of classes and get extensions for two different assignments, but with the chance of getting rid of Nika for good, I was more than willing to make the sacrifice.

Even if it meant eight hours stuck on a tin can soaring frightfully through the air.

"Let go."

I faced Nika. "What?"

"You are squeezing my hand. It hurts. Let go."

I looked down at my hand, which had somehow made its way into hers. Squeezing as hard as I was, I had made her fingers go white.

"Oh." I let go and crossed my arms to keep them contained. "Sorry."

I stared at the seat in front of me as we took off. I was feeling cold and hot at the same time, as my hands grew clammy. Eight hours of this. I was almost certain that I could see Nika looking at me like I was a particularly unique shade of odd. I would somehow have to keep up the pretence of being a manly, unafraid, Tanzanian man. If Nika discovered how truly afraid I was of flying, I had a sneaking suspicion that she would not find it endearing, or charming, watching her little ginger friend squirm in his seat in fear. She would laugh at me. I could not allow my dignity to be further lost to her clutches. I straightened in my chair and resolved to appear as carefree as possible as we reached cruising altitude.

I was given – or rather, I demanded – the aisle seat, because I felt as though I had the chance to flee if the opportunity arose. The fact that dozens of seats and bodies lay in between me and any door, was, to my mind, entirely beside the point. The fact that outside of that door there was nothing but air and clouds was also completely redundant. I started to grind my teeth together, and as I began to believe that I had, potentially, worn down my molars to stubs, Nika smacked me with a backhand.

"Ow!" I hissed. "What was that for?"

"Stop it. It's disgusting." She cringed.

"What is?"

"That sound."

I sighed and rubbed my arm. "I need to go for a walk." I threw off my seatbelt and jumped out into the aisle. Unfortunately I fell directly into a flight attendant and her trolley, knocking her to the ground and flinging hot tea all over the passengers opposite me.

"Oh my goodness. Oh no." My first instinct was to cover my mouth with my hand like a four-year-old child. But when adulthood crept back into my psyche, I turned to the people to whom I had potentially given third degree burns. "Are you all right? I'm sorry." I grabbed serviettes from the toppled trolley and began passing them feverishly to the three stunned, and wet, passengers. "Are you hurt?"

I didn't wait for a response before I bent down to help the stewardess to her feet. "I am so sorry. I'm so terribly sorry."

The woman, whose name badge said Julie-Anne, was, understandably, infuriated with me. She rejected my hand and instead opted to bring herself to her feet using the chairs around us. I felt her rejection was undeserved, and I was unwilling to allow her to get away without realising I was a gentleman and was required to assist her. I reached for her shoulders, but, just as I did so, there was a sudden jolt from turbulence and my hands landed directly on her breasts.

Before I realised that I was groping a random stranger, I squeezed. I had been trying to get a tighter grip on her shoulders, to lift her properly to her feet, but evidently I was doing something dramatically different.

"Get your hands off me!" Julie-Anne screamed.

I withdrew my hands with urgency, a stricken look of terror across my face as I realised what I had done. "Oh no. Oh no. I didn't mean to."

"You groped me!" she accused.

"No, no, no, no, no," I whimpered. "I didn't. No. It was an accident. I didn't mean to. I…I…I…"

The woman glared at me furiously. "Sit. Down. Sir."

I swallowed hard and looked around at the hundred or so passengers that were now staring at me, enjoying British Airway's surprise inflight entertainment. Slowly, I sank back down into my seat.

Nika reached across and petted my knee, almost lovingly. "I'm sorry," she leaned across me to the stewardess. "He's a terrible flyer."

I dropped my head into my hands and tried to disappear. Suddenly my fear of flying was gone. If the plane's engine had given out and we suddenly started to free fall towards the earth, I didn't think I would mind. In fact, I may have even preferred it.

Thirty-Seven

My first instinct was to kiss the ground as soon as I stepped out of the airport. Not so much for having landed safely, but for having finally been out from underneath the rude and judgemental stares from passengers, Julie-Anne, and her protective posse of flight attendants. Apparently, my name had been written down somewhere, in a file or a book or something that said I was to be watched. I imagined if ever again I spilled hot beverages on random strangers, or knocked over a trolley or unsuspecting flight attendant, I would be handcuffed and tied to the underside of the plane's right wing. My desire to kiss the ground with unbridled glee, however, was short lived. The smell was the first thing I noticed; potent and extreme, a mixture of spices and pollution.

Immediately, I was swept up into a fast paced crowd, and that was when I noticed the colour. It was, by far, the most intoxicating thing, beyond the smell, the noise, the clamour. Bright colours were everywhere, clouding my vision in the most spectacular of ways. I wanted to stop and take it all in, but Nika had a firm grip on my arm as we were hurried along in the crowd.

When we arrived at the train station, I felt a sudden wash of nausea. There was a sea of people, dashing from left to right, and as we waded our way towards our train, I tried not to focus on the fact that we were going to be stuck on it for the next twenty or so hours. It was a long way to Rajgir, where we would find Uncle Oswald.

I followed Nika onto the train. She seemed perfectly at ease in the hustle and bustle, the chaos and strangeness. We squished ourselves into a seat.

From the looks of it, we were lucky to find one.

"Might I just say this one more time?" I started, as an old man shoved in beside me, an unwelcome third addition to a two seater bench.

"Say what?" Nika said, undisturbed.

I cleared my throat. "The obvious. That this is crazy!" I hissed.

"Crazy?" Nika turned to face me, folding her arms crossly.

"Yes! It's crazy to be off gallivanting after Uncle Oswald. This is ridiculous. We should never have left London."

"You're the one that wanted to get rid of me."

"I... No. I…You are the one who wanted to go find him. I was perfectly happy in London."

"With me sitting around the house, waiting for you to come home?"

"That's not what I meant."

"Well, what did you mean, then?" she snapped.

I deliberated for a moment, wondering if I would tell her that, though I was severely displeased at our random trip to India, I was not at all displeased to be ridding myself of her constant presence. "Nothing," I sighed. "Nothing at all." I thought it best to attempt to change the subject. "Twenty hours and counting, hey?" As if on cue, the man beside me began to snore, his head lolling over onto my shoulder. His beard tickled my arm.

Nika snickered. "It's going to fly by."

I leaned my head back and stared at the sooty ceiling. The smell of body odour was overwhelming, but not more so than the noise. We were surrounded by people, each engaged in vigorous conversation, chattering away in a language I hadn't a hope of understanding.

"We should try to sleep."

I shot Nika a look of bewilderment. "Sleep?" I looked around me, utterly perplexed. "How do you suppose we do that?"

"Close your eyes." Nika leaned against the window and shut her eyes, leaving me alone in the land of consciousness. While Nika had the window for support, I had nothing to rest my weary head upon.

The old Indian man beside me smiled, as if enjoying my conundrum, revealing yellowed teeth spread intermittently throughout his mouth, which was itself, hidden behind a straggly white beard. The very same beard that had been tickling me just moments earlier when I had mistaken the man for one who was sleeping. I tried to smile in return, but I was afraid it fell rather flat.

My eyes grew heavy, weighted as they were with jet lag. I closed them slowly, and before I knew it my head was resting comfortably on Nika's shoulder.

When I awoke, the cover of night had fallen over the Indian landscape that we scooted past. I sat up clasping my neck and moaned in pain. It was then that I noticed that the train had become considerably fuller. It was so full, in fact, that the floors were covered with sleeping people and every bench had at least four people squeezed onto it. The train had become a veritable sea of people.

A fourth person had even squashed themselves onto my bench.

I looked over at Nika, seeking support, but she was lost to me, fast asleep. I was taken, for a moment, by the sweetness of her face. She looked so gentle and soft, and I could almost overlook the fact that she was a villainous and wily creature. Her dark hair was brushed back over her shoulder, her mouth was closed, her lips slightly pursed.

There was no denying the blatant truth – she was stunning. Simply beautiful. I could walk the earth for a thousand years, watch the sun set a million times on a million empty days and never find someone who was, to me, as beautiful as she.

I adored her.

In the most hateful way.

How could someone so truly fantastically wonderful be so…so…so… malicious? And immoral. And dastardly. How could such horrible words come out of such a beautiful mouth, such lovely lips?

I could think of it no longer. Instead I decided to enjoy the moment. The moment where she was at peace. The moment where, in my mind, I chose to believe that she was the most real.

Suddenly unconcerned by the smell of the train, the sounds of snoring passengers, the closeness of a hundred strangers, I nestled into her shoulder once more and enjoyed the peculiar moment of familiarity between me, Nika and my new Indian friends.

Thirty-Eight

We were there.

Sort of.

Rajgir, India.

I sighed. "Where the bloody hell are we?"

Even Nika looked slightly confused. "I don't know."

Before I could speak again, a woman dressed in a full sari, of electric blue, walked up to me and smacked me on the arm.

"Ow!" I shouted. "What was that for?"

She immediately went into a rage, spluttering what I guessed to be her frustration with my existence. Nika came up beside me, her bags in her hands. She appeared to be as confused as I was, which actually provided a small amount of relief.

"Do you have any idea what is going on?" I asked Nika, fending off aggressive fingers that pointed in my direction.

Nika laughed. "No clue."

The woman must have been in her late sixties, with long grey hair wound neatly atop her head. She had a small red dot in the centre of her forehead and a ring in her nose. She moved her fingers from my face to Nika, where she pointed at the bags Nika held in her hands.

We stared at her blankly.

She stopped speaking abruptly, clearly gathering that we did not, in fact, speak her language. She went for our bags.

"Ah, excuse me," I said, trying to remain polite. "I'm going to have to ask you to leave those bags. Leave them please. Leave…leave them."

157

The stranger paid me no heed. She unfurled Nika's hands from around her bag, and shoved them against my chest.

It was then that I got the idea. I should be holding her bags.

So, of course, I took the bags. The woman stopped speaking and patted me on the cheek, a broad, sweet smile appearing on her face. She pulled back and bowed with a dip of her head, then walked away.

Now unburdened by a single bag, Nika grinned. "You should have more respect for women."

"Excuse me?" I choked.

"More respect for women. Why haven't you been carrying my bags all along?"

I growled and headed for the bus that would take us onward to the ruins of Nalanda University, where Uncle Oswald was. The ruins were once the home of one of the world's first universities that offered accommodation, but was destroyed sometime in the 1100's. Or at least that's what I researched before we left for India.

I didn't like the look of the bus. I suspected that, at any moment, it could possibly explode. Or tip over from the large collection of people that had swarmed over it like ants. I saw Nika pause and realised that it was an opportunity to have her see that I was unafraid, confident, and poised under pressure.

Everything I had not been so far.

"Come on," I encouraged. "What's the problem?"

"Is it safe?" she asked.

"Of course!" I chuckled like she was being ridiculous. "It is sturdy as anything." I stepped onto the bus and reached a hand down to her. "Coming?"

Tentatively, Nika placed her hand in mine. I suddenly felt like Aladdin, asking Jasmine to step up onto his magic carpet. It seemed fitting since we were heading into a whole new world.

There was nowhere to sit.

More than that, there was nowhere to stand.

I now understood what was glaringly obvious. The people on top of the bus were not there to get a little extra breeze. They were there because there was no other option. The bus driver smiled.

"You come on bus?" he asked.

"Uh, is there…is there any room?" I asked.

The driver continued to smile. "You come on bus?"

Nika grabbed my sleeve. "We could catch next bus?"

"The next bus."

Nika slapped my arm. "Alfie!"

"Look, the next bus will be exactly the same, and it could be hours away for all we know. Let's just…you know. When in Rome."

"We're not in Rome," Nika said, her brows furrowed. "We're in India."

"It's an expression."

"You come on bus?" the man asked again.

"Yes, yes, yes," I said. We stepped off the bus and, following the instructions of the wonderfully friendly passengers sitting on the roof, we made our way to the back of the bus where there was grating for us to climb up.

I looked up at the people staring down at us and laughed. Some waved us up and the others threw their hands down to help lift us up. I was touched for a moment at the unquestioning friendship, and the spectacular joy written across each of their faces.

I held up my hand and grabbed the one nearest to me, yanking myself up. Nika was slow to follow behind. I placed my hand on her back and helped push her up. There was no room left on the top of the bus, so we were required to stay hanging on the back. As the bus took off, rickety at first, then gaining speed, I felt the hot wind blow through my hair. For the first time in years, I felt truly alive.

I was away from stuffy libraries, difficult classes, and Wandsworth. I was in India. I admitted it, I was reluctant at first, being far away from London and everything I knew, but hanging on the back of a rickety old bus in the middle of India, off on an adventure like Bilbo Baggins, I couldn't imagine being anywhere else.

I leaned back, my arms outstretched and felt the sun on my face. I opened my eyes to see Nika hugging tightly to the bus, fear on her face, her eyes tightly closed. With my new found joy, I decided to be brave. I threw my left leg out, and moved my arm to the other side, so that Nika was tucked safely in between me and the bus. If she fell, she would fall onto me, and hopefully, I would be able to catch her without losing my grip. If not, we would both plummet to the ground, lost in a cloud of dust, but at least she would land on me first.

"Nika," I called. "Open your eyes."

Reluctantly, she followed my request. I smiled at her what I hoped would be a reassuring smile. "I've got you."

We shared a moment. An actual moment. Like the ones the main characters experience in movies. We held each other's stare until Nika began to smile. In that instance, everything felt completely brilliant.

Thirty-Nine

Everything was not brilliant.

The bus, the rickety old bus that Nika had been so afraid of getting on, had broken down. The drive from Rajgir to the ruins was only supposed to be around ten minutes. Five minutes in, the bus came to a grinding halt.

Without complaining, everyone simply stepped off the bus and started walking. It would take at least half an hour to finish the journey on foot. Fortunately, I supposed, we didn't have to do the journey alone. We were accompanied by every single passenger who had found themselves equally without transport, yet seemed to take the news far better than me.

Nika and I had been swallowed in a cloud of colour. My feet hurt ten minutes into the walk. We had been travelling for thirty or so hours and the last thing I wanted was to be on my feet, lugging all of our bags out of fear of another beating.

The solace, however, was how truly beautiful it was. The undulating hills created a spectacular view, and despite how the sun beat down upon my ginger brow, it only served to warm me. There were countless trees, casting shadows this way and that; the potent green of their leaves caught me entirely by surprise.

I made the mistake of not looking where I was going, transfixed as I was by the landscape. I bumped into someone in front of me and immediately apologised.

However, when my eyes caught up to my body, I realised it was not a person I had bumped into, so much as it was a cow.

A cow.

In the middle of the road.

"Oh." My head tipped to the side in confusion. "What are you doing here?"

"Uh, Alfie." Nika's voice sounded worried.

"Look," I said, pointing at the cow. "It's just wandering around. It must have gotten loose from some farm somewhere. Poor thing. Go back home, dearie, or someone might make a hamburger out of you."

"Alfie," Nika hissed.

I was laughing at my own joke. "What?"

Nika's eyes were flickering. "I think you did something wrong again."

The entire crowd of people had stopped and were staring at me with horrified expressions on their faces. The cow started to moo. I chuckled half-heartedly.

"Cow," I pointed. "Look."

"Alfie, stop."

I turned to Nika in a panic. "What's going on? What have I done now?"

"Cows are sacred in India, Alfie. You just bumped into one. Hard. And then you mentioned…you mentioned hamburgers!"

"Oh." My stomach dropped. "Oh. Oh dear."

"Yeah."

I struggled to breathe as anxiety made my heart beat quickly. "I'm very sorry. Very, very sorry." I reached out and stroked the cow on the back, hoping my gentle touch would show the cross people around me that I meant the cow now harm.

It appeared to work.

The angry mob relaxed ever so slightly, and even a few of those who were slightly bolder came up to the cow and joined me in petting the creature. However, they seemed to be focused mainly on the cow's tail, for reasons I felt too flustered to attempt to discover.

Nika slapped me on the back. "I think you made an impression." She leaned in close, as I feigned a smile at my petting comrades, and whispered in my ear, "Welcome to India."

Forty

I stayed at the very back of the crowd, unwilling to get too close to the passengers for fear I would further insult their traditions or humiliate myself beyond repair. So far, I was not making a very good impression on India.

Nika was up ahead, walking beside two women with whom she seemed to be having a swell time. They were laughing and chatting, and I wondered how she had managed to find people who spoke English so quickly, when the only people I had spoken to so far couldn't understand a single word I blurted out.

My feelings of freedom and happiness and whatnot had vanished, needless to say. I started to sweat, baking underneath the sun, with the absence of a strong breeze created by the movement of the bus. I felt myself slowly resenting all the colours splashed around me and hating the smells and sounds.

I just wanted to go home. I wanted to be in my apartment in Wandsworth, watching an episode of Firefly. I wanted to be sitting on the couch, Aslan preening my hair. I could only hope that Hugh was taking good care of her. It turned my stomach in knots to consider the fact that she could be going without food and water. Hugh could barely take care of himself; no one knew this better than I did, and yet I was left with no other choice than to leave my beloved monkey in Hugh's fatuous paws. I half imagined I'd return to find her stuffed and sitting on the mantelpiece over our fireplace. I cringed at the thought.

I kicked a stone on the ground and readjusted the bags with which I was heavy laden. Watching Nika laugh and wave her hands around in animated conversation filled me with rage. I glared at her through squinting eyes and began to mock her, mouthing out a conversation in gibberish and flailing my hands about in an overly effeminate manner. It was childish, I knew, but it helped me to feel better.

That was, of course, until I noticed two men to my right staring at me confusedly.

I immediately stopped and gave them a wilted smile. I couldn't even mock the woman in peace.

I decided to be better. I would breathe in patience and exhale my hatred. I drew in a deep breath, filling my lungs with the warm air around me, and blew it all back out again. The process appeared to have failed. I still felt hatred.

I tried again, this time making myself dizzy with oxygen. Again, there was no difference to my state of mind. It was at that point that I gave up. I hated her and no amount of new age breathing would change that.

We were nearing the town, to my relief. Rajgir, India, a city located in the Nalanda district of Bihar, had a population of only 41, 587 people. Given that Mumbai had more than 11 million people, Rajgir was not exactly a bustling metropolis. But this was where Uncle Oswald was. As soon as we arrived at his hotel, I could pass the Nika shaped baton over to him and be done with this nightmare.

"Having a nice walk?"

I jumped at Nika's sudden presence beside me. I hadn't noticed that she had bid farewell to her friends and joined me once again.

"Oh. The best," I muttered.

"Isn't it beautiful?" she asked, sighing.

"Lovely," I murmured.

"Oh, come on Alfred. Be happy. Look at where we are."

"Alife," I said, through gritted teeth. "That's the name on my birth certificate. And I am looking at where we are. That's the problem."

"You know, you would be a lot happier if you just accepted that we are

164

here now, and there's nothing you can do about it. You might even have a good time."

"A good time? A good time? Here? With you?" I scoffed. "Nika, I have blisters the size of pancakes on my feet, I've been lugging your bags and my own around so much that I think that my spine may permanently tilt to the right from now on, and I'm out of pocket thousands of dollars because you decided it was time to go on a merry goose chase. I'm hot, I'm tired, I don't speak a word of Hindi and I just want to go home."

"Wow."

"Wow what?"

"Is this what it is like to be you?" she asked. "Bitter about everything? Never looking for positives? You do nothing but complain and so you miss it."

"Miss what?" I snapped.

Nika looked at me and I saw something strange in her eyes. Something like pity…or sadness. "You miss…life."

I slowed, shocked by her words, and Nika tottered on ahead of me. That simply wasn't true. I didn't miss life. I had a life. Back in England. I was working towards being someone, working on creating myself, one day at a time. I had a plan. I didn't miss life. It wasn't true.

Was it?

Forty-One

"I'm sorry," I whispered, before clearing my throat so that my voice would be audible to humans. "Could you please repeat that?"

"But of course, sir," the skinny man behind the counter said in a think Hindi accent. "Mr Oswald is no longer staying with us, sir."

"No…longer…staying with you?" I croaked.

"No, no, no. He was a very nice man, but he is now gone, sir, yes, very much gone indeed, sir."

I wiped sweat from my forehead. "Did he happen to say where he was going?"

"Oh, yes, sir, yes, indeed he did, sir."

I waited. "Will you tell me, please?"

"Oh, yes. He is gone, sir." The man blinked at me and smiled.

"Ah, yes, yes, I got that." I cleared my throat and tried not to panic. "But where?"

"Oh, yes, yes. He has left India altogether. He is now in Nepal, sir."

I stared at the man, unmoving, for a considerable amount of time. It was only when Nika shoved me in the ribs that I spluttered out my horror. "Russia?" I swallowed hard. "As in…vodka and snow and Anastasia?"

"Oh, yes, sir. Very good, sir."

"Did he happen to say where in Russia he was going?" A droplet of anxiety induced sweat dripped into my eye. "It's quite a large place."

"No, no, no. He did not, sir."

I closed my eyes and dropped my head onto the counter.

The stranger patted a hand on my shoulder. "Are you all right, sir? That sounded very much painful, indeed, sir."

I straightened and forced a smile. "Thanks for your help. Let's go, Nika."

He called out for us as we neared the front door. "He did leave a letter, sir. Would this be of assistance to you?"

I turned around to face the man again. "A letter? For me?"

"That depends, sir."

"On?"

"On what your name is. I cannot very well hand out a private letter for someone who is not him. If you are not him, sir, then I simply cannot give you the letter."

"My name is Alfie," I said, slapping my hands eagerly against the counter. "Alfie Alvey."

The man smiled a broad, infectious smile. "Then you are very much indeed him, sir." He bent down and retrieved a letter from somewhere. "Here you go, sir."

I tore open the letter. Hopefully, this was another of Uncle Oswald's increasingly infuriating jokes, and this letter would confirm that he had not left the country, but was hiding behind a pot plant or a sand dune or something.

Alfie, my boy!

Sorry to leave you stranded here, but I simply had to rush off! Russia calls! I was here for the ruins of Nalanda University, but I got all that I could out of it before I had to scoot over to Russia. Sorry for the inconvenience, old chap.

I have supplied some money for you and your fiancé to travel, as I understand the financial strain caused by my absence. I have purchased tickets in both of your names. They await you at the New Delhi airport. Once you arrive in Moscow, a friend of mine will meet you at the Borkyenka Hotel, and bring you to me. We have much to discuss.

See you soon, old boy!

I searched the envelope for the money and was grateful to find what I hoped would be enough to support us in Moscow. At least he'd had the decency to buy us plane tickets.

Russia! Bloody Russia! How much further away could he possibly have gone?

I scrunched up the letter in frustration and shoved it into my pocket.

"Let's go then," Nika said, trying to usher me out the door.

"Uh, I don't think so."

"Why not?"

"We have been travelling for nearly two days straight. I need sleep. Proper, actual, sleep. In a bed. We will leave tomorrow." I turned to the helpful man behind the counter. "One room, please."

"One room?" Nika gasped.

"Yes. One. We are saving money. A concept you clearly have never quite grasped."

Nika sighed angrily. "And just what are we supposed to do for the rest of the day? It's not night out there. Sun is up!"

"The sun," I corrected.

"I know!"

"Oh, excuse me, excuse me, sir," the man behind the counter said to Nika.

"I am not a sir," Nika spat.

"Oh, my most sincere apologies. But if you do not mind me saying so, the ruins of Nalanda University are truly spectacular. Yes, truly very spectacular indeed."

"Yes, my Uncle was here for that." 'Was' being the operative word. I groaned internally.

"Oh, yes, sir, he said so, sir. He thought it was truly very spectacular."

"Well, why don't we go look at that, then?" I suggested.

"At dusty old ruins? In heat of day?"

The fact that Nika seemed unimpressed with the idea made my heart swell with happiness. "Yes. I hear that it's truly very spectacular indeed," I added in my most serious voice.

"Oh, yes, sir," the man added joyfully.

"Besides," I added, "you wanted something to do for the rest of the day."

Nika rolled her eyes.

"It's decided then!" I beamed. "We'll get settled into our room and then we'll go see the ruins."

Nika threw me a sarcastic smile. Seeing her so perturbed had ensured my sour mood had drastically improved.

Forty-Two

"Oh. No."

Nika's voice reflected my own concern. "Oh, dear."

"This is our room?"

I looked around. "So it would seem."

Although, the title room seemed to be quite the misnomer, for there was a substantial lack of just that – room. There was a toilet to my immediate right, from where I stood in the doorway, and exactly two feet from the door was the bed, which took up the entirety of the rest of the space.

"There's barely room to swing a cat, is there?" I said, baffled.

"Why would we want to swing a cat in here? I'm allergic."

"All the more reason," I muttered.

"What?"

"I said, no reason. It's just a saying." I attempted to look on the bright side, something I had been accused of never doing. "It's very…cosy."

"How are we going to sleep?"

"We'll just have to make do."

"I cannot believe your stupid Uncle isn't here. I could kill him," Nika growled.

"For once, we agree," I said, surprised.

"You are not close to him? Is that why he did this to you?"

"Well, I thought we were close. But seeing as he didn't think twice about throwing my life into a chaotic whirlpool, I think I might have been wrong."

"Does anybody in your family like you?"

"What's that supposed to mean?" I asked angrily.

"Your mother seems pretty upset with you."

"Thanks to you," I muttered,

"I like your sister though."

"Yea. So do I. And she definitely likes me, thank you. I mean, not so much when we were growing up, but that's normal."

"Must be nice to have a sister."

"It is," I agreed.

Nika walked forward and dumped her bags on the bed. The springs made a frightening groaning sound.

"Shall we go?" I asked.

"Fine," she sighed.

Tired as we both were, the room was not somewhere we wanted to spend the rest of the day. Leaving our belongings behind, as well as Uncle Oswald's letter and funds, we embarked on the short journey from the hotel to the ruins.

Forty-Three

I was definitely not in Wandsworth anymore.

I had never seen anything quite so eerily beautiful. The sun was hanging lower in the sky, casting a haunting shadow across the crumbling walls of a building that had, according to Google, been an extraordinary University, and one of the first to have dormitories. I tried to imagine students, bustling to and fro, in the furrows of yesteryear.

"It's difficult, isn't it?" I said, forgetting that Nika had not been privy to the thoughts wading through my mind.

"What is?"

"Just imagining people here. That this place was real, and that there were students. I mean, this could be like Oxford, or Yale, or anywhere, if it hadn't been destroyed."

"I heard that there were so many books that it took months for it to burn." Nika's voice was low and quiet.

"It's so sad." I felt a chill course over my body. A sudden melancholy caused my eyes to sting. I abruptly turned away from Nika so that she wouldn't be able to see me quickly wipe my eyes.

It had been destroyed in 1200CE by ran-sackers who clearly had no regard for knowledge or the written word. The University, however, was very recently recreated about twelve kilometres from the ruins.

"It is beautiful, is it not?"

I jumped at the new voice. "Yes," I said, somewhat warily as I took in the stranger. "Quite."

Nika stayed still and quiet as the man wound around us. He had scraggly hair, a few days growth on his chin and piercing blue eyes, which seemed remarkably anomalous, given his dark Indian skin.

"This is your first time in India, correct?" he said as he continued to slither around us.

"Yes. Yes, actually it is. Does it show?" I stiffened slightly as he brushed past me.

"I am so familiar with this country, that I can tell those who have never set foot in it before."

"Well, you pegged us. Just visiting. Actually, we were about to leave here. Thought we would maybe go and have some tea in one of the local restaurants. Can you, uh, can you suggest any?" I had to hold myself still when the dastardly man stopped in front of Nika and took hold of a thick strand of her hair, lifting it to his face.

"Coconut?" he asked.

"Yes," she said quietly. "Shampoo."

He took another whiff of her hair and let it go. "You mustn't leave yet."

"No?" I squeaked.

"No, you must first watch the sunset. An Indian sunset over the ruins of Nalanda is truly one of the most beautiful things you will ever see."

"Ah. But… I've never been one for sunsets." I pointed to my eyes and scrunched my face. "Hurts my eyes, all that staring at the sun."

"Oh, but you must brave it. For the pleasure of the sight will outweigh the sorrow of the eyes."

"That's, uh, that's very poetic," I said. "Did you make that up yourself?"

The man scoffed a laugh. "I must introduce you to my friends."

"Friends?" I croaked. The man gave me an ill feeling, sinister and snake-like as he was. "I'm not so sure that we have the time. We really do have to go."

"Make time." His voice suddenly had a much harsher edge, as two other men came out of the shadows.

"Nika," I said firmly, "come here, please."

She hurried to my side without complaint as the three men encircled us.

"I'm afraid that we are going to have to relieve you of your belongings now." The same man who had appeared sinister before, now seemed completely terrifying, surrounded by his friends, closing in on us.

I stood tall, trying to appear strong and unfazed. "We have nothing of value."

"Nothing?" The man laughed. "You are tourists – you are carrying all of your belongings on you. Now, give us your money before we have to take it by force. But then of course…" he paused and reached out a hand to touch Nika's cheek. "I wouldn't mind taking you by force."

Nika jerked away from his touch and buried herself into my side. The men laughed at her sign of timidity, and I felt a protective anger rise forth from within me.

"Don't touch her," I growled.

The man chuckled. "Don't touch? Maybe she wants me to touch. We don't see such a pretty flower like this one every day."

I emptied my pockets onto the ground, throwing the contents at their feet. "Here! This is honestly all I have. Now, we'll be going."

The man crouched down to rifle through the bus tickets, plane tickets, a stick of gum and some lint. He stood up again and moseyed towards me with his hands in his pockets. Suddenly, like a flash of lightening, his hands shot out of his pockets and his fingers wrapped around my cheeks. "This is nothing!" he shouted. Droplets of spit slapped my face.

"I told you, we aren't carrying anything of value." My knees began to feel like my mother's infamous custard tarts.

"What about you?" he asked, turning to Nika, eyeing her up and down. "I am sure that you have something that we want." He let my face go and redirected his dirty fingers to Nika's neck. I watched as he caressed her throat, making his way lower and lower as he headed towards her chest.

My stomach dropped. Suddenly, something ferocious, and if I do say so myself, downright heroic, came over me. Overwhelmed with the prospect of such an injustice taking place, right before my eyes, I took a tight hold of

Nika's waist and spun her around, yanking her out of the man's reach. "Do not touch her again."

I watched his eyes go dark with anger. At the precise moment he reared back to slog me in the face, I drew back my leg and kicked the ground, scuffing up sand and dirt into his face. He gargled in pain, holding a hand over his eyes.

"Run, Nika!" I shouted.

She took off at a sprint, with me following closely behind. I looked over my shoulder, only to see the man start towards us and order his friends to follow suit.

"Faster!" I shouted. "Run!"

I had never been athletic. I had always come dead last, having fallen over at least once, in every forced running race from grade one until I graduated. The races were, in my opinion, designed to put children in their place, to embarrass them, and separate the little weaklings from the glorious strong, who would carry on to be the popular kids, beating up the puny ones, and getting all the girls.

But on this day, with my actual life on the line, I was running faster than I ever had before, and as I overtook Nika, I got a glimpse of what it would have been like to be one of the kids who actually won.

"Alfie!" Nika shouted.

I stopped and saw she had fallen. For a moment, I swelled with pride in knowing I wasn't the only one who usually face-planted the ground while running. But as I saw the men approaching her, I dashed back to her aid.

Unfortunately, I wasn't quick enough. One of the men accompanying our attacker threw himself on top of her, holding her down with his knee. Pulling out a knife he held it up menacingly. As it glinted in the sun, I panicked, running ever faster towards her.

Nika screamed and started to thrash underneath his considerable weight. The other men were catching up, and I could only imagine what they would do if they took her. Frantic, I looked around for my options. Seeing a large rock on the ground, I picked it up and came at the man from

175

the side. I had never really hit someone in the head with a rock before, so it was new to me, but I managed to muddle through. I held it in both hands and brought it down across the side of his face, knocking him to the ground. He lay there in a dazed puddle with, no doubt, a very memorable headache.

I bent down and lifted Nika to her feet. "Can you still run?"

"I think so," she whimpered through tears.

I took her hand in mine and squeezed it tightly. "Together."

We took off as fast as we could, leaving the men behind in our dust. I was so afraid, and yet, running through India, with villains on my tail, while fleeing for the honour of a woman, made me feel like a hero in an action film. I felt like I wasn't missing anything anymore.

I was almost having fun.

Almost.

Not quite.

I decided to ponder what that meant about my character later.

For now I was in a foreign country, running from bandits, with Nika. Who, I noticed, looked rather fetching shimmering in the setting sun.

As we neared the town, the bandits slowed and let us leave, unwilling to carry out their hooliganisms in front of many witnesses. Nika and I kept running. I looked at her and smiled and then marvelled at her strength when, despite what she had just been through, she smiled back.

Forty-Four

We burst into the hotel, and the familiar face of the man behind the counter, whose name badge indicated his name as Rajesh, was an instant comfort.

"Oh, dear, sir. What happened to you?"

I gasped for air, resting against the counter top. "These men…attacked us… we ran."

"Oh no, sir, oh no. When the afternoon grows late, many unsavoury characters come out around the area of the ruins, sir. You shouldn't go there once the afternoon gets on, sir."

I looked up at him and growled, "Why didn't you tell us, Rajesh?"

"Oh, sir, you did not ask, and I did not think to tell."

"Great," I muttered.

"Sir, for this grave error, on behalf of this hotel, I would very much indeed like to offer you both a free evening meal. At our restaurant."

When I stared back blankly at him, he saw it as his cue to carry on.

"Oh, sir, we have the most wonderful meals here for you. If you come down here at six o'clock, I myself will lead you to our dining room for the most pleasurable of dinners."

Rajesh stepped out from behind the counter and looped an arm around Nika and me, leading us to the stairs that would take us to our room. "We have the most exquisite food here, and you will find it most gratifying indeed, sir."

"Six?" I sighed.

"Precisely, sir." Rajesh gave us a little shove up the stairs. "I shall eagerly await your return, sir."

"Pushy, isn't he?" I muttered.

"I like him," Nika said, still breathless.

The first thing we did when walked into our room was collapse on the bed, side by side.

"Wow," I said, "that was intense." My blood was still pumping wildly through my body, adrenaline making me hyperaware. "I mean… we were nearly goners. They were bad guys. Did you see them? Hey? Nika?"

I turned to see a small tear trickling down her face. Her lips quivered and her chin puckered.

How had I been so insensitive? Nika was terrified, and I was on some sort of twisted high.

"Nika," I whispered. "Are you all right? That must have been very frightening for you."

The tears came much quicker now, rolling down her face in rapid succession.

"It's okay, Nika. We're safe now."

"I was so scared," she whimpered.

"I know." I shifted onto my side and faced her. "But we're safe now."

Nika rolled over and buried her face into my neck, pressing herself right up against me. "There was nothing I could do. I couldn't stop him. He came right at me, and touched me, and I couldn't stop it. And then the man with the knife. He was going to kill me!"

"Oh, I'm sure you could have fought them off," I reassured her, trying to comfort her in some small way. "You are strong. You can take care of yourself. You have a belt. A black one. Doesn't that mean something?"

"Oh, come on, Alfie!" she snapped. "I don't have a black belt. I was lying."

I deliberated for a moment about what to say in response. "Why did you lie?"

"Because I was mad at you!"

She began to cry harder. I was at a loss for what to do. She reached up

178

and wrapped her arm around my neck, but instead of squeezing until my head popped off, she just held on tightly, as if for dear life.

My shirt was soggy with her tears, but I didn't mind. I placed my arm around her and held her in a warm embrace. Time suddenly went all wibbly wobbly, and I had no idea how long we stayed like that in such an intimate moment, just holding each other. The smell of her hair was intoxicating, her warmth against me invigorating. I had never felt so strange – fervent, confused and slightly sick – before. What was happening to me?

Slowly Nika pulled far enough back so that she could look at me. "I'm sorry."

"What for?" I asked.

"For losing it a little bit. And for ruining your shirt."

"Oh, it's not ruined. Just a little salty if anything."

She smiled weakly and sat up. She looked quite fragile, like a cherry blossom holding onto its branch when heavy winds try to blow it away. The rays of sun that made it through the window threw a regal gold glow across her, highlighting flecks of red that I hadn't noticed were laced throughout her hair. When she turned to face me, with the sun's light adorning her just so, her eyes seemed almost sandy, a light and beautiful colour I had never seen before.

And then, just when I was in danger of losing myself entirely, she stood up and walked away.

Forty-Five

Rajesh met us at the bottom of the stairs at exactly six o'clock. I was grateful for his presence because it allowed me to regain my composure. Nika looked ravishing. There simply was no other word for it.

She wore a long black dress, with a plunging neckline that tantalised my imagination. I hated her for her beauty. Surely she knew what she was doing to me, when she cried on my shoulder, nestled into my side, then appeared before me looking like that. What was I supposed to do? I was only one man!

I had only stuttered a few sections of an unformed sentence since she emerged from the bathroom looking like some dazzling Trojan princess. The sentence would have stated, if I was functioning on a proper human level, that she looked quite elegant and I was pleased to accompany her for dinner.

What I ended up saying however, resulted in her questioning my health. Was I feeling ill? Did I want her to bring me back something to nibble? Did I need to lie down?

I had waved her words away like I was swatting at a fly, which only further served to make me appear somewhat unstable.

Now, though, as Rajesh walked us to our table, I felt as though I stood the chance of making it through dinner without looking like a total pillock.

The dining room was rather overstated. Everything was gold plated, or, more likely, painted yellow. On the walls were various different artworks, slightly more eccentric than my taste allowed for, and the lighting was so dim that I walked directly into a chair.

"Ah, sir, here is your table, sir." Rajesh stopped by a table, intricately adorned with what appeared to be their best dinnerware, as the plates, which were in their own right pieces of art, were vastly different from the plain white plates and cups that occupied every other table.

"Thank you," I said, taking a seat.

"Please, sir, enjoy your evening here with us, and once again I very much am sorry for not making mention of the potential danger for you and your beautiful wife, sir. Enjoy your meal, sir."

Before I could correct him on his grievous error as to the nature of mine and Nika's relationship, Rajesh scuttled off and disappeared.

The dining room consisted only of six patrons, myself and Nika included. A family of four sat to our immediate left. A mother and father, a small boy who must have been about six, and what appeared to be a relatively new born baby.

They looked happy and I found myself smiling at the simplicity of a family eating a meal together. Without drama. Or emotional explosions. Or me crying like a little girl in the loo. That, I was ashamed to say, had happened…more than once.

"You look very nice."

I turned abruptly from my view of the lovely family to Nika, from whom the unexpected compliment had undoubtedly originated.

"Oh. Thank you," I said, mentally giving myself a wedgie. How had I allowed Nika to compliment me before I complimented her? I was, without a doubt, the most useless man on the earth. And that included the man who lived across from us who collected his own burps in little jars and displayed them on his window sill in chronological order.

"You…you…" I said, floundering slightly, "you look good. Beautiful! I mean, beautiful."

Nika laughed. "Thank you."

I felt my face going red. No matter, I tried to console myself, I could recover. "It's a lovely dress. That one. That you're wearing. On your body. Uh, Now."

Perhaps I should excuse myself, run into the kitchen and just plunge my head into a deep fryer.

Nika laughed, a lovely little sound that gave me goose pimples.

"Thank you," she said again, smiling a small, sweet smile. Her face suddenly turned darker. "Listen, Alfie, I wanted to thank you."

"What for?"

"For what you did back there," Nika said quietly, looking down at her hands. "At the ruins. You saved my life. You came back for me when you didn't have to. I just wanted to say thank you."

Before I could respond, a waiter appeared at our table and dropped off two plates.

"Oh," I said, slightly confused. "We hadn't ordered yet."

The waiter looked at me and smiled politely, pressing his palms together in front of his chest. "Thank you very much."

"I think there's been a small error." I pointed at the plates to try to get my point across.

The waiter did a little bow and repeated what I guessed were the only words of English he knew. "Thank you very much."

"Well," I said, staring at the suspicious meals in front of us. "I suppose we should dig in?"

Nika leaned in close to the bowl in front of her and sniffed, before recoiling. "What do you think it is?"

"I believe it would be safest if we just think of it as chicken."

"Chicken?"

"It's better than the potential alternatives."

"Which could be?" Nika asked hesitantly.

I stared at Nika, and we both started to laugh. It was a nice, happy moment, which made me feel comfortable and warm. We had been at each other's throats for so long that sharing a laugh and a meal seemed like the most important thing in the world right now.

I just hoped I wouldn't screw it up.

Forty-Six

I screwed it up.

It started after the main course, when we had enjoyed a solid hour of good conversation and mysterious foods. I had allowed myself to believe that I had been misled about Nika. Perhaps I had judged her too quickly, and failed to understand how afraid she must have been when she knocked on my door.

But Nika had proven once again that she was the egotistical, schizophrenic megalomaniac that I had assumed she was.

If Nika had taught me anything, it was to trust my gut.

Admittedly, I had been the one to be a classic knob and put my foot in it, but her reaction reminded me that we had absolutely nothing in common and the sooner I could hand her over to Uncle Oswald, the better.

Our waiter had placed our desserts in front of us, and repeated his famous last words. "Thank you very much." Nika was smiling as he walked away, and the soft lighting in the room made her glow.

"This is nice, isn't it?" I said, picking up my spoon in preparation for dessert.

"What is?"

"Us. Sitting here, eating dinner together. It's nice."

Nika smiled. "Yeah, it is."

"A lot better than how we started off, eh?" I let out a small chuckle.

"Yes, well, you're much nicer now."

"Me?" I scoffed.

"What is that supposed to mean?"

183

"Well," I shrugged, "I think we both know that the one who was the most...unapproachable...was you."

"Me?"

"Yeah. You. You told my whole family we were getting married! In a matter of weeks!"

"You treated me like I was an object to be bought and sold! And you rejected me!"

"I didn't reject you, Nika," I snapped. "I just didn't even know about you."

"Oh, my mistake. You do want to marry me, then?"

I was silent, unsure how to respond. It was true that I had begun to not hate Nika quite as much as I had before, but I couldn't marry her! I would wake up every morning, see her face, and know that she was there out of obligation, rather than desire. I would know, every moment that I fell more in love with her, that she felt nothing at all for me.

"I didn't think so." Nika stood up from the table and threw down her napkin. "You're such a pig."

"Excuse me?" I spat. "I'm not the one with the mental problems!"

"I'm leaving," she hissed.

"No!" I shouted, shoving my chair back and getting to my feet. "I'm leaving. You're...you're...you're just cruel."

"I'm the cruel one? I didn't reject you, remember, Alfie. It was the other way around."

"Cow," I muttered.

Nika smirked. "We're in India. That's a term of endearment."

I scowled at her and marched out of the dining room.

"I was the one leaving, Alfie!" Nika said, trying to overtake me.

I shoved my arm out to block her way. "No, I'm leaving. I want to get away from you."

"Oh, that's very mature, Alfie. Let me through!"

I started to jog. "No!"

Nika kept my pace.

I suddenly fell face first onto the stairs. Nika had stuck her foot out and tripped me. As I watched her take the lead, my eyes narrowed and my game face appeared. I threw myself up the stairs and caught up to her, grabbing her waist and spinning her around until she no longer faced the right direction. I was gaining ground. With our room only ten feet away, I was sure that victory was mine.

However, Nika was not to be so easily defeated.

Her face was almost purple, enraged as she was. She let out an almighty screech and launched herself at me, landing solidly on my back. She wrapped her strong legs around me and squeezed, supporting herself so that she had free hands with which to repeatedly hit me on the head and back.

I waved my hands in the air, attempting to grab her flailing arms. This proved only to exacerbate her anger. She screamed again, yanking her weight this way and that. I began to stumble, my less than manly frame unable to support the banshee on top of me. When my knees hit the ground, I tried to use the time to swing her around to my front so that I could tear her off me. I growled in exertion, inhibited by the vice-like grip she had on me.

At the very moment that Nika took fistfuls of my hair in her hands, one of the doors along the corridor opened, revealing an old woman in her night gown.

We froze.

I couldn't imagine the sight we must have been; me down on all fours, trying to get her off of me, while Nika clung to my back with my hair between her fingers.

"Oh, h-hello," I stuttered. "Lovely evening, isn't it?"

The old woman began to scowl at me. Could it be that she thought that I was abusing Nika? It was, in fact, the other way around, but with the glare I was receiving, I couldn't help but think that she didn't see it that way.

"We are just…looking for my contacts." I tried to smile, and straightened up off my hands and back onto my knees. Nika's grip had somewhat relaxed since the woman had appeared, and consequently, she slid down my back until she plopped onto the ground with an oof.

"We can't find them, though," I rambled. "Tricky little things."

The woman refused to move. Nika stood to her feet and I followed. I half expected the onlooker to run back inside and phone the police. I smiled awkwardly and abruptly turned around, trailing behind Nika as we headed to our room.

India and I were not getting along.

Forty-Seven

I spent the night getting acquainted with the dust bunnies on the floor, crammed between the toilet and the door. I wasn't in the mood to force Nika to share the bed and I didn't want to be anywhere near her, anyway.

I just had to make it to Moscow, where I could finally say goodbye to her. I feared my relationship with Uncle Oswald would be forever tarnished. How could he do this to me? Did he enjoy the thought of me writhing through the emotional hurricane currently whooshing through my life?

The insanity of it all was beyond my comprehension.

I pulled out my phone and decided that I was going to take control of the situation. The trip was getting out of hand. I had bought a data packet before we left, and I set to work on booking a hire car to take us back to New Delhi, where we could get on a plane to Russia and this nightmare could end.

With my phone in my hand, I marvelled at how much simpler it would be if Uncle Oswald owned a mobile phone. But he didn't believe in them. He claimed they tore people further apart, instead of bringing them closer together, though of course he lacked proof for his idealistic theory.

I found myself silently resenting him. Perhaps I had been wrong all this time to care so much for him. I thought I knew him best in this world, and yet I never thought him capable of this.

How was it possible to be so wrong about someone?

I had been naïve. Foolish.

The hire car was waiting out the front of the hotel. It was extremely small, though I could hardly complain, given the size of my own car at home. Nika, still sour over the events of the previous evening, stood with her arms folded by the passenger door as I loaded our bags into the boot.

After carefully stacking my bags in, I picked up Nika's bag and then dropped it into the dust.

"Be careful!" she hissed.

"My mistake," I said smoothly.

I bent down to retrieve her last bag and dropped it, too. This time, however, as I reached over to pick it up, I stood on it.

"Alfie!" she shouted.

"Sorry," I said earnestly. "I'm just ever so clumsy."

"I don't think that clumsy is the word you are looking for. I think evil would be better suited to your personality, which, if I am honest, is somewhat lacking."

I stared at her in disgust.

"Oh, what now?" she sighed.

"You are such a liar. When I first opened my door to you, you could barely speak a word of English. Now, look at you. My personality is somewhat lacking? You're absolutely full of it."

"Fine. You want to know the truth?"

"Uh, yes." I slammed the boot and got into the driver's side.

As Nika followed suit, she huffed loudly. "Truth is I am excellent at English. Except, as you have seen and never fail to point out, I sometimes forget words like the. But, when I arrived at your doorstep, and when I was at your parent's house, I was nervous. So, I thought that it would be better if you, and they, thought I couldn't understand, that I was just some poor foreigner who needed you to take care of her."

I was, for a moment, stunned by the honesty. "You don't need to pretend, Nika. The black belt, the language. What is wrong with you? Is anything you have said to me true?"

"Of course," she said defensively. "You try coming to a new country, leaving everything you know behind." She paused for a long moment before sighing. "Look, do you know what the worst thing is that can happen to someone like me?"

I snorted. "The airline loses your luggage?"

"No. That the person – the stranger – you are going to meet rejects you."

I swallowed hard.

"So, don't pretend that you know anything about me, Alfie. I am alone in this world and I was promised that you would take care of me. But you hate me and you are throwing me away. What will happen to me now? I go home? To live on the streets? Or I follow your Uncle around the world?"

"There are worse things than going on adventures with Oswald, Nika."

"I know," she whispered. "And I have lived them all."

Forty-Eight

The flight to Moscow consisted of many smaller flights, hopscotching from one airport to the next until finally we landed in Moscow, sore, tired, and ready to commit murder.

Bags in hand, we trudged out into the torrential rain to find our hire car, located somewhere in the vast maze of cars.

The woman at the reception desk, a waif-like creature, with white hair and prominent bone cheeks, went through the motions of handing us our keys and vaguely pointing in the direction of carpark D4.

I was pleased to note the car was a lot larger than the one we had in India. I slipped behind the wheel after placing our bags in the boot, with room to spare. The wheel was large and leather, in front of a dashboard full of lights and buttons and knobs. I felt like Captain Kirk aboard his ship.

Nika must have sensed that I was enjoying myself and set out to stop it immediately.

"Are you going to drive, or sit here all day?" she snapped.

"I haven't decided," I answered curtly.

"Do you even know where we're going?"

I realised in that moment that I didn't. I had absolutely no idea. "I don't need to know. That's why we have maps."

I keyed in the Boryenka Hotel, hoping Oswald's friend would meet us there like the letter promised.

I eased out into the traffic like one half-blind and began the journey to the centre of Moscow, a place I'd never expected to visit. The rain was slushing against the windscreen, obscuring the world before me. Cars whizzed past us, drivers leaning on their horns as they went by.

"The locals seem friendly," I murmured.

"Speed up!" Nika shrieked.

"I am going at a perfectly acceptable speed. If I go any faster, we'll crash into something. Now be quiet and let me drive. Unless of course, you would prefer to take over."

The roads felt sloppy and sticky and there were at least a dozen moments, in the last thirty minutes, where I had become more than slightly afraid for our lives.

"What was that?" Nika squirmed in her seat.

The loud bang had carried with it an ominous weight. I knew, even with my limited knowledge of cars, we had just flattened a tire. This meant only one thing.

We. Were. Buggered.

I steered the car to the side of the road, and it rolled to a stop. Now that we were stationary, the rain sounded tinnier as it stabbed at the roof protecting us from the insipid downpour.

"Why did you stop?" Nika asked, fright rising in her voice.

I groaned. "I can't very well keep going, can I? We have a flat tire!"

"Alfie!"

"What? It's not my fault! I can't do anything about it."

Nika's mouth popped open in horror. "But…but…but… you are a man!"

"And the award for the Most Observant Woman of the Year goes to the charming woman beside me," I spoke into the air.

"You are a man!" she said again, this time her voice in a venomous hiss.

"Careful, if you keep saying it that might change. I hear the doctors are warning people. Men everywhere are just – poof – turning into women. Left, right and bloody centre."

"Alfie!"

"What, Nika? What does my being a man have to do with anything?"

"You are a man; this is a car. Get out and fix it."

191

I started to laugh. Perhaps something inside of me snapped, but I found myself laughing hysterically. The combination of my simply preposterous situation, intertwined with this gigantic failure of a trip, had potentially robbed me of my sanity.

"What is wrong with you?" Nika bellowed. "Why are you laughing?"

I gathered myself, grasping onto whatever shred of lucidity I had left. "Nika, I can't fix this car."

"Why not?"

"Not all men drink bear, watch sports, pick their noses and scratch their gentleman sausages in public. Likewise, Dominika, not all men are mechanics. We aren't born with a wrench in our hands. Or jump leads. Or…whatever."

"Then…then… we are stuck? Here?" she gulped.

"It would seem that way."

Nika clasped a hand over her mouth and stifled a small sob.

"Oh, relax," I sighed. I pulled my phone out of my pocket and turned to her with what I almost hoped would be a reassuring smile that would comfort her. "I shall simply call the car company and have someone out here to fix it or give us another car. Keep your knickers on, Nika."

A solid punch landed on my arm.

"Ouch! What was that for?"

Nika pointed an accusing finger in my direction. "You think that just because we are stopped in this car that I will be having the…" she looked around as if she could be heard, then whispered, "sex?"

"Uh…pardon?"

"I am not taking off my knickers! You are a pig!" She punched me again, harder this time and I really had to protest.

"Nika! It's an expression. It means relax. It means calm down. Not let's have the sex."

"Oh." Nika looked confused, but quickly recovered. "That is a disgusting expression. You British people. All about the sex and women and… and… the sex!"

192

"Okay, I for one would feel much more comfortable if we could all stop saying the word sex. All right? I apologise on behalf of all British people for that expression. Can we move on to the slightly more pressing matter at hand?"

"Yes. Please."

"I'm going to step out of the car and call someone, okay?"

"Okay. Okay. Good idea."

I stole one last look at her, bemused by the way she had contorted her face into a mask of concern. Whether the concern was for her own well-being or mine was yet to be determined, but were I a betting man, my money would be on the former.

I slipped out of the car and was immediately pelted by the rain. I closed the door behind me to keep Nika dry from any rain that may gush in and started up the road. I tried to keep my phone as protected as possible, but within mere moments I was drenched from head to toe. I tried to use the fact that the water was quite warm as my consolation for becoming the human embodiment of a drowned rat, but to no avail. Still, it was better than being in the car with her.

I held the phone up to my ear.

Tilting my face to the deep grey sky, I took a moment's pause to evaluate my situation and consider my next move.

That was the moment we heard a gunshot.

Forty-Nine

It was a terrible thing to have the car break down in what could only be described as a deeply unpleasant area. Whether it was due to the rain or the location, there was no one walking down the streets, therefore no one to rescue us from our current predicament.

My feet were glued to the ground. There was nothing I could do to save myself as I watched a man, who had clearly been shot in the leg, beg for mercy from two menacing figures.

Nika ran out of the car and stood beside me.

"Alfie! What was that?" she asked. "It sounded like a gunshot."

I couldn't respond, so Nika was left with no choice but to follow my gaze and watch the scene unfolding.

I had no idea what was going on, but the two men didn't seem intent on killing their victim. After the gunshot, they seemed to be content with having a conversation. A conversation I was glad I couldn't hear.

As the man on the ground, bleeding and wounded, nodded profusely, making promises in Russian, the two gargoyles turned away from him to head back to their car, only to pause when they saw me, open-mouthed, staring at them like a guppy in need of feeding.

"Oh no," Nika breathed. "We should go."

Nika tried to tug on my arm, and she was right to do so, for this would be the moment I should run to the car and zoom away, flat and all. But I couldn't move. I was paralysed with fear. They were going to kill us. Most definitely. She froze when they appeared before us.

"Having car trouble?" one of the men asked in English, clearly aware I was no countryman.

"Uhh," I spluttered. "Yes. Flat tyre."

"Dangerous place to get stuck," the other added.

"We just got here. I'm afraid I don't know my way around very well." My heart was racing in my chest. I was confident this was the moment I would projectile vomit all over them.

"What do you think, Mikhail. Should we give these poor tourists a lift?"

"I think so, boss. Can't very well leave them here alone. Anything could happen to them."

"T-t-that's okay," I said quietly. "We're q-quite fine."

"Really," the one Mikhail called boss closed the gap between us and slammed a firm hand on my shoulder. "I insist."

We sat opposite the boss, in a stately car, with no way out other than flinging open the door and hoping the road took mercy on us.

I watched the boss look us up and down, wondering what to make of us. He stared at me for some time, as though he had intentions of de-vouring my soul, before his lips stretched into the widest of grins. "Hello!" he all but shouted. "It is our pleasure, of course, to offer you a car ride in this most horrible of weathers. We are just doing our civic duty – helping strangers in need."

"You're very kind," Nika said quietly.

"Oh, well, you simply could not have stayed where you were. This is a very dangerous road. All sorts of unsavoury characters all around."

"It is very likely you would have died," the man driving piped in.

I twiddled my fingers in my lap. "Then we are even more grateful for your aid. We have families to get back to. And…monkeys." I read some-where that one should try to remind one's kidnappers that one was human. It was supposed to make it more likely they would spare one's life. I hoped sincerely it would work in our current situation if we were indeed in grave danger. Emphasis on the grave.

"I like the way you talk. Where are you from? Australia?" The boss asked.

"Kangaroo!" Mikhail yelped. "Koala!"

"Uh no, actually. I'm from uh…from Britain."

"Ah, you are Irish?"

I pursed my lips. "No, no. English. England." I took a nervous breath. "I'm English."

"Oh! England! Big Ben!" the driver said.

"Prince Harry!" the first added.

"Yes," I laughed. "That's right. Prince Harry."

"I like him," the driver said. "I like his red, red hair. Just like yours. So you are both from England then?"

"No," Nika said. "I am from the Czech Republic."

"Ah!" the driver bellowed. The long stagnant silence remained empty for several seconds. "Actually, I do not know anything about that place."

"What are your names?" the other asked.

"Well, I am Alfie and this is Nika."

"Alfie and Nika." He reached over to slap each of our knees enthusiastically. "We are Pavel," he placed a hand delicately to his own chest, before pointing at the driver, "and Mikhail."

"It's a pleasure to meet you," I said croaking.

Pavel was a broad-faced man, with ice-blue eyes and clear skin. His hair was black, and his broad shoulders hinted at a strength that far exceeded my own. Behind him, Mikhail was even larger. A large scar ran down the side of his bald head, and his features were thin and ghostly.

I sank back in the seat and squeezed my eyes closed, wondering if I tapped my heels together three times and thought there's no place like home, I might find myself back at my flat in Wandsworth. Unlikely.

"What brings you to Russia?" Pavel asked.

"Uh, just visiting a family member."

"You have Russian family?" Mikhail asked, suspicious.

"No. My uncle is here for work. He's waiting for us. He's an archaeologist." Maybe if I told them about Oswald, they'd know someone was waiting for us, someone would know if we were shot and thrown in a birch forest or something for wolves to enjoy.

"Archaeologist," Pavel said, testing the word on his lips. "I do not know this word."

"Uh, archaeologist. They uh, they explore old things. Dig stuff up," I wondered how to explain, then thought of Uncle Oswald's own description. "Lara Croft. Tomb Raider? Know of it?"

Pavel's blank expression twisted into a smile. "Tomb Raider! Lara Croft! I love her movies."

I smiled weakly. "Good, good. Yes. He's like that, only he's… well… he's a man."

Pavel smiled at us, seemingly satisfied. His thick lips stretched back over perfectly straight teeth. "You know, I have a feeling about you two."

"A f-feeling?" I stuttered.

"Yes. I feel as though I can trust you."

"You can," I said reassuringly.

"I feel like I can trust both of you not to say anything about what you just saw. Or," he laughed, "actually, about anything you see at all while you are with us."

"Of course," I said, nodding vigorously. "We shan't say a word."

Nika shoved her hand into mine and squeezed until the tips of my fingers were white.

"Good." Pavel smiled. "Because I like you. I like you both very much. And I would hate to have to make Mikhail come and find you. It would make my heart very sad."

"We wouldn't want that," I said.

"Of course, I will need you to prove your loyalty to me. So that I know I can trust you, yes?"

"Oh, uh, right. What can we do? Pinky-swear?" I laughed weakly, but Pavel didn't seem to see the humour.

Pavel shrugged. "I have a job for you. Easy. You do this for me, I know that I can trust you."

197

"A j-job? What sort of job? We're just tourists. We don't have a visa to work here."

Mikhail laughed. It was an unexpectedly joyful sound, with a slight wheeze at the end, suggesting he was a smoker.

"Not that kind of job," Pavel said, a hint of humour in his voice.

"Oh. Right."

The car came to a sudden stop and my stomach almost fell through my feet.

Pavel nodded towards a café outside. It was quaint and lively, with striped awnings and metal seats outside, abandoned due to the wet weather.

"Inside is a man who would like to join me in my business ventures. I don't know if I can trust him. You are English. You can help me."

"How?" I spluttered.

"I want you to pose as a spy and try to get him to turn on me."

I stared back, unblinking. Surely, I had not heard what I had just heard. "I'm sorry, what did you say?"

"I want you to pose as an MI6 agent and try to get the man inside to turn on me."

"How am I supposed to do that?"

Pavel shrugged his large shoulders. "I am sure you will find a way. I want to trust you. I don't want to hurt you. You do this for me, and I know that we can be friends."

"But I—"

"Alfie. I would hate to have to hurt you. I like you. You understand, no?"

I breathed out a shaky breath. "I understand."

"I will stay here with Nika and enjoy her company while you do what I ask."

I looked from Pavel to Nika and knew what he was saying. Two hours in Moscow and I had already been recruited for the mafia. If I ever made it back to England, I wasn't going to travel ever again.

"Okay," I said, attempting a tone that resembled confident.

"Good!" Pavel cracked his hands together and laughed. "His name is Luka Morozov."

Pavel held up his phone and showed me a photo of a thin man, who couldn't have been more than twenty-five. He had bleached blonde hair, and tattoos on the side of his face.

I nodded and reached a shaky hand to the door handle to let myself out. My blood was pulsating through my body at rapid speed, and I felt sweat mingle with rain as I walked towards the café.

Was I really going to do this?

But then, what choice did I have?

How had I managed to get myself into this situation? If I didn't follow through, there was no doubt that Pavel would kill Nika. I couldn't let that happen. I had no choice but to forge ahead.

Everything I knew about being a spy came from watching James Bond films, so I knew the first thing I needed was a suit jacket. I looked around the room and saw one hanging on the back of a chair. The man occupying the chair was engaged in raucous conversation with his guests.

I walked past the table and swiped the jacket off the back of the chair. A rush of adrenaline coursed through my veins. The only thing I had ever stolen was my mother's heart the day I was born. I waited until I was far enough from the table to slip the jacket on, wiping sweat from my brow as I went.

I had to calm down or this was all going to go very badly. I darted into the bathroom and turned on the tap, letting cold water wash over my hands. I washed the sweat off my face and eyed the reflection staring back at me.

"You can do this," I encouraged, pointing an angry finger at the face staring back at me. "You are James Bond."

I straightened and slowed my breathing. I took a moment to neaten my hair and dry my face. With one last steely glare, I left the bathroom.

Feeling slightly more together, I surveyed the café, looking for my target. I saw him sitting by himself at a booth, eating a positively enormous sandwich. I slowly glided towards him, the very picture of cool and calm.

I saw down beside him, without saying a word.

He grunted something at me in Russian.

I tilted my head to the side and waited.

"What are you doing at my table?" he asked again, this time in English.

"I'd just like to have a conversation with you, Mr Morozov." I raised a hand to the passing waitress. "Two olive martinis, please. Shaken, not stirred."

"What do you want?" Luka asked, wary. "Who are you?"

"Me? I'm nobody. But you? You're somebody special."

"Get the hell out of here," Luka spat.

My heart slammed in my chest. But Nika needed me. She was going to die if I couldn't pull this off. "I'm afraid I can't do that. See, you work for a very dangerous man. A man that we'd like to know more about."

"You are not from here. You're English. What are you, a spy?"

I remained silent.

"So, you are a spy," Luka said, drawing his own conclusions as our olive martinis arrived.

"I just want to know about your boss, Pavel. See, he's a very dangerous man, and I'm sure he wouldn't be happy to know we are having this conversation. He might even think you turned on him." I took a sip of my first ever martini and tried not to spit it straight back out again.

"He will kill me," Luka said.

My stomach lurched. "I don't want that to happen."

"You can offer me protection?"

"See, I—" I was starting to fall apart. If Luka turned on Pavel, then Pavel was going to kill him and that would make me an accessory. I couldn't be a part of this. My façade was starting to crack. "I, uh—"

"I'll talk. I'll tell you anything you want to know. Pavel is a top player in the mafia," Luka said quickly, spilling his words out across the table.

"You should really stop," I said, but he didn't hear me.

"He owns half the police force. Please, you have to make sure you get me out of Russia safely. He'll kill me!"

I was going to pass out. This was not going well.

Luka gulped down his martini in one mouthful. I stood to my feet and started pacing in front of his booth.

This was going very badly. What was I going to do?

I could see Luka flailing his arms beside me, lost in total panic.

"Oh no," I said to myself quietly. "Oh, no, no, no. I can't do this. I can't be a part of this."

I spun around to face Luka, whose eyes were wide with panic. "He's going to kill you, you total moron!"

Luka was speechless, grasping at the air like a madman.

"You turned on him! Just like that! I thought the mafia were supposed to be tough! You just folded like a paper towel!"

I started to pace again, with no idea what to do now. "He's outside, right now, and he's waiting for me to come back and tell him if you turned on him. What am I supposed to do now?"

I wore a hole in the carpet, pacing in front of Luka as he panicked. "I could lie!" I spun around, elated with my idea, to notice Luka was a strange shade of purple.

"This is no time to lose it, Luka. I need your help or we're both going to die."

Luka slumped back in his chair and stopped moving. Finally, he was calming down. "Thank you," I said, sitting down opposite him. "All we have to do is lie. And you have to never betray your boss again. You really should have thought harder about your career choices."

Luka stared into space, unspeaking.

"Luka?" I said, not understanding his sudden silence. "Luka?" I reached out a hand to touch him and he slumped forwards, his head slamming down on the table. "Luka?" I repeated weakly.

I reached a tentative hand to his neck and felt for a pulse. I dry-heaved when my fingers felt no rhythm.

He was dead! How the hell had he died? I looked around for some sort of clue as to how he had died, only to notice his martini glass was empty and his olive was gone. The memory of a panicked Luka gulping back his entire martini flashed across my eyes.

"Oh," I breathed. "Oh dear."

I looked around, but no one seemed to have noticed us yet. I stood up and quickly walked across the floor to the exit. I burst out of the café into the rain and threw myself into the back of Pavel's car, never more grateful to be stuck in a car with mobsters.

"What happened?" Pavel asked.

I was breathing heavily, bordering on panic. "He turned on you," I spluttered. I realised I was still wearing the stolen jacket and whipped it off as quickly as I could.

"I knew it. That lying snake," Pavel hissed.

"I killed him!" I shouted.

Nika jumped back in surprise and Pavel's eyes went wide.

"What?" Pavel chuckled.

"You were right. He folded on you in no time. And… and… I killed him. He's dead."

"You killed him? How?" Pavel asked.

"He… choked," I croaked.

"You choked him? In a cafe?"

Mikhail and Pavel stared at me, their expressions unreadable.

"I—I…" I was going to be killed.

Pavel erupted in laughter. He clapped his hands as Mikhail started laughing.

"This guy!" Pavel said, turning to Mikhail. "I love him!"

Pavel reached across and put two hands on either side of my face. He kissed my cheeks, one then the other, and then slapped his hands against me.

"You have earned my trust, Alfie! Now, we are brothers. Our bond is forged in blood."

"I…" I sat back in the seat, stunned.

"Come. Now we drink. Mikhail, get us out of here."

Mikhail pulled the car out onto the road and sped away. I watched the café disappear behind us.

Fifty

How we had gotten from the outside of the café in which I had accidentally been party to a man's untimely demise at the hands of an olive, to the inside of a bright, noisy, and somewhat cluttered restaurant was beyond me. Perhaps I had slipped into some sort of comatose state, whereby I lost my sanity, and my brain could not hold onto even the simplest of audio or visual stimuli.

Standing at the entrance of the restaurant, we were greeted quickly by a nervous looking man, who seem overly friendly and welcoming. I figured it was not my own intimidating figure that cast a ghoulish light upon his brow, but rather that of my company.

They conversed quickly, then Pavel turned to me and smiled. "You will love the food here. It is the best."

I had to do something. I had to act, or Nika and I could end up just like the man currently dead in a café half an hour away. Now was the time. I summoned my courage, like Samwise Gamgee as he carried Frodo up the mountain. "Oh," I chuckled weakly. "That's a lovely offer. Really. But I am afraid we must be going."

Pavel's eyebrows were drawn until they met in the middle of his face. He then waved his hand at me and laughed. "Nonsense! You will come."

I dug my heels in. "I truly thank you for your hospitality, Pavel, but I must insist."

Pavel pursed his lips and looked to Mikhail, whose face was drawn. I regretted my decision to be bold the moment that Pavel turned back to me and wrapped, quite firmly, his arm around my neck. His face was remarkably close to mine, to the point where I could smell exactly what he had eaten earlier in the day. Chicken. Or some form of poultry. I didn't want to think about it.

"Alfie." His voice was lower now than it had been before. I felt a chill. "You must let me provide you with dinner. My mother, she taught me to take care of people, like they are family. I feel that I know you, Alfie. Like we have been lifelong friends. What you have done for me, it makes us brothers. You and me, united forever. You must allow me the honour of a meal together. Don't you feel the same way?"

I let out a pitiful laugh and nodded. "I do." Not.

"See? We are family. Nothing is more important to me than family. I do not let anything come between me and my family. Anything. Do you understand?"

I nodded again. I felt Nika grip hold of my shirt as if at any moment she was going to make a run for it, tugging me along as she went.

Pavel released me and threw his arms up in the air. "Excellent! It is settled then. You will join us for dinner."

I looked at Nika in what I hoped was a reassuring way. "We would love to, Pavel."

This seemed to brighten the face of Mikhail. I couldn't shake the thought that he looked like some kind of crocodile who was giddy about finding out some unwitting tourists were going to go swimming in his lake. Every single giant sea creature film I had ever seen quickly flashed before my eyes.

I could only hope that our evening would end in a slightly less gruesome way.

We were led past the rest of the patrons, into a back room, prepared, I assumed, especially for visits such as this. All eyes were on us as we disappeared from view. Seven or eight other men were already in the room waiting. Pavel greeted them loudly, and equally as vocal greetings were thrust back at him. Clearly, he was beloved by whoever all these men were. Pavel grasped both my shoulder and Nika's, and began, I guessed, explaining who we were in his native tongue.

Abruptly, one at a time, the men popped up and shook our hands fervently, like we were old friends they hadn't seen in an age.

The shock of it all was quite disarming.

"Do you understand what they're saying?" I asked Nika.

"I am not from Russia. I'm from the Czech Republic. It's not the same thing," she whispered.

"Oh. Right. Sorry."

Ushered into my seat, I sat completely unprepared for anything that was to come. I was so far from home and in a situation so far removed from any reality I had ever known. My stomach was rolling tumultuously, partly from nerves and partly because I was feeling guilty about offering what would turn out to be a deadly martini to a man I didn't even know.

There was only one thing to do.

I held out my glass as the man to my right filled it with what I could only guess was vodka. In one fell swoop, I downed it. My throat burned like fire, which told me that it was potent. Nika looked at me, deliberated for a moment, and then gulped down her own drink. We were either going to enjoy an unexpected evening out with some mobsters or we were going to die. Either way, alcohol seemed like the right choice.

Admittedly, it wasn't exactly the best plan, but devoid of any others, I rolled with it.

The man to my right laughed when I held out my glass for a refill, my face still mangled in distaste, as the burning refused to cease. As I finished my second glass and the entrees were served, I didn't feel quite so scared anymore.

In fact, I was feeling pretty groovy.

Fifty-One

The night became a flurry of rich, sumptuous foods I'd never seen before, head spinning drinks and amusing conversation. Even Nika seemed more relaxed than I had seen her in a long while. Whether this was attributed to the fact that she was becoming more and more intoxicated, or to the fact that she was warming up around our company, I wasn't sure, and in my current state, I didn't much care.

The entire trip so far had been one gigantic mess, and for the first time, surrounded by people who were definitely skirting the law, I was actually… happy. Truly happy. I didn't have to worry about assignments or essays or whether or not Hugh was going to wear trousers that day or just wander around in his underpants. I didn't feel any residual anger or bitterness towards Uncle Oswald, or Nika. She, in my eyes, seemed positively radiant. I found myself letting go of everything she had ever said or done to me that had caused me to want to wring her neck until her little head plopped off her shoulders. I felt light and happy. I felt… splendid.

Something told me it wasn't the alcohol, of which I had rather uncharacteristically consumed plenty, that was responsible for my joviality. I felt loose and free, like the stuffing that had been keeping me rigid all these years was pouring out of me. I didn't need pretences in the company of criminals. It didn't matter that I was poor or that I lived in a crappy flat in the dodgy end of Wandsworth. It didn't matter that my family was certifiably insane or that I was here with a woman who I was supposed to marry, yet barely knew. All that mattered was that I was here, and that everything was just fine. Ish.

I looked to Nika and smiled. She grinned back, her face flushed red. I felt the sudden urge to lean over to her and kiss her beautifully plump lips. She was the embodiment of perfection. She was beauty in its finest feminine form. I could search a thousand cities on every continent, and I would never see another face that was as stunning as hers. I was going to do it. I felt like I was the Han Solo to her Leia, the Captain Wash to her Zoe; the Doctor to her River Song. How could I possibly get rejected?

Just as I started to lean forward, ready to kiss her and make her my own, Pavel appeared behind her, took her hand, and yanked her up to her feet. She laughed a beautiful musical sound, as Pavel started to spin her around in time with the music.

They were quickly joined by others, who lined up around them and started to dance. Apparently, now that dinner was over, it was time to dance.

Disheartened as I was at my golden opportunity being robbed from me, I couldn't help but be swept up in the moment as I watched Mikhail and Pavel teach Nika how to dance like a Russian.

My newest friend, an extremely muscular man named Oleg, took both of my hands in his and stood me up beside him. He walked me through a few steps and before I knew it, I was dancing like I was born there.

Or, more likely, dancing like I was very, very drunk.

I slammed into Nika and she laughed, and it was the best feeling in the world to be holding her. I couldn't remember why I had ever been angry at her. Why did I hate her? There was no reason, surely. She was an angel. Nothing but an angel.

Pavel appeared beside us and shouted something, causing an eruption of laughter and cheers. He passed Nika and me a glass and held our hands up in the air. "Zazdaróvye!" he shouted, and the night vanished into a blur.

Fifty-Two

I had awoken into a nightmare.

As the night grew late and the sun was close to rising, we somehow found our way to a hotel room above the restaurant and collapsed on the bed, fully clothed, right down to our muddy shoes. I had drifted off into a peaceful, dreamless sleep, swallowed by the fluffiness of the bed and the warmth of Nika's close body.

The night was a blur, but one I remembered, for the most part, quite fondly.

I heard a loud thump that roused me from my sleep. My arm was draped over Nika's waist, and she was snuggled closely into my side. I quickly pulled my arm off her, unsure exactly how I had ended up in this exact position.

While I was debating how to get out of the bed without waking her, our door burst open.

Nika and I flew into an upright position, bleary eyed and substantially hung over. Mikhail stood in the doorway, panting and sweating.

"You have to get out of here," he hissed.

"What?" I groaned.

Mikhail closed the door quickly and flicked the lock. "The police. It's a raid. You have to run."

"The police?" Nika shrieked, crawling off the bed. "What do they want with us?"

My eyes almost rolled back in my head as I drifted into a state of shock.

"Pavel told me to warn you. Hurry. You must leave. Meet us on the outskirts of Moscow, at Ivanovich Hotel."

While I wanted to ask why we would do that, Mikhail was otherwise preoccupied running to our window, opening it wide.

Before I could ask what exactly was going on, Mikhail threw himself out of the window.

Nika screamed.

Getting to my feet, I rushed to the window to survey the damage of what we had just witnessed. But, instead of a body splattered all over the ground below, I saw a sopping wet Mikhail clawing his way out of the swimming pool below, before taking off at a remarkable speed.

"He's fine," I assured Nika calmly. "There's a swimming pool right below us."

Nika dropped her hand from her mouth in relief. "What was he talking about?"

Another loud thud, this time much closer, and followed by the shouts of what I could only imagine were Russian police officers, threw into sharp relief the situation in which we had found ourselves.

"Never mind," Nika said. "We have to go." She ran to her bag, and threw it over her shoulder. She threw my rucksack at me and I caught it with my face. "We'll have to leave the rest behind."

"I'm going to spend the rest of my life in a Russian prison, aren't I?" I gasped.

"No, you're not," Nika said, leaning out the window.

"What on earth are you doing?" I asked.

Nika was halfway out the window, her legs dangling over the side. "I am running."

My bleary eyes widened. "You cannot be serious. You can't jump out the window."

"Alfie, you killed a man, remember?"

"No, no, no. Wait. It was the olive. I didn't mean to. He choked. Do I feel responsible? Yes. Did I technically kill him? No."

"Alfie," Nika said seriously, taking hold of my hand. "We have about five seconds before they burst into this room and take us to jail. Do you want that?"

"Well, no, but…"

"Then jump."

Without giving me the chance to further explain my view of the situation, Nika plopped straight out of the window and splashed into the pool below.

"Please tell me this is a dream," I muttered.

Just as the words escaped my lips, the door to our room was thrust open yet again and dozens of police officers stormed in.

Looking down, I saw Nika wave me down to join her. I didn't have time to consider any other course of action. It was this or go to jail. I slung my rucksack over my shoulders and crawling out of the window, I took a deep breath jumped.

Fifty-Three

The water below was ice-cold, and I immediately regretted the dozen or so alcoholic beverages I had consumed mere hours ago. My stomach was churning like the torrents of a raging sea, as I plummeted to the bottom of the pool, entirely enveloped.

I paddled my way to the surface of the water, gasping for a breath when my face hit the air.

"Hurry up!" Nika yelled over the angry shouts from the policemen above us. "We have to go!"

"I don't feel so good," I spluttered as I doggy-paddled my way to the side of the pool.

Nika was already out, so she assisted in lugging my lethargic body out of the water. As soon as I was on my two feet, she took my hand and started to run. Without looking back, I followed her. I felt like the Doctor and Amy Pond, running from some new alien threat. Only, I supposed, rather embarrassingly, in this scenario I was Amy Pond and Nika was the Doctor.

Running into the breeze, while sopping wet, made both speed and stability an issue. Speed, because the heaviness of my now drenched clothes weighed me down, and stability because I was battling the urge to vomit with every step.

Shouts that drew nearer behind us made Nika run faster, dragging me along. I looked over my shoulder to see seven or eight men chasing after us.

Oh dear.

"Faster, Alfie!" Nika shouted, though why she bothered I wasn't sure. I needed no encouragement to outrun these men.

We rounded a corner and almost collected a father and son who had the distinct misfortune of walking in our way.

I stopped, unable to simply continue and abandon all chivalry, no matter the circumstances. "I am so sorry," I spluttered. "I truly apologise."

"Leave them, Alfie!" Nika shrieked, already ten feet in front of me.

Flustered, I awkwardly petted the child's head and, as he began to cry, I took off in a flurry to chase after Nika. I had never been more disappointed in myself. I had forsaken them in their moment of need.

Nika was turning me into a true scoundrel.

Whether it was being drenched in icy water or the sudden, unwelcome smell of some unnameable food coming from a nearby stall – or perhaps even a combination of the two – the nausea I had been feeling became an immediate hindrance to our escape.

I was running in line with Nika when I raised a hand to my mouth and stopped dead in my tracks, unable to continue a single step further.

As she turned around to yell at me once more for slowing us down while we were busy outrunning the authorities, Nika's face developed a blurry hue.

"Oh my," I mumbled through my fingers.

"Alfie?" I was certain Nika had intended on speaking to me in a much harsher tone, and the fact that she didn't served as an indication of how I must have looked.

Without a choice, I turned to the side and was fortunate enough to bend over in time for it to be the gutter, and not the woman in front of me, to catch the projectile vomit that catapulted from my mouth.

"Alfie!" Nika squeaked.

I wrapped my arms around my stomach and coughed yesterday's dinner out of my throat. Warm hands touched my back soothingly. Still bent over, I opened my previously tightly squeezed eyes, expecting to see Nika's feet beside me, as she stood near and rubbed my back. I shot up in surprise, however, when small feet, encased in black leather, was all I saw.

213

A sympathetic looking old woman, with tufts of grey hair sprouting underneath her colourful babushka, took her hand from my back and gave me an encouraging slap on the shoulder and a heartening smile.

"Oh," I moaned, before clearing my throat of sick. "Thank you. Thank you very much."

"Alfie! Run, you idiot!"

Nika's voice reminded me that I was currently a wanted man, in manner of Roy O'Bannon, and the shouts to halt brought my attention to the police who had almost caught up to us.

However, hastiness was never a reason to be outright rude to strangers. "Have a nice day, ma'am," I said, before taking off as quickly as my weak and shaky frame would allow.

I followed Nika as she wound her way through the streets, navigating seamlessly on sheer instinct. Either that or she was getting us hopelessly lost. I tried to keep up with her, but the rhythmic pounding of my feet against the ground and the jostling of my body proved to be too much, time and again. I lasted about thirty feet the first time, when I was overcome by the urge to, once again, empty my stomach. Seeing a nearby bin, I paused momentarily to throw my head inside it and blow cookies.

I didn't allow myself more time than absolutely necessary to finish heaving, before I took off once again. It was the most unpleasant of circumstances, but I tried to remind myself that ending up lost in a Russian prison would be far, far worse.

I made it about a quarter of a mile the second time, when heat rose again to my cheeks and my stomach warned me that I was about to relive last night's fluid intake once again.

I fell to my knees and coughed violently into the gutter.

I couldn't take much more of this.

I looked up to see that Nika hadn't stopped for me this time, and she was quickly getting away from me. Forcing myself to my feet, I jogged after her for another hundred or so feet.

"Stop!" I shouted as we ducked down a small lane. "Let's just take a breather."

Nika, equally as breathless, mercifully agreed and threw herself into an alleyway, taking cover behind a collection of rubbish bins. I parked myself beside her, raking in air.

"Are you alright?" she asked.

What a stupid question. "Fine," I muttered.

"You threw up in technicolour back there."

I sighed, unable to speak for fear the words threw up would bring on another picturesque performance.

"A few times," she added.

"Please," I rasped, waving a hand to swat away her words.

"Quiet!" she hissed.

At that very moment, the unaware police officers ran straight past the mouth of our little hideaway lane and continued on a path that we were no longer following.

The coast was clear.

"They're gone," she whispered. "We're fine now."

My stomach lurched, and not in the way that indicated I was about to try for another attempt at emptying my belly. Rather, I was filled with a sudden, unavoidable sense of dread.

"Time to get the hell out of Russia before they alert the train stations and airports and we are stuck here forever."

"Let's go," Nika said, rising.

"Wait," I said.

"What is it? We don't have time for this."

Promptly, I threw up again.

Wiping my mouth, I stood up. "Now we can go."

Fifty-Four

If there was one thing I knew, it was that being on the run from police in Russia is pretty much the worst-case scenario. It's no secret that Russia is a communist country, and they don't take kindly to people, particularly foreigners, running from the police.

The airport wasn't far from where we were, so we were able to high-tail it to the airport and catch the next flight out, without the luxury of caring about the destination. This meant that a fifteen hours later we arrived in South Korea, incredibly jet lagged and considerably poorer.

I had spent the entire plane ride questioning my life choices.

Landing at Incheon Airport, I had never felt more relief to have ended up in a random country, that wasn't of my choosing. We had successfully made it out of Russia, and there was no way I was ever going to go back.

Sitting outside the airport, the fresh, cold rain a relief to my cheeks burning with shame, I sat down on a bench and tried to evaluate our situation.

I couldn't be farther from home if I had tried to be. Worse than that, I was nowhere near Uncle Oswald, who was still, as far as I knew, in Russia, awaiting my arrival. Worse, I was running out of money. Oswald had paid for our flights to Russia, but he hadn't paid for the flights for us to escape and getting home to London was looking less and less like a possibility.

I had limited savings that had all but been used up, and a credit card with a miniscule limit. What were we going to do?

South Korea was a place I'd only ever seen when I partook in my very secret guilty pleasure – watching Korean dramas.

216

It was thanks to that that I had a vague idea about where we were.

"Well," Nika said, sitting down beside me. "I've never been here before."

"No," I sighed. "Neither have I."

"Might as well enjoy it, right?" Nika shrugged her shoulders, seemingly unperturbed by the events of the last forty-eight hours.

"Nika, we've lost most of our belongings in Russia, we just fled the police, we have no money, and now we're a million miles away from Oswald, in South Korea! You know what we're going to do?"

"What?"

"We're going to figure out what we're going to do!"

"From a bench outside the airport?" Nika rolled her eyes. "Come on, we may as well get a train into the city and get something to eat. We can make a plan on the way."

Nika stood up and held out her hand for me to take. I looked at it, and then at her. "Come on. We're here. Nothing is going to change that right now. We may as well have a good time."

I laughed. Not a small snicker. Not a weak chortle. A full, stomach-aching laugh. I had either gone insane or I had realised that there was no better reaction to the situation in which I had found myself. This trip had so far pushed me beyond my limits, but I would be lying if I did not admit that somewhere deep inside, I was starting to like it.

I had no money, no way of contacting Oswald, no idea how to speak Korean and no clue what to do next.

I took Nika's hand and we headed for the train.

217

Fifty-Five

It took me mere minutes to realise I really liked South Korea.

The train was clean. Like, unbelievably clean. There was no graffiti, no weird smell. No gum stuck on the seat, no hoodlums intimidating elderly women. I could live on this train, quite happily.

Once we disembarked our pleasant train ride, we were in a cacophony of noise and people and busyness and I felt a buzz of excitement prickling my toes. We took to walking, since spending money on a cab felt like a luxury at this point. But walking proved to be an excellent choice.

If the signs – which very conveniently, were also written in English – were to be believed, we had found ourselves in a place called Insa-dong and I was not displeased. There were countless stalls selling a variety of strange (to me) foods, and I found myself abandoning my cherished rule of never buying food off a street vendor. Not simply because the cost was so low, but because the food was so good.

"Want one of these, too?" I asked Nika, pointing at some sort of fish-like substance on a stick. "And these ball-things, too?"

Nika agreed happily, and we munched on our first meal in hours.

"I didn't realise how hungry I was," she sighed happily. "I love this place."

"I can't believe I've never been here before," I exclaimed, as we walked past brightly lit shops selling everything from homewares to croissants, and everything in between.

The road turned to cobblestones, and open streets became alleyways, with stairs leading up and down. Tiny little restaurants poked through holes in the wall, and everywhere you looked was life itself.

I realised, with alarming intensity, how small my world had been before Nika had entered it.

"I'm glad I met you," I blurted, surprising even myself.

"Really?" Nika said, possibly more shocked than I was at what had just come out of my mouth.

"Yeah. I am."

Nika hesitated a moment, taking a bite into her mystery food-stick. "Me, too," she finally said.

We must have walked around for hours before I finally saw it. I stopped in the middle of the street, and stared.

"What is it?" Nika asked. "What's wrong."

I simply pointed, unable to speak.

Nika followed my outstretched finger. "Oh," she said. "Ohhh."

Without another word, we marched through a set of doors to find ourselves surrounded by meercats.

Meercats.

As a few of the curious little fellows toddled up to me, I dropped to my knees like a broken man and allowed them to investigate me.

"I had no idea you were such an animal lover," Nika laughed.

"The monkey didn't give it away?" I lay down on the floor, and meercats crawled all over me.

Nika sat down beside me and a meercat crawled onto her shoulder.

"Tell me this wasn't worth it all," she said.

I looked at her face, elated in a way I had never seen before and nodded. "Worth it."

<h1 style="text-align:center">Fifty-Six</h1>

Once the sun began to set, I realised we were going to need somewhere to sleep.

I choose a small, traditional looking restaurant with outdoor seating and plunked down, pulling out my phone. "We don't have a lot of money left," I said, a little embarrassed.

"Surely there is somewhere cheap to stay," Nika encouraged, looking at the large menu she couldn't read.

I did a quick internet search as a waiter came to ask for our order. Nika pointed at a variety of random items, enough for the both of us, as I stumbled across what felt to me like an excellent solution. "I think I've found us somewhere to stay, but I don't think you're going to like it."

"Why wouldn't I like it?" she asked.

"Well, you don't have a room, per say. You have more of a… shelf."

"A what?"

I turned the phone around and showed her photos of hotel that had dorm rooms, lined with cubes in which the guests could sleep.

"Oh, no." Nika shook here head emphatically. "No, no, no."

"I'm sorry, but it's the cheapest I can find."

Nika whipped the phone out of my hand and embarked on her own search.

"We have to keep the cost low, Nika. We have to get back to London somehow."

"You have to get back to London," Nika corrected. "I don't."

"I don't think the South Korean government is just going to let you stay here forever. There are rules."

"I'm not going back to the Czech Republic, Alfie. And you said it your-self, we have no idea how to find Oswald."

"I could call my mother. She might have a way to contact him."

"Then you would have to tell her why you are in South Korea and why you are trying to find him. Are you ready to do that?"

"I don't really see an alternative at this point. We are dead broke, on the other side of the world."

"Here," Nika said, sliding the phone across to me. "Look, these nice-looking people have a guest house we can stay in. Pretty much same price."

"The same price. Fine," I conceded. "Don't sleep in a cube. Have it your way."

"Thank you," she said, satisfactorily.

Our meals arrived and the table was filled with colourful dishes that smelled like heaven. We immediately dug in.

"What exactly do you want, Nika?" I asked gently.

"I want a home," she said, simply. "I've never really had one before. I want to belong somewhere. Somewhere safe."

"Anywhere in particular?" I scooped a heap of kimchi onto my plate and shoved it into my mouth, unaware of how spicy it was. My eyes began to water.

"Anywhere that will have me," she responded.

I wondered what it must feel like to have such a simple request feel so out of reach. She was right – I had been ungrateful for what I had. For all their eccentricities, I had a family who loved me. A home. A life.

I put my chopsticks down and leaned across the table. "I'll help you in any way I can."

"Really?" Nika asked.

"Really. Not begrudgingly, this time. Genuinely. I want to help you."

"Then what's our next move?"

"I make a call. One I never thought I would."

Nika tilted her head to the side, wondering what I meant. I took another bite of kimchi for courage.

Fifty-Seven

The phone only rang twice before an answer.

"Alfie!"

I smiled at the sound of home. "Hugh!" I returned with equal enthusiasm.

"Where the bloody hell are you?" he asked.

"Not India."

"What?"

I looked over my shoulder to Nika who was sitting at our table in the restaurant. I took a few more steps away, to ensure she couldn't hear me.

"Well, right now I'm in South Korea. Seoul, specifically."

Hugh laughed and the sound crackled through the phone line. "You must be happy!"

"Why would you say that?" I asked.

"Seoul! The home of all your Korean dramas."

My cheeks flamed. "How did you know about my Korean dramas?"

"You can't hide anything from me, mate."

I cringed at how far that statement could reach.

"Having a good time?" he asked.

"Yes, actually. But, I'm afraid we've hit a small snag."

"Since you're supposed to be in India, I should think you have."

"Look, it's a long story, involving the death of a mobster and a lot of vodka, but I am out of money and we are stuck here."

"Ah," Hugh said in a sage-like tone. "So you have come to your Jedi master."

"Something like that."

"You need money."

"I do." I squeezed my eyes shut, sick at my request. "You know I'd never ask unless it was an emergency. But we are literally stuck here, Hugh. I don't have enough money to get home."

"Mate, say no more. I'm here for you. I'm gonna take care of everything."

The relief was instantaneous.

"Text me the address of where you're staying so if you die, I'll know where to send the police. I'll call you in the morning. Your morning, I guess."

"Thank you, Hugh. I… I can't… I don't…"

"I know, mate."

The line went dead.

I quickly texted Hugh the address of where we would be staying, then dialled a second number.

"Hello?" my mother's voice trilled on the other end of the line.

"Mum, it's me," I turned around to make sure Nika was still where I had left her. She was happily enjoying the feast set out before her.

"Alfie, darling. I was just talking with your father, and I must say, I think we are going to have a great deal of trouble staying under a guest list of three hundred."

"That's not why I--," I paused. "Wait. Three hundred? Three hundred? I don't even know that many people. How could there possibly be three hundred people to invite?"

"Well, of course we've got our family, the members of all my different social clubs, the people at church, all your school friends, your father's gardening club—"

"Mother," I interrupted, "I do not need to invite Dad's gardening club to my wedding."

"Well, you're breaking that news to him, not me."

"You can't have your social club guests, either."

"Alfie!" My mother scoffed, gasping in breaths of rage. "How could you say such a thing?"

"Look, that's not even why I called."

"I am your mother. I birthed you. Labour was aptly named, I can tell you! Laborious! All to get you into this world! And after your display at your birthday, I should think that you would want to make it up to me in any way you can." She sniffed.

I sighed. "Fine. Whatever. Invite whoever you like."

Instantly cheered, she clucked, "Wonderful! It's going to be quite the affair."

"Mum," I interjected.

"Does Nika have a colour scheme in mind?"

"Mum!"

"I was thinking yellow. Baby yellow if there is such a thing."

"Mum!" I shouted, causing numerous passers-by to look my way curiously. I smiled in what I hoped was a reassuring manner.

"What is it, Alfie?" she said impatiently.

"I need to know how to get in touch with Uncle Oswald."

"Oh, you can just call him, darling."

"He doesn't own a mobile phone," I admonished.

"No, but his assistant, Ling, does. Lovely chap. Chinese. Sent me flowers on my birthday."

If I was an emoji, it would be the facepalm.

"Thank goodness. Can I have his phone number?"

"Of course, I have it here somewhere." After she had finished rummaging around in her drawer for her address book, she recounted the number and I added it to my phone. "Why the rush to find Oswald? Is everything all right, darling?"

"Everything's fine."

"Where are you? It sounds noisy."

"I'm… it's a long story."

"Darling, you're making me nervous. Your voice sounds all funny. Tell me where you are this instant."

I faltered. I couldn't handle one more lie to my mother. Lying was not in my nature. "Well, I'm in Seoul."

"What about your soul, Alfie? You're not making any sense."

"No, no. Seoul. As in, South Korea."

Mum was silent. I could hear her breathing on the end of the line. Finally, she broke the silence. "You are in South Korea?"

"Yes."

"Right now?"

"Yes."

"Right now, you're in South Korea?"

I drew in a deep breath. "Still yes."

"Well, what in heaven's name are you doing there?" Mum's voice reached that high pitch that made my eyes roll back into my head.

"I told you, it's a long story."

"Well, you better tell it anyway."

"I can't. I'm here with Nika, everything's all right. We're safe. No one has died," I pursed my lips, "that I personally know, and we're okay. We're fine."

"Are you coming home?"

"Yes."

"When?"

"I'm not sure."

"Is this it?"

"Is this what?"

"Your rebellious phase. You never had one. Is this it now? Are you finally rebelling at 25 years old? What else are you going to do? Are you going to quit school and become a painter?"

Mum was bordering on hysterics, but I was in for a penny, in for a pound at this point. "I don't know. Maybe. Not the bit about being a painter, though."

"What?" she screeched. "You cannot be serious! You have six months to

226

go, Alfie!"

"I know that, Mum."

"I cannot believe what is happening. George!" she wailed. "George! George, where is Queenie! Queenie!"

I held the phone away from my head to save my hearing. "Calm down, Mum."

"Queenie! Come here! Did you know about this? George!"

"Okay, I've got to go now, Mum," I said as cheerfully as I could.

"Don't you hang up on me, Alfie Alvey!"

"Have a good night. Uh, day. Or, whatever."

"Alfie!"

I hung up the phone and stretched my lips into a grimace. "Well, that went well." I turned the phone on silent to ignore the barrage of return calls I would no doubt receive, and slipped it into my pocket.

I walked back to the table and sat down.

"Who was that?" she asked. "What call did you have to make."

"I got Oswald's assistant's phone number. We should be able to call him and get through to Oswald."

"Okay," Nika said, less enthused than I was expecting.

"I called Hugh, too."

"What for?"

"Money."

She scoffed. "You called Hugh for money?"

"His parents are very wealthy. He's never asked them for money before, but he's going to now. For me."

"Oh."

I picked up a slice of barbequed meat and ate it. "Wow, that's good."

"Yeah," Nika said, an expression on her face I couldn't read. "That mustn't have been easy, calling Hugh."

"No, it wasn't. I didn't think I'd ever have to put him in that position."

"Thank you."

"Well, it's not just for you. I've got to get home somehow."

"Right."

I watched the corners of Nika's lips turn upwards into a small smile as she returned to her food.

Fifty-Eight

It turned out that the guest house Nika had booked for us was more like their house than a guest house. We knocked on the large gate that was the central feature of the brick façade. A man came out to meet us and let us into what looked like a good-sized courtyard. The house was simple and neat, with a flat roof and a table outside the front door. The windows were warmly lit from inside. The man smiled and called out for his family. They emerged moments later. There was an elderly woman with white hair, and what I presumed to be her daughter and two teenage sons of her own.

"Hello," I said, returning their bows. "Pleased to meet you."

The elderly woman said something in fast Korean, that I didn't have a hope of understanding. I simply smiled and nodded, as they led us inside. They ushered us into a small living room, with a low set table, a small lounge chair and an adjoining kitchen.

The man asked us a question, but I was lost.

"I'm sorry?"

He made an eating gesture with his hands.

"Oh, no, no. Thank you. We already ate," I said, shaking my head.

He simply repeated himself, then steered me by the shoulders to the table. I sat down on the ground, and Nika followed suit.

The two women placed a dozen plates of dishes onto the table, and I suddenly regretted having spent most of the day eating.

"Oh, wow," I said, wondering what to do.

I looked over to Nika for help, but she just grinned like a Cheshire cat.

The family sat down around us and gestured for us to dig in. One of the

229

teenage sons poured something into my glass and as their father raised his glass, I had little choice but to do the same.

I coughed when I realised it was alcohol. Strong alcohol.

They laughed at my pathetic, English tolerance, and my glass was re-filled.

How could I tell them that nothing good ever comes from me drinking? How could I tell them that a very short while ago, I was running through the streets, vomiting?

I couldn't, of course, so I simply prayed for strength and took another drink.

Despite the fact I was not even almost hungry, I found myself happily indulging in the food. It was delicious. I wanted to stay here forever.

I was astonished by the hospitality these strangers showed us. They opened up their home, laid out an enormous spread of food, and were full of laughter and life. As the night wore on, we developed some sort of coded way of communicating, and I took to teaching the young boys the English words for simple things like table, plate, cup, spoon.

The women took Nika under their wing and doted on her like she was their long-lost daughter. Nika looked happier than I had ever seen her. Seeing her with these women gave me a small insight into what it was that Nika had been missing all these years and what she hoped to find.

At the end of the meal, I carried the dishes back to the sink, and it was as if I had just healed a broken leg, right in front of them. The grandmother hugged me tightly, and I wondered what would happen if I washed them, too.

But Nika shoved me aside and took a tea towel from the bench and began drying the dishes as they were washed. I could tell she didn't want me stealing a single moment that could have been hers.

I watched her happily, warm with the buzz of what I had discovered was called soju. I realised in that moment, that I would be quite happy to live in this moment forever.

Everything I had worked so hard for all these years seemed pointless.

Dull. The man ushered his sons to bed, leaving me alone in the living room for a moment. I watched the women in the kitchen and wondered how their skilled hands had made such intricately flavoured food. I wondered what their story was, who the grandmother had been when she was young. Who would the teenage boys grow up to be? I wondered if they would remember me, or if I was just another tourist in a long line of people who took advantage of their hospitality.

Was there anything about me that was memorable?

I tried to see myself through their eyes, but stopped when I couldn't see anything good. Maybe Queenie was right. Maybe I had studied law just to be the sensible one. But what if I didn't want to be the sensible one anymore? Was it too late?

It was at that moment, sitting on the floor in a living room in Seoul, South Korea, that I knew I wouldn't go back to finish my law degree.

I felt both terrified and free. In front of me, my future stretched out like a blank canvas and I was both afraid and excited to see what was going to happen.

I had nothing to go back to. I had been studying law full time for years. There was room for very little else. Now, my time was my own.

Nika laughed her musical laugh and as I thought about my future, I wondered if she was going to be a part of it.

<h1 style="text-align:center">Fifty-Nine</h1>

I got a small sense of wicked satisfaction when we discovered we would both be sleeping on the floor.

We were given two soft mattresses, rolled tightly into cylinders, to unfurl and sleep on. Nika watched me stretch mine out, and I laughed when she stared at me blankly, not sure what to do. I took hers and laid it down next to mine, as far apart as the small room would allow.

Nika sat down on her bed and lifted her bag onto her lap. She started searching through it, and grew increasingly more distressed.

"What's wrong?"

"I can't find it," she said.

"What are you looking for?"

Without answering, she upended the bag and tipped the contents onto the mattress. A single change of clothes, her passport, and a random assortment of odds and ends spewed out across the bed.

She searched through them until she found what she was looking for, and clutched it to her chest.

"What is that?" I asked.

"It was my mother's," she answered, lowering it down for me to see. A small hairpin, adorned with gold flowers sat in her hand. "For a moment I thought I lost it in Russia."

I looked over her belongings. There was a pair of old spectacles, a collection of browning photos, and a small book with withered pages.

"What is all this?" I asked.

"It's… everything I own. Especially now since I lost my suitcase in Russia. These belonged to my parents. These were my fathers," she held up the spectacles, "and they used to read this book to me before bed. It's a collection of poems."

She handed the book to me and I took it gingerly. It felt breakable, like at any moment all the pages might come spilling out. "This is everything you have of theirs?"

"It's everything I have at all," she corrected. She shrugged. "It's okay. When you don't have a lot, you realise you never really needed a lot."

"Are they photos of your parents?" I asked.

Her face brightened. "Yes. Do you want to see them?"

I nodded eagerly, and she took the pile of photos and held up the first one. A bearded man with kind eyes and the same spectacles stared back at me.

"He was a professor," she explained. "This is my mother," she continued, handing me a photo of a woman in a yellow dress, holding a baby. "That's me she's holding. The woman was beautiful. Nika was almost a carbon copy of her.

"You look just like her."

"Do you think so?" she asked.

She smiled and tucked a lock of her hair behind her ear. The moment hung between us, thick and heavy. I couldn't look away from her. Her smile faded, and her expression became soft and delicate. I felt the overwhelming urge to reach out and touch her face. Her lips were soft and red, and I knew what they tasted like. I wanted to crush my lips against hers, but doing so would surely be an irrevocable mistake.

She hated me, didn't she? Nothing had changed that.

The whole reason we were here was so that she could get away from me. So, why was she looking at me like that? Or was I imagining it?

I cleared my throat and willed myself to look away. The moment dissipated.

She handed me the stack of photos. "Here, you can look through them. I'm going to go find the bathroom."

233

I sat motionless on the bed for a full minute before I could shake myself out of my state. Everything I had been wanting suddenly seemed a little less agreeable now. I wasn't sure I wanted to find Oswald now. Maybe we could just stay like this forever.

I was officially insane. Nika wanted to go back to Oswald. This was sleep-deprivation and stress, winding me up into a ball of knots. I just had to find Oswald, and everything would be fine.

I looked down at the photos in my hands and looked through them. There were a few of Nika as a very young child, but the photos were mostly of her parents. That was when I saw it. Time and space froze around me. I could hear my heartbeat slamming against my ribcage. My head pounded like a drum, and my blood turned to ice in my veins.

I held up the photo and examined it in better light to make sure that I wasn't seeing things. The light revealed the truth.

The photo was taken in front of a mountain, on a dirt road. Nika's mother was smiling, holding Nika's tiny hand. Her father was grinning wide, his arm wrapped around the neck of a man who, though much younger, was undoubtedly Oswald Basil Montgomery.

<h1 style="text-align:center">Sixty</h1>

When Nika walked back into the room, I hadn't moved from my stunned position.

"What's wrong?" she asked, sensing a disturbance in the force.

I held up the photo. She took it carefully and examined it. She smiled. "This is one of my favourites. It was taken at the Wielki Szyszak, this huge mountain where the Czech Republic meets Poland."

"And the man?" I pressed. "The man with your father?"

"That was my father's closest friend. I don't remember a lot about him, just that he was very kind and I used to call him Monty."

"Nika," I breathed, "that's Uncle Oswald."

"What?"

"In the photo, that's my Uncle Oswald."

"No, it can't be. His name is Monty."

"Oswald Montgomery. Montgomery is his last name. That must be why you called him Monty."

"I don't understand," Nika said, shaking her head. "This doesn't make sense."

"Oswald knew your parents," I announced. "That's the only explanation."

"Did he know that when he arranged for me to marry you?" Nika asked.

"I don't know. But if I know anything about Oswald, my money is on yes."

"Why would he do this?"

"I don't know. But we're going to find out."

I pulled out my phone and called Ling.

Nika was quick to fall asleep, but I kept thinking about Oswald. Our conversation was brief, as he was knee deep in a cave or tomb or something, so all I could do was tell him we weren't in Russia, and we were instead in South Korea. He told me that he had been requested to assist with work in Japan, and had previously declined, but since we were so close, he would take it. Therefore, if we could get there, we would be able to see him. He told me the address to meet him in three days, and then the line crackled and went dead.

If Oswald had known Nika's parents, what were the odds that he didn't know that when he selected her to be my bride? I was convinced the chances were slim. Why would he do this? There had to be more to the story, something that I was missing. This evening I had felt hesitant to catch up with Oswald, content to enjoy Korea and Nika for a little longer, but now I was eager to find him. I wondered how Nika must have felt, but I couldn't even begin to imagine.

I rolled over and watched her sleeping. She was breathing peacefully, her face serene. My eyes grew heavy, and I slowly let them close, and sleep took me.

Sixty-One

I woke up to the sound of a loud, joyful voice. At first, it incorporated itself into my dream, but as the voice grew louder, I stirred awake and sat up. Still mangled with sleep and exhaustion, it took me a minute to realise I recognised that voice.

I stood up and walked out of the room, sure I must have been mistaken, but there, standing in my Korean hosts' living room was Hugh Dabney.

I could have kissed his chubby cheeks.

"Hugh!" I bellowed.

"Alfie!" he returned.

"What are you doing here?" I closed the gap between us and embraced him in a bear-hug. It felt like it had been an age since I had seen his stringy beard and stained shirts.

"I said I was gonna call you in the morning, but I thought this was better."

"You didn't have to come all this way."

"Why would I want to be stuck in class, when you're gallivanting around the world?"

I laughed and did my best to introduce Hugh to my obliging hosts. They greeted him affectionately and began laying out a hearty breakfast on the table. Hugh watched them lay out breakfast, eyes wide and mouth open.

"Oh, Alfie," he said, wrapping an arm around me. "I think I'm going to like it here."

I slapped his back. "I think you will, too."

Nika appeared in the doorway, and when she saw Hugh, she ran up to him and leapt into his arms. A stab of some nameless emotion came over me. I couldn't imagine her ever greeting me that way.

"Come on," I said, sitting down, "You've never tasted food like this. They're geniuses."

Hugh seemed to be a hit, as always, especially with the grandmother. After breakfast, we helped clean up, and then packed up our room. Saying goodbye to our hosts was harder than I had expected. I had discovered something about myself here, and I was afraid that if I left, I would lose it.

Though we had only just arrived here, Nika and I were excited to show Hugh around. Hugh had travelled more than I had, but even he had never been here, and the street food was, of course, his favourite thing about the place.

When we stopped for lunch, Nika and I decided to fill Hugh in on what we learned about Oswald while we waited for our meals to arrive.

"You mean Oswald knows Nika?" Hugh blurted, as a variety of complementary side dishes were placed in front of us. The colours were deep, and you could almost see the flavour.

"It would seem so," I replied gravely.

"Do you think he knew Nika was the… you know… the one…he was sending?" In an unusual display of discomfort, Hugh struggled with how to delicately call a spade a spade.

"Do I think Oswald knew I was the bride being sent to Alfie?" Nika said flatly. "I don't know."

"What are we gonna do?" Hugh picked up his chopsticks and attempted to situate them comfortably between his fingers. "Where is he now?"

"He'll be in Japan in a couple of days. We're supposed to meet him at an address in Nagato, wherever that is."

"What are you going to say when you see him?" Hugh asked.

"I don't know."

The food arrived and we were immediately taken by the smell, and not in a good way.

"Wow," Hugh said, covering his nose.

"What did you order?" Nika said, gagging.

"I don't know!" I whispered hoarsely.

"It smells like mouldy cheese and vinegar," Hugh added. "What is it?"

I looked at the menu and read the Romanised version of what I'd ordered. "It's called Hongeo," I attempted, butchering the pronunciation.

"It smells like a public toilet!" Nika groaned.

"Maybe it tastes good," I offered.

Nika scoffed. "You first!"

I looked down at the plate of what could only be raw fish of some kind. I was ill-prepared for this moment. But Nika and Hugh were watching me, and there was no way I was going to chicken out now.

I picked up my chopsticks and placed a large dollop of kimchi on top of a slimy slice of dead fish. I clumsily scooped it up and held it in front of my face, willing myself to open my mouth. Up close the smell was even worse. It was like dirty laundry and public toilets at a music festival. My eyes started to water. I couldn't do this. I was going to back out.

"You can do it, Alfie," Nika said, in a rare moment of encouragement.

I sighed internally. I couldn't back out now. I opened my mouth and shoved it inside before I could change my mind.

The first thing that hit me was the texture. Chewy and unnatural, it was hard to break down. The taste was next. If it smelled like a toilet, it tasted like what you would find inside.

The unpleasant taste slashed at my tastebuds, and before I could stop myself, I was gagging.

Once I started gagging, I had a great deal of trouble stopping.

Nika and Hugh, ever the supportive companions, erupted in spasmic fits of laughter. I refused to give in, and continued chewing, as more of the ammonia-like taste exploded in my mouth like a bomb of urine. I covered my hand with my mouth, unwilling to allow the food to escape. I rustled up every ounce of willpower I had left in my bones and swallowed.

The food attempted to claw its way back up my throat as I gagged on the heady flavour and unbearable texture. I poured myself a shot of soju and downed it in one gulp. When I was satisfied that the food had landed in my stomach, and there was little threat of it returning, I raked in deep breaths and slapped the table with my hands. "It's good," I croaked. "Tastes fantastic."

Sixty-Two

Thanks to Hugh, we made it to Japan without sending me bankrupt. It would have been best to fly into Osaka, but Hugh declared there was no way he was going to Japan without seeing Tokyo.

A rabid fan of anime, he had a life-long goal of seeing Akihabara, a famous shopping district with an electric culture. Standing between enormous megastores, with neon signs and thirty-foot high characters presiding over the anarchic streets below, it was easy to forget we were here to meet Oswald.

The streets were swarming with tourists and locals alike, and the vibrant buzz was tangible. We spent a good chunk of the day wandering from store to store, until Hugh saw the opportunity of a lifetime, and dragged us along for the ride.

Apparently, it was quite a popular experience to dress up as your favourite character, and go-kart around the city. Amongst the cars. And the motorbikes. And the trucks.

As I selected an outfit and slid my feeble frame into the go-kart, I marvelled at the irony of a law student never having made a will.

"We could die, you know," I shouted over the engine to Hugh.

"But at least we'll die living!" he shouted back.

I looked over to Nika and saw the smile on her face. Maybe it was time to let go of that predetermined need to be overly cautious. Had this trip taught me anything but this? Life was found right on the very cusp of comfort, right when you're about to tip over into the unknown. It was second nature to me to be sensible, and cautious and, well, afraid. I had been living my life like that. Every decision, from nursery to law school, had been bow-tied with common sense. But maybe I wanted to be a little less common. And maybe I wanted my life to make a little less sense.

I lowered my goggles and turned back to Hugh.

"A tenner says I beat your arse."

Hugh squinted, his eyes narrowing, assessing my nerve. "You're on."

"I want in on that," Nika shouted. "Twenty says I beat you both."

"Deal!" Hugh and I hollered in unison.

With that, we took off and zoomed down the street with surprising speed. Nika was an early leader, and I felt my male pride swell in my chest. I could not, would not, be beaten by her. I pressed my foot to the floor and nudged past Hugh, who was disappointed to learn that it seemed he had the slowest go-kart.

Nika looked behind her, to see me gaining speed. But she was nimble, and her ability to drive a go-kart far exceeded mine. Luckily, however, we were approaching a red light, and race or no race, we were still on the streets of Tokyo, and unless we wanted to be chased by the police in another country, we would have to obey all traffic laws.

She screeched to a halt and allowed me the chance to catch up to her. We sat beside each other, our little engines rumbling like tiger cubs.

We eyed each other, and I revved my engine, egging her on. My attempt to psych her out was successful, and I launched off the line a second earlier than she did. But a second was all I needed. I zoomed in front of her, and then all I had to do was make sure she couldn't pass me.

Somewhere in the back of my mind, I wondered how I could be so blessed. Sitting in a go-kart in Japan, with the only two people I would want to share this experience with. It surprised me how much I had been enjoying time with Nika, how little I wanted to see her gone.

Since she came into my life, all sense of normalcy and sanity seemed to have vanished, and life without her was a picture I couldn't really see anymore. I wanted every day to be like today. I wanted to be the kind of person who wasn't afraid, or anxious, or addicted to sameness. I wanted to be someone Nika could like. Maybe even love.

As we crossed the finish line, my chest was bloated with pride and joy. It was a small victory, in the grand scheme of things, but to me, it was like defeating my old self. I stepped out of the go-kart and held my hands above my head like Rocky, elated with victory.

Nika laughed, a gracious loser, but as Hugh sputtered to a stop, his loss was taken with less humility.

"I cannot bloody believe I was beaten by your ginger arse!" he shouted, flailing wildly as he attempted to get out of the kart. He tripped on the edge of the door and caught himself with his hands before his face kissed the road.

"But beat you, I did," I gloated.

"Admit it," Nika said conspiratorially to Hugh. "You're kind of proud of him."

"Never," Hugh proclaimed.

"Lunch is on you losers."

"This time I pick the place," Nika interjected quickly. "I don't want a repeat of the toxic fish."

"Fair point," I nodded.

We stripped off our costumes, and headed for lunch. Nika and Hugh walked ahead; I lingered behind them and looked up the sky. Everything felt fresh and new. Different.

The world around me was big and beautiful and insane. I didn't want to miss a moment of it.

Hugh and Nika were talking animatedly, and I wanted to drink in the moment forever. I realised how long it had been since I felt truly happy. I had to admit the role that Nika played in my newfound outlook on life. She had challenged me and robbed me of my sanity. She had pushed me, chased away my logic, and forced me to face uncomfortable things about myself that I had hidden deep down. As I watched Hugh regale her with a story, flapping his arms around like a dying bird, I wondered if Nika realised that she had become the sun which we all orbited around.

I stopped, my feet freezing beneath me. My body glowed hot, my face erupting into flames. My heart fell into my stomach and the world around me grew quiet. A realisation crawled up my spine and into my brain. How had I missed this? I was at once a fool; my blind and ignorant eyes opened into dazzling light.

Nika.

It was Nika. From the moment she knocked on my door, I was doomed. My decisions were made for me, my choices stripped away. I had no armour that she could not penetrate, though my defences had put up a good fight. But the unassailable truth remained. It was always going to be Nika.

I was in love with her.

When did that happen?

Nika and Hugh turned around, suddenly aware I was no longer following them.

"Alfie, you all right?" Hugh asked. "You look like you're going to be a bit sick."

"Are you okay?" Nika added. "Do you need to sit down?"

I shook my head weakly and withdrew a smile. "I'm fine," I said, as convincingly as possible. "Let's go."

Hugh and Nika shrugged and Hugh continued his story.

In that moment, I promised myself things would be different. I would devote myself to the pursuit of happiness. Nika's, and my own.

Sixty-Three

It turned out that Nagato, the prefecture in which we were to meet Oswald, was an eleven-hour drive from where we were. We decided to hire a car and set out first thing tomorrow morning. Hugh selected a dramatically tall hotel, with a view of the Tokyo Tower, to be our place of respite for the evening and after the experiences I'd had so far, I was in no position to argue. The room even had a shower. When was the last time I had showered? I shuddered at the thought.

I was sharing a room with Hugh, and Nika had her own room directly across the hall. I took longer than was strictly necessary in the shower, washing away the events of the last few days. When I came out, Hugh was already passed out on his bed, his shoes still on his feet.

I padded quietly over to the bed and gently took off his shoes. I lifted the corner of the blanket and stretched it out over him as far as it would go. He snorted his appreciation.

I walked over to the window and gulped in the view. The Tokyo Tower was lit up, and the expanse of the city stretched out before me like a crumpled blanket. I was feeling strangely invigorated. It was early evening, and sleep held no appeal for me. I wanted to be out there, not stuck in here.

I grabbed my jacket off the bed and quietly exited the room. Nika's door was right in front of me. I wondered what she was doing. I knocked quietly. When she opened the door, my breath caught in my throat. Nika, wet hair dripping raindrops down her back, was standing in naught but a towel.

"Hi," she said.

"H-hello," I stuttered. "I see you took advantage of the shower, as well."

Nika turned around and walked back into the room, leaving the door open for me. "I don't remember when I showered last."

"Me neither. It's been a wild few days. I'm honestly not even sure how long we've been gone."

"I'm sure you're looking forward to getting back to normal," Nika said, slipping into the bathroom. She left the door slightly ajar so she could still hear me.

"Not as much as you would think," I sat down on the chair and tried to be a gentleman who did not attempt to look through the door.

"Oh, come on. I know this has been a nightmare for you. As soon as we find Oswald, you're free of all this. Free of me."

Nika emerged from the bathroom, dressed in a jeans and a jumper that we had bought from a department store earlier that day. It was a simple outfit, but she looked anything but. She was towel drying her hair, and I had to look away to be able to speak.

"What if I don't want to be free?" I asked quietly.

Nika lowered the towel and hung it on the door handle. "What do you mean?"

I stood up. "Let's go to dinner. Just you and me. Hugh's asleep anyway."

"Okay, sure. Now?"

"Now," I said eagerly.

"All right. Let's go."

"Great."

As we left the room, I realised I felt nervous. I had just asked Nika on a date, but I wasn't sure if she realised that it was a date. If she did know, would she have agreed?

Outside it was cold. We started down the street with nowhere in particular in mind. I wondered what she was thinking. Did she feel the same electricity running up and down her arm as it swung close to mine?

"I wanted to say thank you," she said, taking me off guard.

"Thank you? For what?"

"For doing this. I know none of this is what you had planned. When I arrived at your door, I was afraid that you would be a horrible person. That's the only kind we really get. But… I was lucky. You are helping me find my place."

"What do you want to do, Nika?" I asked gently.

"I was thinking sushi, maybe? We are in Japan, after all."

"That's not what I mean." I bolstered all the courage I could. "When was the last time you thought about what you wanted to do with your life?"

"Uh, never, I guess. I haven't really had that chance."

"You have it now, don't you?"

"Do I?" Nika scoffed. "Aren't we doing all this so you can hand me over to Oswald. Are you forgetting that we don't even know if Oswald is willing to take me?"

"You're not a stray dog, Nika. You don't need anyone to take you."

"I don't have your citizenship, Alfie. The world isn't as open for me. I can't just decide where I want to be, and stay there forever. There are laws. I don't have any money, any job experience. I'm nothing."

I couldn't believe what I was hearing. "You're not nothing. You're everything."

Nika stopped walking. She stared at me in disbelief. "What?"

"You're everything," I repeated lamely. "To me, you're… everything."

"You hate me," she said, her voice hollow.

"No. No, I don't."

"But… but, I…" Nika looked around in search of support, but all she found was an empty street.

"I don't want you to leave, Nika."

"Isn't that why we're here?"

"It doesn't have to be. Not anymore."

"I don't understand."

"Look, I don't claim to be a very good catch. I know I've been horrible, and boring and cruel. I know that you look at me and all you see is a grumpy law student with nothing to offer you, but I don't want to be that person anymore. I want to be different. I will be different. I'm not going to go back to university. I'm done with all that. I don't know what I'm going to do, but I want to do it with you."

Nika stared back at me, not sure what to say.

I took her silence as my opening. I cupped her face with my hands and kissed her with alarming intensity. She was stunned at first, but soon she relaxed and her lips moved in time with mine. Quietly, I was quite impressed with myself. I had been brave enough to kiss her. For real, this time. Not to get revenge or keep up a pretence in front of my family. I kissed her because I wanted to kiss her.

And she kissed me back.

It was an almost euphoric moment. I was calm and quiet on the inside, lost in tranquillity and joy. I suddenly understand all the romcoms Queenie had made me watch, and had a sudden urge to watch more. Sade's songs now made sense and for the first time, I was the hero of my own story.

I was kissing Nika and she was kissing me.

Until she wasn't.

With shocking abruptness, Nika pushed me back. Our lips made a popping sound as we parted. I stood there, mouth open like a fish, in surprise.

"What's wrong?" I asked dumbly.

"This is a mistake," she murmured.

"It is?"

"You don't know what you want, Alfie."

"But I do," I protested.

"No. You think you do, but tomorrow you're going to wake up and regret this. What you want is to get me out of your life."

"Is that what you want?" I asked.

She paused a moment, then nodded. "It is. You have your life, and I need to find mine."

With that, she turned and walked back to the hotel. I stood there, deflated and depressed, as she disappeared into the shadows.

Sixty-Four

Sharing a car with Hugh, we were subject to his best karaoke voice. Nika sat in the backseat, and I sat beside Hugh, staring out the window. We had been driving for at least two hours, and Nika and I were yet to speak a word to each other.

Suddenly, the blaring music switched off. I turned to Hugh, who slapped his hands against the steering wheel.

"That's it," he boomed. "Someone tell me what's going on."

"Nothing," I balked.

"I might not be the most astute of all people. I did not see the whole Brad and Angeline break up coming, and even though I know quite a lot about the British monarchy, every episode of The Crown still takes me be surprise. But I can tell that something is different about today, and it's not coming from me. So spill it, or I'll fart and lock the windows."

"All right, all right," I shrieked. "Nobody wants that."

"Then, get on with it. What happened?"

"I…Nika…" I floundered, not sure what to say. "I suggested that perhaps we don't need to worry about finding Oswald. Nika disagreed."

"Well, of course she did. I would, too. We need to know how Oswald knew her parents."

"Quite right," I agreed. "Quite right."

"So, can we move on, please?"

"Of course," I nodded emphatically. "For the sake of our nostrils."

"Alfie, we have nine more hours of driving ahead of us. I'm still going to fart. I just won't lock the windows."

"You are nothing if not generous, Hugh."

"It's one of my best qualities."

"I couldn't agree more."

"Do you want another of my best qualities?"

"Please."

"I'm excellent at surprises."

"What are you talking about?" Nika asked.

"See, I did a little research last night, when I woke up in the middle of the night and couldn't get back to sleep. Since we're going on this here road trip, I thought it would be a wasted opportunity not to add a few sights to our itinerary."

"We have to meet Oswald on time, Hugh," I objected.

"Yes, yes, we will. Stop stressing. But you'll thank me for this, one day, Alfie. Maybe even this day."

"Where are we going?"

Hugh pulled over and switched off the engine.

"Hugh? Hello? Where are we?"

Hugh grinned and pointed out the windscreen. My eyes followed his finger until I saw what he was pointing at.

Mount Fuji.

We stepped out of the car, and looked up at the enormous mountain looming down on us like a sentinel, immune to time.

"See?" Hugh chortled. "Aren't you glad we stopped here?"

Nika walked up beside me. "It's beautiful," she said.

"Yes," I agreed. "Beautiful."

It was immensely painful to be standing beside her, wearing the undignified cloak of rejection. I had put myself out there, thrown caution to the wind, and bared my soul to her, only to come face to face with stone cold dismissal.

Still, I couldn't bring myself to regret the events that led me to that brutal moment. I was feeling freer and more alive than I ever had. The agony was a sensation I had never felt before, true, but it was a sensation, nonetheless. I had spent so much of my time feeling nothing at all, other than grey hair inducing stress and anxiety. Thanks to Nika and this unbelievable experience, I was a new man, as dramatic as that sounded.

I wouldn't change it for the world.

And whether my feelings for her were reciprocated or not, I wanted the best for her. If she felt the best thing was for her to find Oswald, then that was what we were going to do. I was glad to be a part of her journey, even if the role I played was a small one.

Hugh shoved his way between us and looped his arms around our necks. "What a bloody sight, eh?"

"What a bloody sight," I agreed.

Sixty-Five

We had a quick pit-stop in Nagoya, but we didn't stop again until we hit Kyoto. I had driven from Mount Fuji, and I was grateful to get out of the car and stretch my legs. It was my turn for surprises, this time. There was no way I was going to come all the way to Kyoto without seeing the bamboo forest.

Nika walked ahead of me, and I saw flickers of her face as she passed through the shadows cast by the ancient bamboos. It was calming, quiet. Until Hugh opened his mouth of course.

"Well, this is great and all, but you know what I'd like to see?"

"What would that be?" I asked.

"Geisha. Real life Geisha." Hugh's face lit up with a joy that only the thought of women could create. "Do you think a Geisha could fall in love with me?"

"Why wouldn't she?" I asked. "What's not to love?"

"See," Hugh said, wagging a finger in my face, "that's what I thought!"

It turned out that Hugh was actually quite a hit with the Geisha, a fact which shouldn't have surprised me. We sat at a traditional matcha tea ceremony, with Geisha both instructing us on the proper way to make tea and dancing to the music played on a traditional guitar-like instrument I was informed was made of cat skin.

While this fact made it slightly less appealing, it was quite entertaining to watch Hugh attempt to woo a Geisha. He was embarrassingly dumbstruck at one particular woman, who did seem to dote on him more than anyone else.

Hugh left the room floating on a cloud, and I felt a little bad that we couldn't stay longer for him to pine over her.

When I was younger, I just assumed that one day I would fall in love and get married, like it was a given. I just imagined that one day I would wake up married, and that would be that. I'd have the whole picture – a wife I loved, a house, children. It wasn't until now that I realised that doesn't happen for everyone. Maybe there was no one for me, or for Hugh. There was no guarantee we would meet someone who actually loved us back. Perhaps we would spend the rest of our lives like this – weird best friends, living together in a flat in Wandsworth.

The thought left an acidic taste in my mouth. Wandering through the streets of Kyoto, lined with traditional looking houses, I felt about as far away from Wandsworth as physically possible. It was difficult to imagine that back in England my house was still sitting where I left it and my desk was still covered with random papers. Everything that was mine was waiting there for my return. But I wasn't filled with feelings of homesickness, I was filled with claustrophobia. That world seemed too small now. It wasn't mine anymore.

I wasn't the same person I was when I left, and the thought of returning felt like putting my feet into shoes that didn't fit me anymore.

We stopped for food at an ancient-looking restaurant, and were served a variety of dishes, one of which appeared to be not quite dead. Nika seemed to be having the time of her life, and Hugh was as happy as she was. I absorbed every second of her smile that I could, knowing all too soon I wouldn't be seeing it again.

My phone buzzed in my pocket. I pulled it out and saw the name Ling flash on the screen. I answered it quickly.

"Hello?"

"Alfie, my boy!" Oswald's voice boomed on the other end of the phone. "How are you?"

"Oswald," As I said his name, Nika and Hugh looked up at me like rabbits who had heard a fox. "I'm fine, thank you." My voice was clipped.

"Where are you right now?" he asked.

"Kyoto," I answered. "We're on our way to you."

"Never mind coming to Nagoya. Change of plans. Wait in Kyoto and I'll come to you. I'm not far. I'll be there by dinner. I'll have Ling text you the address of my favourite sushi restaurant. Delicious. Fish like you've never had before. Meet me there at seven."

"We will."

"Is everything all right, lad?" he asked, his ostentatious voice softening a little.

"Fine, Oswald. Everything's fine."

"Right. Okay. Well, then, I'll see you at seven."

"See you then." I ended the call without another word. Hugh and Nika were staring at me, waiting for me to speak.

"Well, you'll be pleased to know our road trip ends here. Nika, you're saved from having to drive another six hours with us. Oswald will be meeting us here, in Kyoto. We are to meet him at a restaurant tonight at seven."

I wasn't sure if it was something in my voice, or just that neither of them were quite prepared to have our adventure end so suddenly, but Nika and Hugh didn't seem happy.

I poked at my plate, my appetite suddenly gone.

I could feel Hugh's eyes on me. The room seemed to shrink in size. I resisted the urge to gasp for air.

"Well!" Hugh clapped his hands together, startling Nika. "I guess that means we've got a few hours to kill, eh?" He slapped a hand down on Nika's shoulder. "Who wants to have some fun?"

Sixty-Six

I was glad Hugh was here. Both Nika and I were difficult to get out of our funk. I knew the reason for mine, but I couldn't understand why she seemed so unhappy. Hugh was determined to have a wild afternoon with us, and he always got his own way.

We started with Ninja lessons, something I wasn't aware was an actual thing. But a thing it was, and we were outfitted in the official uniform of a ninja, and were taught to throw knives, use swords, and otherwise inflict bodily harm. From there, we went to the Fushimi Inari Shrine, which I was astounded by, but was a little too slow for Hugh.

At this point, Nika asked how long we had until we had to meet Oswald, and when I told her we still had a few hours, she tentatively asked if we could do something on her wish list. We both quickly agreed, and drove the short distance from Kyoto to Nara, where we went to Deer Park.

The animal lover in me was in heaven. Hundreds of wild deer called the park home, and we were allowed to roam around, feeding them. They were surprisingly friendly, butting their little heads against my leg to ask for more food to nibble.

I almost forgot that we were about to meet Oswald, and that would mean walking away from Nika.

"If this was England, they'd all be venison by nightfall," Hugh said.

"Then it's a good thing this isn't England." Hugh and I were sitting on a bench while Nika wandered around not far from us.

"You realise you have made an atrocious mistake." Hugh sat hunched, trying to look wise and old like the Dalai Lama.

"Do you even know what atrocious means?" I quipped.

"See? That, right there. A classic self-defence mechanism."

"A what now?"

"Self-defence mechanism. I accidently took Professor Walter's psychology class the other day. It was very informative."

"I can only imagine."

"See, what it means is that you are feeling sad and sorry for yourself because you are letting literally the only chance of happiness you are ever going to get walk right out of your life, without so much as a whoopsy-daisy."

"No," I said, shaking a finger at him. "No, you're wrong. That's not it at all."

"When are you going to admit it?"

"Admit what, Hugh?"

Hugh looked at me with a knowing stare. "That you love her. Are you going to do something about it?"

"About what?"

"About the fact she's about to walk out of your life forever, without knowing how you feel about her."

I chuckled dryly. "Well, she does know, and she's not interested."

"Ah," Hugh rubbed his beard like a genie. "I see. That's what the whole issue in the car was, right?"

"Right."

"Ouch."

"Yep."

"Look, I've been talking to Nika a lot since I got here, and it's obvious, mate."

I scoffed. "Nothing is obvious about that woman."

"Trust me. She likes you."

"If that were true, she would not have said the exact opposite."

"Did she say she didn't like you?" he asked.

"No, not exactly. She said more that she didn't think I liked her."

256

"Well, I wonder whatever could have given her that impression?"

"What's that supposed to mean?"

"Well, it's not like as if you got off to a very good start," Hugh admonished.

"I know. I've been trying to undo that, but I mean, how would you have reacted?" Hugh gave me a knowing look and I sighed. "Right, yes, okay, well, I know how you would have reacted. I admit I haven't handled things well. But things have changed. Or, at least I thought they had."

"You should talk to her again. Make her see how you feel."

"It's too late. Oswald is coming tonight."

"If there's one thing I know, Alfie, it's that it's never too late." Hugh stood up. "I'll let Nika know it's time to head back."

Sixty-Seven

The restaurant was less glamourous than I had expected. There was something warm and comforting about the wood panelled walls, stone floors, and dim lighting. We sat at our table, waiting for Oswald to arrive. The tension was palpable.

Hugh kept watching dish after dish arrive at other tables, and sighed longingly. "Is it seven o'clock yet?"

"Almost," I answered. "We were a little early."

Nika shifted uneasily in her seat.

"Are you all right?"

"I'm nervous," she admitted. "I don't know what to expect."

"Well," I began, as Oswald walked through the entrance, "we're about to find out."

Oswald was dressed in a three-piece suit. His vivacious face was crinkled with a smile, and his cheeks were flushed with too much sun. He didn't look anything at all like my mother, or anyone else in our family for that matter. His black hair was streaked with silver, one of the only signs he was aging. He was a head taller than me, and I was far from short. His broad shoulders hinted that he was certainly in better shape than I was, but I supposed he had to be in his line of work. Crawling through caves, and cracking open sealed tombs was physically demanding.

I stood up to greet him, and Nika and Hugh followed. "Good evening, Uncle Oswald," I said stiffly.

"Alfie!" he boomed, embracing me in a tight hug. "Ah, it's so good to see you. And with your darling bride-to-be. Such a pleasure."

"I'm afraid the pleasure is all yours," I retorted coolly.

"I see," he answered back calmly. "Hugh," Oswald nodded his greeting.

"Evening Mr. Montgomery," Hugh replied happily. "Good to see you, as always."

"And Dominika," Oswald plucked her hand from her side and kissed it, as if she were a queen, and he her loyal subject. "It's a pleasure."

Upon releasing her hand, Oswald sat down, and we joined him at the table. I wasn't really sure where to begin, and I was grateful to discover I didn't need to take the lead.

"Thank you for meeting me here," Oswald began. "I was sorry that we couldn't meet in Russia. Was everything all right?"

"Well, depends on your definition of all right. Can we ever go back there? No. Did we make it out alive? Yes." I took a sip of sake and tried to steady myself.

"There's quite a story there, I can tell."

"Another time, perhaps," Nika said softly.

"Of course." Oswald cleared his throat. "I presume you are here to discuss the reason I brought you two together."

"Since you jumped straight into it, yes. What the hell were you thinking?" I hissed. "A mail order bride? Are you sick?"

"I understand your anger," Oswald said calmly. "And I am here to explain everything."

"I've always known you're a little unhinged, but this was too far. My entire family believes we're getting married. It's not just Nika and I you have hurt, it's them, too. Mum. Dad. Queenie. Do you not care about them at all?"

"Of course I care, Alfie. And I had no idea that you would tell your entire family you were getting married if you had no intention of doing so."

"Well, we got off to a pretty rough start. Nika was under the impression I was going to marry her and understandably, she was a little upset when she found out I had no idea about any of it!"

Oswald tried to interject but I was on a roll.

"Do you have any idea what we have been through since we left London? Do you know what we lived through? It cost me every pound I had! That's why Hugh is here!"

Hugh raised a hand and gave a little wave. "Happy to help. Honestly. I've had a lovely time."

"And Nika! She thought she was coming to England to have a home. For the first time since her parents died. And you send her to a poor university student, with no idea who she is. If you don't care about me, surely you would care about her."

"I do care," Oswald exclaimed.

"I want to know how you could do this to me. How you could do this to Nika."

Oswald sighed. "I didn't do this to you, Alfie, I did this for her."

"What are you talking about?" I asked.

Oswald gave me a dissatisfied glare and shifted in his seat to face Nika. "I don't know if you remember me, Nika, but I knew your parents."

Nika pulled the photograph of Oswald and her parents out of her pocket. "I know. Alfie saw this, and told me who you were."

"So, you do remember me?"

"A little, yes."

"Then do you remember that your father was my best friend? We met on an archaeological dig when we were young boys, still studying. He went on to be a professor, of course, and I took a more…hands-on route. I was best man at his wedding to your mother. I was also your godfather."

Nika looked up in surprise. "Then where were you when they died?"

"I was overseas on a dig. I was in the jungle, no way to contact anyone except via radio. It was a different world then. No internet messages on your phone, allowing you to talk to anyone anywhere in the world. By the time word of their deaths reached me, it had already been three weeks. I took the next flight to the Czech Republic, but you were gone. I spent a year looking for you, but all my searches proved fruitless. You were nowhere to be found."

Nika held a hand over her mouth to hide her quivering lips. I reached under the table and took hold of her other hand. "I was taken to an orphanage out of the city. I tried to run away a few times, but I had nowhere else to go."

"I am sorry, Nika. That was never supposed to be your fate. I have continued to search for you all these years. Finally, I found you. Well, I should say Ling found you, bless him. I was quite disheartened to discover the situation you were in and I did the only thing I could do to ensure your freedom. I arranged for your marriage to Alfie. I didn't know where I was going to be from one day to the next, but I knew Alfie would be home, and he would keep you safe. He was the only one I could trust with you until I managed to meet you both to explain everything."

"Oh," I said pathetically.

"That's beautiful, Mr Montgomery," Hugh said. "Quite a story."

"You bought my freedom?" Nika asked shakily.

"Look," Oswald said, uncharacteristically quiet. "I never meant to lose you, Nika. If I had been able to find you, I would have raised you. Kept you safe. Please believe that I tried."

Nika nodded, unsure what she could possibly say.

"And Alfie," Oswald continued, "thank you for bringing her to me. I'm sorry I didn't explain everything in the letter. I guess I wanted to tell you – and Nika – myself. I am sorry for any trouble I've caused."

I sat there dumbly, wishing I had more of a right to be angry. But if Oswald had just been trying to get Nika a new life, could I really fault him for that? After all, it was his decision to send Nika to me and for that I would always be grateful. Even if the road had been bumpy.

Oswald sat uncomfortably in his chair, looking smaller than I had ever seen him. Nika reached out her hand across the table and took hold of his. He looked up at her, stunned by the gesture.

"Thank you," she said quietly. "Thank you for saving me."

Oswald sniffed back his emotions and tightened his hand around hers. "I'm sorry it didn't come sooner."

Oswald placed a hand on my back. "Thank you, Alfie. Thank you for taking care of her until now."

Nika's eyes met mine. Something nameless passed between us. My chest swelled with pain. "It's been my pleasure," I said softly.

"Should we order?" Hugh asked, breaking the silence that had fallen over the table. "You said this was your favourite place, right?"

Oswald's darkened face brightened. "Yes. Yes, I did."

Oswald spent most of the night telling stories of his adventures over the last few months. He had made surprising discoveries and fought off bandits. He had discovered new ways to look at old things, and old ways to look at new things. I found myself relaxing into the evening, enjoying the night in a way I didn't think I would. When Nika asked about her parents, Oswald threw himself fervently into telling her stories of his adventures with her father.

As I watched her laugh at his tales, I realised that this is where Nika belonged. It was only right that Nika leave me behind and explore the world with Oswald. He had been an uncle to me, but he could be a father to her.

She deserved that, after all these years.

Sixty-Eight

Outside the restaurant, the night air was frigid. I had excused myself for a breath of fresh air, and fresh it certainly was. Standing alone in the street, I tried to figure out what I was supposed to do next. Nika was about to leave with Oswald, and I was to… what? Go back to Wandsworth? How could I do that now, when I had tasted life outside the walls of my flat.

I wished my sister were here. This was the kind of moment where Queenie would say the right thing and make sure everything made sense again. She had always been my lifeboat. Maybe being the stable one was never my calling. Maybe it was hers, all along.

I tried to think of what she would say, but then I realised maybe she had already said it.

Why hadn't I followed in Oswald's footsteps? My drive to be steady and secure for my family, especially for Queenie, had driven me to do law, but now that I wasn't going back, what was stopping me from going with him?

I had always wished that my life looked more like Oswald's. Maybe this was my chance. But if Nika was going with him, too, I didn't know if that was an option anymore.

I started to pace, weighing up my choices, when Nika walked out.

"Alfie are you okay?" she asked.

I spun around at the sound of her voice. "Fine. Totally, completely fine. Are… are you okay?"

"I am," she nodded. "I'm… happy."

"Good. Excellent. Mission accomplished, captain." I saluted her and felt the immediate need to kick myself in my balls.

Nika chuckled. "What are you doing out here?"

"Oh, you know. Contemplating life and all the choices I've ever made."

"Just another day for you, isn't it?"

"Pretty much."

"Oswald wants me to travel with him." Nika's voice shook a little.

"Ah. Great. That's great." Even I knew that was a poor attempt at sounding pleased.

"Is it?" she laughed.

"It is," I said, a little more convincingly. "This is what you've always wanted. A family. He's your godfather. You can't miss out on that."

"No, I can't," Nika agreed. "And you have your life to get back to."

Nika turned to go back inside.

"I'm not going back to England," I declared.

She paused and turned back around to face me. "You're not?"

"No," I shook my head emphatically.

"Why not?"

"How could I after all this?" I held my arms out and gestured to the world around me. "Travelling with you has been the most insane, infuriating, incredible time of my life, and I'm… different now. I don't fit there anymore."

"What are you going to do?" she asked.

"I'm going with you," I announced, half expecting her to hurl her shoe at my head.

Nika blinked rapidly. "I'm sorry?"

I walked up to her, closing the gap between us in three long strides. "I'm going with you," I repeated smoothly.

"But…you…I… but…" Nika protested, words faltering on the end of her tongue.

"You might not love me now, but you will. And I'll wait." I bent down and kissed her cheek. "As long as it takes."

The corner of my mouth raised to offer a small smile, then I brushed past her and headed for the entrance. "Come on," I called over my shoulder. "I'm suddenly starving."

"Alfie, come back here!" she called, but I was already inside, ready to start my life all over again.

About the Author

Hosanna King is a novelist, screenwriter and children's book author. She is a passionate writer and mother. She can never find a book long enough, a car trip far enough or a country too far away. She is a self-confessed crazy dog lady, and lover of Jesus, travelling, languages, chai lattes and sushi.

www. hosannaking.com
www.chapterspublishing.com